WINTER SCENE

David Berardelli

WINTER SCENE

GRAVESTONE PRESS

Chapter 1 - Sunday

John Callen turned to face the cemetery and shivered despite the balmy heat of the late afternoon.

The past few days had been in the low eighties, indicating a sudden burst of Indian summer for the Ohio Valley, even though October was just around the corner.

John knew why he shivered. As he thought about it, he found himself shivering even more.

Death. It's following me again.

It lost the trail when I was shipped home but somehow picked up the scent again after all these years.

Then he remembered that his aunt was standing beside him, gazing longingly at the grave.

"I really feel bad about not seeing Uncle John for so long, Aunt Meg," he said, putting his other feelings aside. "He was, after all, my dad's only brother. I was even named after him. And with both Mom and Dad gone, there's no one left. Just you and me."

The slender, white-haired woman smiled. Her smile, as always, made her deep-blue eyes sparkle like rare gems. "He understood, Johnny. He always thought the world of you, and since we couldn't have kids of our own, we considered you our own."

"I've always known that. But…leaving me the deed to your house?"

"That's what he wanted. I certainly can't take care of it anymore. Not at my age. I have trouble moving around, my sciatica's getting worse, and I really don't have the desire to keep a place looking spotless. You'll find that when you reach my age, your priorities change drastically. You can always sell it, you know."

"You wouldn't mind?"

"Once I'm gone, I won't care. And I can't say as I would blame you. We both knew you wouldn't want to relocate up here, so..."

John turned to his uncle's marker and realized again how utterly revolting such a stone was, serving as the solitary reminder of someone's death. The more he stared, the more he realized how revolting they all were, no matter how fancy you tried making them. Or what kind of stone you chose. Or how many flowers you used to decorate them.

A marker was simply a marker. No matter what you stuck on its face, it served only as a sad hint that the remains of someone lay beneath it.

And it didn't help seeing his name on its polished face.

JOHN EDWARD CALLEN
Beloved Husband of Margaret

"You're flying back to Orlando tonight?"

He had wanted to head home and get back to his software business, but inwardly he was debating whether he should visit his old friend, Buster Norton.

Buster, who John hadn't seen since Iraq, lived in Bern, Ohio—just two hours west, on the Interstate. Buster had stepped on an IED about three months after the chopper had dropped them onto enemy soil and was shipped home immediately. While he and Buster had corresponded for a while before drifting apart, John always felt guilty about not visiting his old friend after being discharged. John had been in the Pittsburgh area several times during the last couple of decades on business and to see his relatives but had never taken the opportunity to call or visit Buster. And despite the times he reminded himself of his duty to check on his former sidekick, something had always come up to change his plans.

John fully knew the reason he kept putting it off, and it was this reason alone that would forever keep them apart.

"I…have a friend in Bern," he told his aunt. "We were in Iraq together."

"How long since you've seen him?"

He gazed into the deep blue orbs. It was always difficult, lying to this woman. Her eyes and her vulnerable, delicate-boned face made you want to bare your soul. "Fifteen years," he said, his voice constricted.

"Why so long?"

He couldn't tell her the whole story. It was too horrible, for one thing; and he didn't think this gentle soul should hear such sadness so soon after the passing of her husband.

She knew John had spent six months in Walter Reed. That much she learned from John's mother. However, the exact nature of his injuries had been carefully locked away—not only in the files of the U.S. Army, but also in the darkest recesses of John's brain.

"I always found it painful to relive Iraq. Buster was blown up not long after the chopper dropped us off over there. He went home. I stayed."

His aunt shivered. "How badly was he hurt?"

"Lost a leg. But he was lucky. When he got out of the hospital, he started working at the post office. He's also been receiving full comp from the Military. He'll probably be in good shape financially when he decides to retire."

Aunt Meg took his arm. John couldn't help noticing how small and fragile it felt. How her hand seemed to disappear in the crook of his elbow. He remembered how strong and robust she was when he was little, picking up bricks and heavy lumber when she and Uncle John were having their house built.

The same house that would soon be his.

They walked a short way in silence. Then she said, "Your mother told me about your trouble. She was vague, of course. Probably because what the Army told her wasn't that much. But she knew whatever had happened was bad. Very bad. Your father had already passed, of course, so he never knew what you went through. But your mother did,

8

and she told me how difficult it was, trying to be your mom once again after they sent you home."

"How did she know? I never told her. I always tried keeping things — "

Aunt Meg smiled. "She could see it in your eyes. She was your mother; she could feel what had happened to you."

John didn't reply; he was remembering the past. How his mother had aged so quickly after he'd returned home. Aged, then died just a couple of years later.

She saw—felt—what was in my head and knew she couldn't cope with it.

Can't blame her.

Hell, I couldn't even handle it.

"I never liked telling others what to do." Aunt Meg stood with her arms crossed over her tiny chest, looking at him. "But let me say this. Life is too precious and too short to spend it alone. You know that; you probably knew it years ago. Turn around and look what's left of your uncle." She sighed. "A cold stone marker. A chunk of granite, some flowers that will die in a day or so, and a mound of dirt." Her eyes filled, making them glitter. "And I'll never get another chance to tell him how much I loved him."

They hugged one another.

Moments later, she recovered. Her eyes still sparkled. She pulled away and looked at him. "Go see your friend, Johnny. You're not getting any younger. None of us is. Go see him so you can tell him how you feel. Why you stayed away. Celebrate the fact that you're both still alive and well."

"I...don't know if I can..."

"You can, believe me. And no matter what happened back there, it's over now. It happened in another part of the world and in another lifetime, and you made it back. Now go see your friend and tell him what I just told you."

John studied the twinkling blue eyes, saw the hope in them, and the love that would be forever lost on the man lying beneath the stone marker just a few yards away. She would never again hug the man she loved for more than half a century. And she wanted her beloved nephew to bury the past.

By bringing it back.

He suddenly realized how right she was. How incredibly, horribly right.

"I think I understand," he said, giving her one last hug and feeling a coldness that made him tremble down to his toes.

***

The Murphy twins sat in the front seat of the beat-up tan Ford pickup and eyed the blonde coming out of the rest stop bathroom.

"Sharp." Ron sat behind the wheel, finishing the tuna sandwich they had picked up along the way. "I like the way her ass fills those tight jeans."

"Wanna do 'er, Ronnie?" Rich sipped some Coors. "Just bundle her up and stick her in back. For later. I don't think she'd put up much of a fuss. She might *like* it rough."

"You know better'n that." A scowl wrinkled his brother's fair features. "Got a job to do, and you know how much it's payin'. Ain't *no* piece of ass worth *that* much jack."

The blonde unlocked the door of the shiny black Camaro two spaces down. She bent her slim frame and slid inside.

"Just thinkin' out loud." Rich suppressed a belch. "You know how long it's been since I been laid."

"Sure do. Don't forget—*you* don't get laid, *I* don't get laid. But when we're through with this job, we'll get ourselves some top-quality stuff."

Rich grinned and sat back. He felt the familiar twitch between his thighs.

Pittsburgh chicks were about the best. Especially the ones working the Hilton. They cost a bundle but were well worth it. Those bitches really knew how to treat a dude.

Ron switched on the ignition, put the truck in reverse, and backed out of their space. They got back on the Interstate and headed east, where they would soon earn a shitload of money for one night's work.

***

As John Callen headed west, he couldn't shake the icy feeling that had settled in the back of his neck.

This just didn't feel right.

Not at all...

But something kept him going, nonetheless.

11

Maybe it was the hope that, once he saw Buster again, everything would be fine. That whatever had happened back then remained dead and buried. And that the joy of seeing an old friend would overcome any old wounds.

He and Buster had met at Fort Benning, for Advanced Sniper Training. John had taken Basic at Benning, while Buster had been shipped in from Fort Jackson, South Carolina. Benning had been seven weeks of pure hell and, although they all knew their ultimate destination, they'd celebrated their graduation with the same enthusiasm as a kid leaving home to be on his own for the first time in his life.

John was selected for sniper training. Though he'd not had much experience with firearms before his induction, he quickly proved to be a crack shot, and could hit just about anything up to one hundred and fifty yards without a scope. At sniper school, he'd done near-perfect scores with the 7.62mm Knight's Armament M110 rifle, the M2010 in .300 Winchester Magnum, and the Barrett M107 in .50 BMG., and was promptly shipped to Iraq, where he was attached to a squad of scout-snipers working the same infantry unit Buster had been assigned to.

His memories of the nocturnal hunts were sketchy, at best. Keeping the nauseating stench of lingering death from penetrating his pores had been nearly impossible. Despite what had transpired after being dropped off in the Ramadi desert in the middle of the night, he managed to avoid insanity, though even now he couldn't remember how he'd actually accomplished that amazing feat.

He recalled endless days and nights of lying on hard sand for hours, covered in burlap and shattered kindling, his .50 Barrett cradled tightly in his arms. Staying in the same position for forty-eight hours at a stretch, listening to the nearby babbling of the insurgents as they searched the terrain for the evil infidel who had savagely invaded their homeland.

Now, as he headed off for Ohio, John couldn't shake the mixed feelings muddling his mind. Feelings of anxiety for seeing his old friend again. Of utter dread for bringing up the shattered past—which was inevitable.

The closer John got to the small Ohio town of Bern, the more these cold feelings of apprehension ate away at him.

He knew what would happen soon after they saw each other again.

Buster would undoubtedly ask him what had happened to their mutual friend, Bill Sebastian.

Like it or not, this would bring back the nightmare.

In bloody technicolor.

***

At six o'clock, Erika Larson checked the roast.

Looking good.

Now, if Paul doesn't come home late again, it might just prove to be an enjoyable evening.

The roast had been a sort of bribe to make sure the man came home, instead of spending half the night, as usual, in his Wheeling offices. It was his

13

very favorite meal, and Erika had been careful to select the finest cut of meat, as well as his special brand of claret, to ensure the meal would be something very special.

Sipping her port, Erika tried remembering when their marriage had started showing signs of trouble. The more she thought about it, the more she was convinced her two miscarriages had been instrumental.

The first had taken place five years ago, after they had celebrated their second anniversary.

Paul had recently started up Larson & Associates, Ltd., and began spending long days at the office, making sure the software company was given the opportunity to take off.

Within two years, L&A did enough business to warrant a major move from its two-room office on the second floor of the Bern National Bank, to half a floor on Market Street in downtown Wheeling. Not long after, it was employing three other associates, establishing itself as a full-time business venture.

In just three years, it had made over three million dollars, expanded its operation to an entire floor, and boasted more than a dozen associates, producing software packages nationwide and gradually becoming one of Wheeling's top software distributors.

Erika suffered her second miscarriage last year.

She came back from the hospital, spent three melancholy days in bed, and tried desperately to forget -- or, at least, accept -- her ordeal.

Two days later, Paul flew to Tampa for a series of seminars. After a few half-hearted attempts to console Erika, he obviously preferred directing his efforts to his work rather than waste his valuable time struggling to help heal his ailing, despondent wife.

Erika longed for his support. She wanted to talk about their loss, their plans for the future.

Perhaps his detachment was, in essence, what had started the deterioration. And, the more Erika thought about it, the more she realized that this strained silence had been like the slamming of a door.

She tried, during the past few months, to pry the door open. To push their relationship back where it had once been. While her efforts were sincere, she realized, almost at once, that she had been nudging a dead horse.

Their marriage had run its course.

Now, as she sipped her port and contemplated the evening ahead, she told herself that, despite everything, she was going to give it yet another try.

She truly believed their marriage deserved at least that much.

***

The Murphy twins stopped in Zanesville and gassed up at a 7-Eleven just off the Interstate.

Ron was filling the tank when Rich strolled over. "Wanna have some fun with the clerk?"

Ron shook his head. "Got a schedule to keep. Don't think we oughta — "

"He's Indian," prompted Rich, a devilish smile on his handsome young face. "Saw 'im through the front window. Haven't done one of *them* in a while."

"You sure about that?"

Rich grinned. "Looks just like that sucker on *The Simpsons*. Shit-colored skin? One eyebrow?"

Ron tilted his blond head. They hadn't done in a foreigner in a while. He thought of the stupid spic bitch that had cut them off in traffic a few months ago, back in Westerville. He clearly recalled how they'd followed her to the K-Mart and did her in her own car, Rich standing by the opened passenger door, gripping her ankles, Ron on the driver's side, crushing her windpipe with one powerful hand. Watching the people going by, smiling politely as he did her in.

It had been fun, watching her kick and thrash in the seat...

"Guess we got a few extra minutes to kill," he said with a chuckle.

Grinning, the twins ambled to the front of the brightly lit store.

***

At seven o'clock, John stopped at a Holiday Inn outside St. Clairsville and found a pay phone with a directory.

The directory covered the Belmont County area. Since Bern was in Belmont County, he knew Buster's number might be in it, if he hadn't moved. And if the number was listed.

It took only a moment to discover that he was right. On both counts.

Despite his reluctance, he watched as his own hand, feeling as if it belonged to someone else, pulled out his cell and dialed.

His only thoughts were that it would make things so much simpler if the number was no longer valid.

If Buster wasn't home.

If he didn't have an audix.

If --

Despite John's hopes and fears, he heard the familiar voice answer on the third ring. "Hello?"

"Buster?"

There was a pause. "Not many people call me that anymore," came the reply. "Who's this?"

"It's John," he said. "John Callen."

Another pause.

Then a gasp.

"John...*Callen*? Johnny? Is that...is it really *you*?"

"Sure is."

"What -- when did you -- where the hell *are* you?"

"At the Holiday Inn, outside St. Clairsville."

"That's...*fifteen minutes* from here!"

"I take it you're at the same address?"

"Right off Main. Take the first Bern exit, then left at the stop sign. Go five miles and you're in the city limits. Make a left at the Burger King, go up one street and turn right. I'm the first house there. I'll have a cool one ready."

"I'll be as quick as I can."

"You'd better be!"

**

Ron Murphy moved closer to the counter when a pudgy woman and her squealing little brat burst into the store.

He groaned and rubbed the back of his thick, muscular neck. No way could they sour a terrific deal for the sake of a little fun. They could always have fun. This was America: there were foreigners everywhere. And they could always come back after the job if they wanted to.

That was the good thing about foreigners: they were kind of like cats. You could drive out to the country and run over a dozen cats, shoot a dozen more, then drive somewhere else and do the same damn thing.

Seemed like cats and foreigners were made just for sport...

Ron stood behind the woman and waited while she paid for her gas. The kid was fidgety; it seemed like she needed a nap, or a pee. She turned and looked up at him. He smiled and winked at her. The brat turned back to her fat momma and squealed. Fat Momma nudged her with a fleshy hip. The kid lowered her head and went quiet.

Moments later, Ron backed up and let the slovenly woman squeeze through the slim aisle. She nearly knocked over the potato chip rack, which continued to totter long after she left the store.

Ron approached the register, dropped a six-pack of Pepsi on the counter, gave Yanni two twenties, and watched as the swarthy Indian meticulously counted out his change. Ron pocketed it, returned the Indian's warm smile with a cold one, and calmly said, "We might just be back this way in a day or so to cap your butt, Yanni."

The Indian blinked. "Beg pardon?"

Ron continued smiling. "I said, thanks and have a nice day."

The Indian smiled uncomfortably, displaying four glittering gold teeth.

Rich was standing halfway down the aisle, giggling. When Ron approached, Rich said, "He didn't get it, did he?"

"Not a clue."

"I guess we ain't gonna do him now, huh?"

"Too much damn traffic."

The two reluctantly moved outside, into the muggy night.

**

Buster Norton was sitting on the front porch of his two-story frame house when John showed up shortly after seven-thirty.

John noticed that his friend had gained quite a bit of weight over the years, most of it settling around his middle. His hair, which had been light brown, had turned gray around his temples. And, though his face was broad and heavy, Buster's small hazel eyes made him look lost and frightened.

Buster stood awkwardly, grasping the curved wooden arms of his rocker for balance. He carefully turned toward the steps and then shuffled toward the front entrance as John hurried up the walk.

"You bastard!" Buster yelled, laughing. The two men grasped one another tightly. "You haven't even gained any *weight*, for God's sake!" He held John at arm's length, gave his face a quick evaluation, and chuckled. "I doubt if you have ten gray hairs, total!"

They stood gazing at each other. John couldn't get over how his friend had aged. But when he thought of what Buster had been through, he realized what a miracle it was that the man could not only stand on his own, but walk, hold down a job, and maintain a normal lifestyle.

"You're not looking *too* bad, Buster," he said jokingly, yet feeling a strange sadness. It seemed as if a lifetime had passed by very quickly, changing everything he had ever known.

Buster swatted John on the shoulder. "Always *were* a lying son of a bitch." He gestured to a padded wicker chair next to the rocker. Buster fell rather clumsily into the rocker with a grunt. "But that kind of bullshit makes me feel good, anyway."

John sat in the wicker chair. He noticed the half-empty bottle of Jack's on the metal table, and the two glasses beside it. Buster poured two large drinks and handed a glass to John.

"Still like whiskey?" Buster asked.

"You really need to ask?"

"Just trying to be polite," Buster quipped.

John blinked. "Is that *you* in there, Buster?"

They both laughed.

"To Iraq." Buster held up his glass. "Getting the hell out, that is."

They clinked, then drank.

Buster sat back. "So tell me, my friend. What's been happening to you the last sixteen years? And, for Christ's sake, don't give me that stupid 'nothing much' bullshit."

"Actually, a lot." John told his friend what had happened when he went back to Pittsburgh. As in his letters, he omitted the Walter Reed chapter of his life. He wasn't ready to tell it and, despite the strong drink, as well as the knowledge that there would be more strong drinks to follow, shoved that portion of his past back into its file for later.

And hoped with all his heart that "later" would never present itself.

He told Buster about his first marriage, which ended in divorce after three years, and another attempt, which didn't last long enough for the formal announcement.

"That's odd." Buster sipped some Jack's. "You always had good luck with women. What happened? The desert fuck you up as bad as the rest of us?"

"That more or less sums it up."

A tense expression appeared on Buster's face. John could clearly see it, even in the approaching dusk. "What really happened?" he asked softly, shifting awkwardly in his seat. "Something with that sniper unit you were in?"

John shivered.

It was amazing just how quickly "later" popped up...

"It was the same old shit you hear about," he said casually. *Downplay it.* "You know. Going somewhere you didn't want to go, fighting someone else's war, being in a place you weren't wanted."

"I hear that."

John said nothing; his lips were taut as he raised his glass. A sudden heat began crawling lazily up the back of his neck. His hands began shaking.

The nightmare, although simmering on the back burner for many years, had suddenly switched on full.

It was a nightmare that just wouldn't go away.

"Tell me about your leg," John said, the back of his neck damp. "How much did you lose?"

Buster reached down and placed a palm on his right thigh. "Right above the knee. The whole works. But the Army takes care of its own — remember hearing that somewhere?"

"Once or twice."

"Surprisingly, the Army was really good to me. Don't know if it was guilt or what, but they treat you like royalty when you become one of their walking dead. Made me one super-duper prosthetic leg. Knee joint, rotating ankle—the works." Buster tapped his kneecap with the middle knuckle of his right hand. It made a disgusting dead sound.

"How long were you in the hospital?"

"A year, but most of that was therapy. You know, getting used to the new leg and all. It was a bitch at first, believe me." Buster shook his head. "I honestly don't know how I got through it."

"You had lots of company."

"Actually, what saved my ass from that self-pity trip was that day I was being taken to the whirlpool for some quality time. There was this guy in the hall, in a wheelchair, looking out the window. No legs and just one arm, but the hand was gone, and he had one of those metal hooky things that looked like it was taken from a giant insect in a sci-fi flick. He asked me to light his cigarette for him. He wasn't used to the hook yet, and he needed a smoke."

Buster shook his head. "What amazed me was this guy's attitude. The boy was really chipper because they'd told him his new hand and arm had just come in, and he'd be getting it attached within the week. This one had a real appendage—one that looked like a genuine hand and would be hooked up directly to the nerves. He could soon light his own cigarettes, wash and dress himself—even wipe his own ass. All by himself."

John was silent. The memories had made the heat intensify in his gut. "They really made a mess, didn't they?"

Buster was looking down, shaking his head. "What about the generation before us? The one the Boomers lived through?"

"Vietnam. The good ol' days…"

"Remember all those TV shows about Vietnam vets turning psycho and going berserk, killing women and children? I've seen some of those shows on You Tube and on the Classic TV channel.

23

Seemed like every fucking villain in a seventies TV show was a Vietnam vet psycho."

"I remember." The heat had settled in the small of his back. "But at least we were treated a little better than they were."

"Doesn't make any of it right, though..."

Silence.

Moments later, Buster looked gravely at John. "Tell me what happened to Bill, Johnny."

John cringed. His thoughts raced. His pulse hammered. The heat in his gut had intensified. He reached up and wiped his forehead. A large, hot lump filled his throat; he struggled to force it down.

"B-Bill?" he finally said, terrified that the nightmare had indeed returned.

Buster tilted his head. "Bill Sebastian. How many Bills did we know back then?"

Only one who really mattered, John thought dismally, draining his drink.

***

Erika Larson gingerly applied the cold washcloth to her warm face.

She glanced at her watch. 8:45. Facing the bathroom mirror, she pushed the heavy black mane away from her glistening eyes. She blotted them gently and tried to ignore her temples, which throbbed unmercifully.

They were going to have it out, once and for all. Paul was drunk again. He was slouched in the armchair, barely making it through a rerun of *Baywatch*.

Her head buzzed when she thought how her efforts had been for nothing. Rushing to the supermarket after work. Decorating the dining room table with their good china. Lighting the candles for romantic flavor. Displaying the claret on its wooden stand.

But her husband hadn't been in shape for the claret, nor anything else. He'd come home just ten minutes ago and collapsed in the chair. And hadn't budged since—not even when she'd bent to greet him with a tender kiss.

Paul was still in the chair when she came back, her left hand keeping the washrag firmly against her temple. She glared at the widescreen. "I want to know what's happening to us, Paul."

No reply.

"Are you asleep? Or just spaced out? I said, I want to know—"

"I heard what you said."

She waited tensely.

He sighed, stirring on the pillows. "What the hell's wrong now?"

"You don't remember, do you?" The fact that he didn't even realize what was happening infuriated her even more.

He struggled to sit up, then watched her curiously, blinking a few times, trying to get his bearings. It was obvious he'd zoned out. His eyes glistened in the hazy light of the table lamp. She recognized their familiar gloss. "I remember you bitching again. Getting on my case. For nothing."

"How about for not coming home last night? Or is that something I'm supposed to put up with? Something I really shouldn't notice? Because I'm such an obliging wife?"

"Obliging?" He snorted.

The sound grated through her.

"I told you, Erika. The business. It keeps—"

"It keeps you away at the most inopportune times. Yes. I know. The business. It's got to be fed. It's got to be nourished, or it dies. You've told me. At least a hundred times."

"Then why the third degree?"

"Because you stay away for so long. And when you come home, you don't even talk to me, tell me where you've been. How things are going. We don't talk, don't laugh like we used to. Don't kiss, make love—"

"That again?"

She glared. "You find me repulsive? Is that what you're trying to say?"

"Now why would you think something like that?"

"When I mention making love, you look like you want to throw up."

"Not true."

"That's how it looked. To me..."

"Your imagination."

Erika shrugged. "Let's make love, then."

"I thought you wanted to read me the riot act."

"If you don't like the idea of making love to me, being intimate—"

"In other words, you want to tear me apart just because I won't fuck you right now?" His expression was half-anger, half-humor.

"When you say it like *that*—"

"It's how you meant it, isn't it?"

Erika began pacing. This wasn't going well at all. He was half-looped, yet he was winning the argument.

"Not at all," she said finally.

"How, then?"

"We're strangers living in the same house. You're away all day, sometimes all week. When you come home, you eat dinner, watch TV, then retreat to your den. I put in a few hours at the bank to keep myself busy and work my flower garden on weekends, just to have something to do because you're always so busy. You're in your den almost all the time, doing your books, making calls." She shivered. "I'm sick and tired of it."

"And?"

"You don't want me anymore."

"I never said I didn't want you."

"Then say you want me."

"An ultimatum?"

"If you want to call it that."

"It's stupid, Erika."

"So is what our marriage has become."

He didn't reply.

"Is all this because of the miscarriages?" she asked, desperate for answers.

He looked away. "I never blamed you for that."

"Why not? I was the one who miscarried..."

"Women miscarry all the time. My own mother miscarried between me and my sister. It's no big deal."

"Then why haven't we had sex in six months?"

"It hasn't been that long, and you know it."

"You're right. It's been longer."

"You're full of shit."

"When was the last time, Paul?"

"Now you're being ridiculous." He got up stiffly and moved awkwardly to the bar counter, where the cognac stood proudly. He poured an inch in a glass, then turned to where she was standing. "You're gonna bust my balls if I can't remember the last time we fucked?"

"A tender way of putting it, but yes, that's what I intend to do."

He shook his head. "You've changed, Erika. You've gone from being a foxy squeeze to a nagging bitch."

"More tender words. Thank you."

"What the hell do you expect?"

"A little understanding. A little warmth."

He didn't reply.

"Miscarrying is bad enough. Losing your husband because of it makes it even worse."

He finished his cognac and put the glass down. "As I just said, I never blamed you for that."

"But the fact remains, Paul. Our sex life up and died." She clicked her fingers. "Like that."

"You're imagining things. Putting them out of proportion."

"I don't think so."

"All married couples go through dry periods in their sex life."

Erika was silent; his statement didn't rate a reply.

He sat heavily on a barstool. There was a slack, disinterested look on his face.

She knew by that single look that everything they ever shared was gone. There was a time when she could see the love in his eyes the instant he looked at her. It had been a tiny sparkle—something special she saw when those baby blues flashed her way. But now, as she watched him, she realized that the sparkle was gone. And as she thought more about it, she realized that it had been gone for some time.

"Let's go to bed, Paul. Let's make love."

He shook his head.

"Why not?"

He shrugged. "The moment isn't right. We're having an argument about the stupidest things—"

"Our sex life is *stupid*?"

"You're putting words in my mouth."

"Then put them there yourself and save me the trouble."

"What's stupid is the fact that you're basing everything on sex. I'm tired, I've had a rough day, and I need to relax. But because I don't want to jump your bones right this minute, our relationship is dead. Nothing works anymore. I'm never here. And when I am, we're not messing up the sheets the way we used to. All of this seems to be because I'm just not in the mood."

"And because you're a cokehead." She tried not to cry as she watched him. He was sniffing again: wiping his wet, bloodshot eyes.

He got up from the stool. "As I've already told you, I do a line to unwind. It's acceptable. It's good business. If I refuse the hospitality of these people, I'm as good as dead."

"You've decided to let them dictate what you do with your body?"

"I had one fucking line!"

"Maybe on your way home. How much did you snort at the office?"

"Dammit!"

"The fact is, Paul, you're doing things that are affecting our relationship and our marriage. And now you're standing there, denying everything. I don't know if it's because you honestly don't remember or because you're playing dumb. This way, I'll eventually get sick of everything and leave."

"That's the most ridiculous thing I've ever -- "

Paul's cell phone buzzed.

A tense expression appeared on his face. He turned and clumsily reached for it, but Erika had snatched it up before his fingertips came close.

"Hello."

A pause.

A low-pitched female voice. "Uh…hello. Mrs. Larson?"

"Yes?"

Another pause.

"This is…Stacy Hutchinson. Mr. Larson's assist—"

"I know who you are. What do you want?"

Another pause.

"I'd like…that is, could I talk with your husband? This is about work—"

"Of course it is." She dropped the cell noisily on the tiled counter and moved away. "It's for you." She didn't even turn to face him. "Your *assistant*." She blotted her overheated face with the rag, which was no longer cold. "And it's about work, of course."

Paul scooped up the phone and turned. His back was hunched, his voice low. In just seconds she heard him chuckling softly.

She watched him for the next few minutes. He was bent over the counter, talking and laughing with some other woman named Stacy, who had a low voice. She knew full well that he was having an affair with her.

Stacy Hutchinson. She could visualize the woman. Tall. Long-legged. Blond. Blue-eyed. Well-dressed, well-educated, well-informed. Probably worked up a storm in the office as well as the bedroom. No doubt could speak more than one language. And, going by how she sounded, could talk her way out of anything.

But could this talented, ambitious bitch explain how one of her golden strays had worked its way into a tangle around a button of Paul's navy-blue sports jacket?

Could she justify the one Erika had found snagged in his zipper?

"Get off the phone, Paul."

It was that last thought that did it. She'd had enough.

"I'm *talking*." He turned back to the phone and whispered something, chuckling as he said it.

Erika walked over, reached out, and calmly snatched it out of his hand. Then she dropped it on the counter and walked away.

Paul spun around. His face wide-eyed and flushed, he groped for it. But it was too late; the deadness of the line echoed loudly in his ear.

He slammed it down on the counter. "Why did you do that?"

"Because I don't want to stand around while you yuck it up in my home with some bitch you've been nailing on the sly."

"She's my *assistant*, goddammit! What right have you got, interfering—"

"And this is my *home*. I can tell by how you two were talking that you've been intimate with one another."

"Really?" He stopped about two feet from her and stood stiffly, his dark, smoldering look making her tremble. Paul had never been physical with her in their years together, but right now he didn't exactly look like himself. Right now, he resembled a wounded animal more than ready to defend itself. "And how the hell could you possibly know that when you couldn't even hear what I was saying?"

"Did you ever stop and think that lowering your voice might suggest something to me? Or don't you care?"

"It was *business*, Erika!"

"Sounded pretty light to me."

He didn't reply.

"Let me ask you a question."

He stood there, glaring.

"Is Stacy a blond?"

A flicker of surprise showed in his eyelids. "What the hell does *that* have to do with anything?"

"Just the other day, I found a long, curly hair twisted around one of the buttons of your blue sportscoat. A blond hair, Paul. And, as you can see" — she reached up and nudged her black mane over her shoulder — "it certainly wasn't one of these."

He didn't reply. He simply turned and reached for the cognac bottle.

"I found a similar one caught in the zipper of your pants."

This time, he stiffened as though he'd just been shot.

"You're having an affair with her, aren't you?"

No response.

"Aren't you?"

After long moments, he gave a slight nod.

Erika felt her heart skip a beat. "Why didn't you tell me before?"

He sipped some cognac. When he spoke, his voice was unsteady. "It's not something you discuss…with your wife."

33

"It eventually comes out. Then it *has* to be discussed."

He was silent.

"How long has it been going on, Paul?"

He didn't reply.

"How long?"

He frowned. "Does it matter?"

"Yes."

"Why?"

"Because we've been having problems for a long time, now. I'd like to know if it's because of me, or because of Stacy."

"I really don't think—"

"I've been blaming myself for all this, Paul." The throbbing in her head increased. "The fact that I miscarried. I'd let you down. You've always wanted kids, and when I miscarried, I could tell how disappointed you were. I'd *never* wanted to disappoint you. But now I want to know if our marriage is over because of that or because you've been doing the horizontal mambo with your *assistant…*"

"Maybe it *was* because you miscarried that I turned to someone else." It was Paul's turn. A strange calm now enveloped him. He seemed somewhat relieved everything was out in the open. He no longer resembled a wounded animal. "Maybe because I knew there would never be a family with you. With Stacy, there would be a family. She's young—"

"I don't want to *hear* about her!" Erika turned sharply away and forced herself to stop shaking.

34

Paul laughed. Her outburst had clearly established him the victor.

"*You're* the one who wanted to know. Now I'm gonna tell you. Whether you like it or not. Stacy's twenty-six, tall and slender, with long blond hair and a smile that drives men wild—"

"Don't do this to me, Paul Larson..." Head down, Erika moved stiffly toward the front door.

Paul followed her. She didn't want to look at him, didn't want to see his face frozen in some sort of obscene smile shimmering in the living room lighting, "She's got a college degree, knows software like the back of her hand, can go all night, and gives the best—"

Erika spun around. Her head exploded in a mist of red. For one blistering instant she couldn't see and didn't even realize that her arm had come up and sliced brutally toward his face.

The slap caught him viciously across the cheek.

He bent, nearly losing his balance. Then he reached out, grabbed the arm of the sofa, and stood hunched over, his free hand gingerly covering his stinging cheek.

Erika stayed a safe distance away, teeth clenched, hands balled into fists. Her heart was pounding so wildly, she could hear it thundering in her ears.

She hadn't meant to hit him, but his statement hurt too much, and she hadn't wanted to hear what would follow. But as she watched him cradling his face, she knew that she'd heard the worst. Nothing else would have done more damage.

She knew in that single moment that it was over. And now that she knew the whole story, she was relieved she wouldn't have to live with the guilt of being the one who had ended the marriage. Paul had gone to Stacy because he'd blamed Erika for the miscarriages and wanted someone fresh to start over with.

"You...didn't have to do that." His voice was a soft moan.

" I think I did. I had every right to."

"*Damn* you..." He turned to her. She flinched at the sight of his red cheek and the two slim trails of blood her nails had made on his cheekbone. "You ask me about my girlfriend, then try to kill me when I tell you about her."

"You didn't have to give me the juicy details."

"I want you out of here!"

"This is half my house, remember?"

"I want your ass the hell out of here!"

"Get your lawyer and I'll get mine." For some reason, she found that, like him, she had grown quite calm. Apparently the slap had taken much of the sting that had been ripping through her. "I'll bet I can find someone who's seen you and this Stacy together. Then we'll see who gets the house."

He lunged at her, but Erika twisted out of the way. Paul, full of coke, cognac, pain, and rage, moved sluggishly. His foot caught the polished wooden leg of the coffee table, and he fell on his face with a loud grunt.

And lay still.

Erika grabbed her bag from the coat tree, pulled open the front door, and slipped out into the muggy September night.

**

"What happened to Bill Sebastian, Johnny?"

John and Buster sat at the kitchen table, sharing a fresh bottle of whiskey.

John was feeling cold and uncomfortably tense. The memories had returned, making him shiver in the heat of the evening. As he thought of what happened so long ago, he knew that nothing he said could justify that horrible, blood-filled afternoon that had been plaguing him the last sixteen years.

He'd known all along that he'd have to bring it all back one day. But no matter how hard he tried convincing himself, he knew he wasn't prepared. The word "later" had always come up, forcing him to push the ugly truth into the background, making him believe it might be easier to understand after a bit more thought.

But now that he was faced with it, he knew he would never be able to ignore what happened.

"Bill's dead," he finally said in a whisper.

"I was afraid of that. I'd sent him a letter, but it wasn't answered. When did he die?"

"Just a few months after they sent you back home."

"I figured something like that had happened." Buster sipped the whiskey reflectively. He wasn't looking at John when he said, "The insurgents?"

It took John a while to answer. The chill was moving around again, this time settling around his

37

neck. He unbuttoned the third button of his shirt but still had trouble breathing. "Yeah."

"How'd he buy it?"

"They…caught him."

At least that much was the truth. But it didn't make him feel any better. Nor did it numb the heavy throbbing in his gut.

John finished his drink, then poured more into his glass. The anger was coming back, but he caught it and forced it back to where he'd been keeping it locked up all these years.

Buster shook his head. Then he laughed. "The times we used to have. Sebastian was from Cincinnati. But you knew that."

"Yeah." John was gazing at his glass, struggling for some sort of panacea that would get him through this. Despite his efforts, the anger was right there, fighting to stay alive. He knew it would gain a stranglehold if he didn't do something soon.

"He'd gone to Ohio University and almost had his degree when he decided to go on in. I think I remember him saying he'd majored in ─ "

"Engineering," John said quickly, wiping his brow. He wanted to empty his drink, then finish the bottle, but knew that would be stupid. He'd tried many times to forget the past with booze, but it never worked. Booze didn't make you forget. It only set things aside, making you sick as a dog later on, when you sobered up and started feeling again.

"That's right. Both of us had been in the same boat. I was all set to go to grad school, and he was right behind me. I think he had about three credits to go—"

"You never told me what you've been doing." John finished his drink. *Change the subject. Now. Before you explode. Get him focused on other stuff. Try and make him forget about Bill. About Iraq. About what happened after Buster was blown up and sent back home.* "When we were corresponding, you mentioned the Post Office, but we lost touch not too long after that."

"I applied when I got out. As soon as I started getting around on my own. Took the test, got five extra points for being a vet, five more for being disabled, a couple more for spelling my name right, and ended up with the highest score in the class." He laughed. "But when I first started, those assholes gave me a bunch of shit about my bum leg."

"They didn't like you not having two healthy legs?"

"At the time, there was a severe shortage of carriers. You can imagine their predicament when I was brought in. But I told them I could handle anything they could give me in the mailroom. And anyway, I'd lost my leg in the name of democracy, so they could kiss my ass if they didn't like it." Buster shrugged. "I've been there ever since."

John didn't reply. He was thinking of Bill Sebastian and how their friend had spent the last agonizing moments of his life.

***

Erika parked in front of the Holiday Inn and sat in her car for nearly ten minutes, trying desperately to calm down.

She thought of her fight with Paul and suddenly realized that her hands had squeezed into tight fists.

How *dare* that man cheat on her and then have the brass balls to throw her out of her own house!

How *dare* he blame her for their marriage falling apart!

She blistered at the thought of the roast simmering quietly in its crockpot. The beautifully arranged dinner table. The candles, now dripping red wax onto the white cotton spread her grandmother had painstakingly fashioned thirty years ago, when the fragile old woman was still able to use her talented hands.

Erika fought down the overwhelming urge to cry. She didn't *want* to, but there didn't seem to be any logical reason why she shouldn't. Her marriage of seven years had run its course and she wasn't quite ready to accept it.

She remembered the coldness in Paul's eyes, in his words. The hatred and the hurt that had consumed her when he told her about Stacy.

When it had finally come out in the open, everything seemed so bleak. Her life. Her future. The last seven years. The house itself.

She just couldn't accept how the two of them had managed to turn their love into such an intense loathing.

It made her wonder if there ever had been an attraction.

The heat finally subsiding, Erika pushed open the door of the Toyota. Craving a strong drink, a dark place, and some solitude, she rushed across the front lot and slipped through the heavy glass door.

***

The Murphy twins stopped at a 7-Eleven near Cambridge, Ohio, and bought some peppered beef jerky to nibble on until they reached Bern.

Ron was still grinning about the Indian in Zanesville. He loved threatening people—especially foreigners—and was particularly fond of doing it in a subtle way. It made him feel superior—something he knew already, but also something he liked doing as a method of keeping the feeling fresh. It was just like doing pump sets once or twice a week to keep the muscles flushed and looking good for the babes.

Six spaces down, a skinny redhead was getting out of a green convertible with two pudgy jocks wearing football jerseys. Ron watched closely as she bent over at the far island. Her tight shorts were frayed at the ends, barely reaching mid-thigh. Her loose white crop top was opened at the waist as she bent, giving him a nice shot of smooth, tanned skin.

Ron caught Rich beginning to drool and knew there could be trouble if he didn't keep his brother in check.

"Forget it. No time for it."

"It's been so *long*..."

"The job, remember?"

Rich tore his gaze from the redhead. "I know."

"Even more witnesses here than Zanesville."

41

Through the front window, they could see five people lined up inside the store.

"Five K apiece." Ron knew how to get his brother's head on straight. "For one night's work."

"Yeah."

"We'll find a coupla pros in Pittsburgh when we're finished in Bern."

"We'll have enough jack to buy more than two."

"Damn straight." Ron started up the pickup.

***

At ten o'clock, John sat on the bed in the spare room and studied the collage of paintings in the center of the beige plaster wall.

"I collect them," Buster had explained earlier. "Been doing that most of my life. They remind me of the country, where I grew up. Guess I was happier as a kid. A shrink might say something about a damned insecurity complex."

John had noticed a few others scattered throughout the house. Two in the living room, one rather large one in the dining room, and half a dozen others on the wall leading to the kitchen.

John wondered if Buster's collection had helped him through his ordeal. John clearly experienced an instant calm when observing the paintings. And now, as he studied the grouping of five, he supposed that the scenes offered Buster a tranquility that couldn't be experienced from any other means.

The scene in the middle of the grouping was of a small boy and girl pulling a sled up a snow-covered hill. Tied to the sled was a Christmas tree. Beside the sled, a small black dog kept up with the

42

boy and girl. Footprints and paw prints marked the snow behind them, extending to the bottom of the picture. A snow-covered tree stood proudly to their left, a pine forest directly ahead. Smoke coming from the chimney of a distant house on the other side of the hill complemented the picture.

John began relaxing. The painting had obviously done something to kill the restlessness that had built up within him. But despite the comforting warmth, he felt more edgy than he'd been in a long time and had the urge to go out for a quiet drink. Buster had whiskey in the kitchen, but he didn't want to awaken his friend.

John slipped out of the room, crept down the hall, tiptoed down the stairs, and left the house.

***

Erika was enjoying a quiet drink when a man approached her from the bar.

"Want some company?" The glossy-eyed, executive type grinned stupidly. "You look like you've had a rough –"

"No, thanks." Forcing a polite smile, she mentally cursed him for the intrusion and hoped he'd just walk back to the bar and leave her alone.

He continued grinning as though he hadn't heard her. "Like I said, you look like you've been having a rough time, and I thought — "

"What part of 'no, thanks,' don't you understand?" She sent him a glare that would turn off even the horniest stud bull.

He stopped grinning and stood there, swaying. Erika could tell he was just one or two drinks shy of

43

falling flat on his face. He was probably thinking of something clever to say that would help him save face among his drunken friends sitting at the bar.

"I need to be alone." Erika forced an indifferent smile. "Thanks anyway."

The man mumbled something that sounded angry, then turned stiffly and staggered away.

Erika returned to her drink and began wondering, once again, what she was going to do. She hoped Paul had gone to wherever the new love of his life was, to console himself in the warmth of her perky young breasts. Or maybe he'd polished off the rest of the cognac before heading off to bed. Whatever happened, she knew she should not get too drunk. She'd end up killing herself on her way home and Paul would be off the hook.

She decided to have one more drink before driving home. If Paul were home, she'd simply avoid him. She could sleep in the spare room, then pack the next morning and find a place to stay while they worked out a settlement. If he had left, she'd have a much less stressful night and could take it easy the next morning while she made her plans.

She told herself she wouldn't do anything spiteful or vicious. Paul had been cheating on her, but that didn't mean she should do the same to him. Spite just wasn't in her, and she wasn't about to start anything new in this aspect of her life—especially something she'd eventually be sorry for. She was thirty-four years old. She knew she could probably start afresh, if given the time to heal.

Erika signaled for another drink.

***

John entered the air-conditioned bar, climbed a stool, and ordered a double Jack's on ice.

He surveyed the large, dark room. There were about half a dozen men at the bar, and one woman dressed like a hooker at the far end. Three couples lounged at tables. Two moved rather sluggishly on the dance floor, keeping time to the soft throbbing of the juke.

A woman sat by herself on the other side of the room. All he could see was a slim figure and thick dark hair covering her shoulders. She didn't appear to be a pickup; she was gazing at the glass in front of her, suggesting she obviously wanted to be alone.

The bartender brought his drink.

John planted his elbows firmly on the shiny surface of the counter, picked up the glass, and thought about Bill Sebastian.

And wondered once again how he could possibly tell Buster what happened.

***

The Murphy twins reached Bern at a few minutes after eleven.

They parked the truck on Main, in front of the hardware store, and sat quietly, watching the Sunday night traffic.

"Isn't there a bar back there?" asked Rich, jerking a thumb to his right. "Down from the corner?"

"You thirsty again?" asked his brother. "We just polished off that Pepsi –"

"I could go for a shot of Jim Beam right now."

Ron squeezed his sandy brows together. "Think we oughta cool it for tonight. When the job's done, we could — "

"One won't hurt," said Rich. "Help me relax."

"Don't need to relax. Not tonight." Ron was watching his brother closely, knowing he'd have to appease him, or Rich would lose it. When Rich was nervous, it took quite a bit of energy to get him settled down.

Good thing he's got me around to keep his head on straight.

"I guess one drink won't hurt," Ron said finally.

His brother grinned.

"Just one, now. Get it? Only one…"

"All I need, Ronnie."

They got out of the truck.

***

John had nearly finished his drink when the guy next to him began telling his companions what he planned to do with the brunette sitting by herself.

"Bitch looks like she's stuck up as hell," he said, slurring his words. "I know she wants it, and I'm gonna give it to her." He chuckled. "She just doesn't know it yet."

The guy beside him snickered. "Don't think she's your type, Freddie-boy. That hooker over there? She's more like it. Why don't we go on over, offer her more than those good-ol' boys she's sittin' with?"

Freddie-boy shook his head half a dozen times. "Nope. Want that black-haired chick. She's got a nice set, and I know what she wants."

46

Scowling, John finished his drink. Suddenly needing some fresh air, he got up and made his way for the doors leading to the parking lot out front.

***

Erika left the Holiday Inn and was walking to her car when she heard the crunch of gravel close behind her.

She turned, saw the glossy-eyed jerk, and cringed.

"Hi again," he said, sending over that same stupid glossy-eyed grin. "Ain't this a coincidence, us leaving the same time?"

"Almost like it was planned," she said with a frown. "Listen. In case I didn't make myself clear before -- "

"You did, baby. Damned clear, in fact. But you know what? I just can't understand why a broad comes to a place like this and doesn't wanna do what we all know she *really* wants to do-- "

"What do you mean by *that*?" she asked, feeling flushed.

"I mean, this *is* a pickup place, and when a broad like you -- "

"That's twice you've called me that, and I'd appreciate it if you didn't go for strike three. For your information, I came in for a drink and some peace and quiet. But since it's none of your damned business, I sincerely hope you'll just leave me alone and be on your way before -- "

He chuckled. "I like that, baby. Sincerely hope. That's good. That's *real* good."

47

Erika realized right then that further conversation would be pointless. He was too drunk to understand what she was saying and too obstinate to accept the fact that she wasn't interested.

She turned away, but he grabbed her by the elbow and spun her around.

"Leave me be!" She pulled loose and stepped backwards, nearly tripping on the sidewalk. "Can't you understand that I don't want to have anything to do with you?"

He obviously wasn't concerned about her explanation and groped awkwardly for her. Erika wrenched free, pushing his hand out of the way.

Growling, he lunged at her.

Erika sidestepped. The drunk managed to grasp her belt with a pinkie. He pulled, and she nearly lost her balance again. She twisted away and opened her mouth to yell for help.

Then she saw someone quickly approaching.

The man who'd come in just a few minutes ago and sat at the bar. There was a hard look in his eyes as he moved toward them.

"You've had enough to drink, fella."

"This is pr-private," the drunk stammered.

The man turned to Erika. "He bothering you?"

Erika didn't want a fight -- especially for her sake. All she wanted was to get in her car and drive home. "It's…all right." She hoped the drunk would not take her kindness to mean something else.

The man turned to the drunk. Erika could hear the tightness in his voice when he said, "You got a ride home?"

The drunk looked indignant. He stood up straight and nodded frantically, stopping when he looked like he might puke. "I'm...okay-y-y," he mumbled, and turned to the glass entrance.

"Are you all right?" the man asked her.

"Uh...yes." Erika glanced at the drunk, who staggered across the parking lot, nearly tripped on the curb, then struggled to manipulate the glass door. He managed to inch it open but had a difficult time squeezing through the slim opening. The situation was almost funny.

When she turned back to the other man, she noticed that his expression had changed. Before, his face had been a hard mask. But now, as he looked at her, he seemed very gentle. And no matter how hard he had come across earlier, Erika felt perfectly safe.

"I'm f-fine." She suddenly felt foolish, although she couldn't imagine why. "Thank you for helping me."

"No problem. Where's your car?"

She pointed to her right. "Over there." For a moment she feared this man could be the drunk's partner. He *had* been sitting at the bar, hadn't he? Had this little charade been staged? Hadn't she seen something like it in a movie? But the more she thought about it, the more she realized how foolish her notion was.

"Would you like me to walk you to your car?"

She smiled. "No, thanks. I'm okay now. I think he learned his lesson."

"Well, good night." He turned and made his way briskly for a shiny Lincoln Town Car parked halfway down the aisle.

"Good night," she replied, watching him. "And thanks again."

Halfway to his car, he turned and smiled. She smiled in return, thought of Paul, and went right back to feeling foolish.

Suddenly the prospect of returning home seemed more dismal than her confrontation with the drunk.

***

John experienced a strange feeling of elation as he got on the Interstate.

He caught himself wondering if the brunette had been wearing a wedding ring. He tried hard to remember but realized he hadn't noticed. It was dark, there were other things on his mind, and she hadn't been standing still long enough for him to observe such details.

Even so, he couldn't help feeling good about himself for what he'd done with the drunk—or for what he *hadn't* done.

During the confrontation, he'd gone inside his own mind and realized that he had subconsciously gone back in time. And in doing so, he found himself gazing at the forbidden desert, where Bill Sebastian had died so violently.

John had become twenty years old once again, full of piss and vinegar. The moment he had heard the woman's startled voice crying out, everything had come right back. And when he'd spun around at the frantic sound, instead of gazing upon dark-eyed insurgents hiding behind seared husks of jeeps and smoking piles of kindling, what he'd seen was a drunk in a suit, manhandling a woman.

His teeth clenched tightly, John gripped the padded wheel of the Town Car and tried hard to concentrate on his driving.

It had been a decade and a half, but for some strange reason, he realized that only now was he finally able to say it. To admit what had happened without wanting to scream or slit his wrists.

I killed Bill Sebastian.

He sighed, then took several deep breaths as he struggled to keep from veering off the road. It didn't make him feel any better, but at least the queasiness subsided.

It was me.

And all the years and memories in between can't change it.

He could finally admit it.

But how in God's name could he possibly tell Buster?

***

The Murphy twins leaned against the counter amongst the throngs at the crowded bar, sipping Jim Beam and watching the drunken locals.

It was a loud, booming place. Laughing, glossy-eyed folks crammed the dance floor. A trio of sloppily dressed country boys in huge cowboy hats and bib overalls mimicked Hank Williams, Jr., while the two overworked waitresses squeezed through the crowds, their tight jeans and tank tops damp with sweat.

"So this is Bern's waterin' hole!" Rich yelled, lowering his glass from his face.

"From what I understand," Ron shouted over the thundering roar, "it's the only place in town!"

"Have a look at those hookers over there. Seen better heads on rotten lettuce!"

"That's why we ain't gonna stay here any longer than we got to." Ron glanced at the clock on the wall above the smudged mirror. "Once the job's finished, we're outa here!"

"Uh-oh." Rich scowled as a brightly dressed hooker suddenly appeared from the crowd. "We been scoped, Ronnie."

The heavily made-up woman sashayed in their direction. She looked forty-plus and had obviously seen much better days. Her blazing outfit would have looked better on someone twenty years younger and ten pounds slimmer. It wasn't exactly her color, either. The bright yellow didn't go with her hazel eyes, and the platinum blond wig didn't match her skin texture. Her strong cinnamon perfume scent had been splashed everywhere.

Ron's sinuses began to drain.

"You boys ain't from around here, are ya?" She smiled, moving between them and resting her bare lower back against the padded edge of the bar. "How 'bout a double whammy for half price?"

Ron blew his nose with a napkin. "Sorry, lady, we got things to do."

"But you only just got here. I been watchin' the two of ya. Brothers, ain'tcha?"

The twins looked at each other and shook their heads.

Not only is she ugly, Ron thought, *she's also not exactly a rocket scientist.*

"No," Rich said, watching his brother. "We're twins."

"Really?" She didn't catch the sarcastic remark. "Ain't never knocked boots with twins before. Bet it'd be a real trip! Like I said, how 'bout a double whammy? Half price? I'll make you boys feel *really* good!"

"Thanks again, lady." Ron was determined to be polite. He didn't want anyone remembering them. "Like we said, we gotta go. We got business – – "

"What kinda business?" She watched them as she lit a cigarette.

"Odds 'n ends." Rich nervously tugged his right earlobe. "We usually hire ourselves out – "

"What he means is," Ron said, sending his brother a dark look, "we do errands for big businesses that need guys like us, who like to travel."

The hooker puffed away on her cigarette. She seemed interested. "So whatcha got cookin' here in Bern?"

The twins frowned at one another.

Ron took another stab at being vague. "We're doin' somethin for this company in Wheeling — "

"Wheeling?" She perked up. "I'm from Wheeling. Which company you boys workin' for?"

Once again, Ron glanced at his brother. It was obvious Rich was thinking the same thing. There was no easy way to get rid of this nosy, unpleasant woman.

"Know somethin', lady?" Ron grinned. "I think we'd like to take you up on your offer." He winked at Rich. "Yeah. I think we could use a double whammy, right about now."

The woman cackled. "Was wonderin' how long it would take!"

***

Buster, in his flannel bathrobe, was sitting at the kitchen table, his hands wrapped around a glass, when John got back.

"Did I wake you?" John asked. "I tried to be quiet —"

"Siddown, Johnny." Buster's face resembled a closed fist.

John pulled out a chair and sat.

"Like a drink?"

"Just had one, thanks."

Buster gazed at the glass before he spoke. Then, without raising his eyes, he said, "Couldn't sleep?"

"I guess I needed some fresh air."

Buster raised the glass and sipped. When he lowered the glass, he said, "Tell me why you couldn't sleep."

"I usually don't in a strange house —"

"The truth." Buster's voice had an edge to it.

John began to sweat.

Buster watched him closely. The jagged vertical line between his brows looked like it had been carved with a dull knife.

"Remember how close we were? You, me, and Bill? And even though it's been sixteen years, it's all back. A sort of ESP. I felt it the moment I saw you again." Buster looked grim. "There's no use trying to lie to me anymore. You've been lying all evening, and I want it stopped."

John felt a heavy weight growing in his gut. "Whaddya mean?"

Buster laughed, but his laugh sounded more like a grunt of pain. "The fact that you've been changing the subject since we started reminiscing. Not talking about Bill. Being vague. Asking me about myself the moment we started talking about Bill. Not to mention the little slip-ups I caught when you were answering my questions."

"Slip-ups?" John could barely get the word out.

"For instance, when did you get out, Johnny?"

"Iraq? Or the Army?"

"Let's try Iraq first."

"May, two thousand six."

"We went over there nine months before that, didn't we?"

John made no comment.

"Why'd it end so soon?"

John swallowed; the heaviness in his gut grew. "Whaddya mean?"

"Why'd they let you out? You never mentioned getting wounded."

John was silent; the throbbing in his head grew louder.

"Why only nine months?"

John looked down at his lap. The moment had arrived; he could no longer look at his friend.

"Why, Johnny?"

"Because of what happened…in April."

Buster finished his drink. His unblinking eyes stayed on his friend. "What happened in April?"

John reached up and wiped his gleaming forehead. "April was when Bill…when Bill was killed."

"All right. Bill died in April. What did this have to do with your getting sent home so soon?"

"I…wasn't sent home."

"Where'd they send you?"

The room had grown hotter. John tugged at his collar and took a deep breath. "Walter Reed."

Buster's jaw dropped. The look on his face was one of utter shock. "What the hell for?"

John sighed deeply and began massaging his temples. "I was…I'd gone, well, crazy."

A tense silence.

Buster watched his friend, waiting for more of an explanation.

Head down, John sat in silence, elbows on the table as he massaged his temples.

"Tell me what happened, Johnny."

John stopped shaking. He lowered his hands, raised his head, and looked Buster in the eye. A cold, numbing sensation had enveloped him. "I was the one…the one who…who did it."

"Did what?"

John swallowed and looked down.

"Did what, Johnny?"

"I...I killed...I killed Bill Sebastian."

***

Paul wasn't home.

Erika checked the garage window and saw that the Caddie was gone. But she had no idea where he'd gone. And, as she stood in the kitchen doorway, shaking and feeling lost, she told herself that she should do whatever had to be done.

The crockpot was just as she'd left it. She turned off the burner and moved the pot. She'd put it in the fridge later, after it had cooled.

The dining room was also undisturbed. The candles, her good China, and her grandmother's hand-sewn spread all remained unattended. Erika felt a brief pang of regret as she stared at everything, imagining what might have been.

Water over the bridge.

She forced her mind on other things.

Think ahead—of what needs to be done.

She turned on the hall light. Her heart was thumping nervously as she trudged up the stairs.

She quickly discovered strong evidence that Paul had packed. The top drawer of his dresser verified this. Several pairs of underwear and socks were missing. The closet revealed a gaping hole about two feet wide where his suits hung.

Also, his tan leather suitcase was gone.

He probably went to stay with the heavenly Stacy while he schemed with his attorney to get the house.

She began shaking again and forced herself not to cry.

The more she thought of it, the more she realized how vacant the house felt. It was as if it had been unoccupied for quite a while. She knew it was just her overwrought imagination, but she couldn't help thinking this way.

Maybe because it had been so long since two people who actually cared for one another had lived here...

She went back downstairs and collapsed on the loveseat. She wanted another drink. Since she still felt a slight buzz from the Manhattans, she knew she didn't need another. But when she thought of the status quo, she realized that two drinks might not be quite enough.

The overwhelming urge to cry returned quickly.

An instant later, she told herself she would not dive into that well of self-pity so many others had succumbed to before drinking to unconsciousness.

There was just no need.

She didn't want to wake up feeling like shit, all because of Paul. She was made of much better stuff.

Instead, she decided to relax on the loveseat and evaluate, think of what needed to be done.

That was the right thing to do. She would relax, apply her brain.

Maybe then she'd be able to figure out something.

And if she wanted a small glass of port later on, she'd have one.

That seemed sensible, didn't it?

***

The Murphy twins sat in the truck, contemplating the dead hooker lying on the floor in the back.

"We need to bury her," Ron said. "She's local. Someone'll miss her."

Rich took a swig from the Pepsi bottle. He let out a tired sigh. "Why the fuck did this bitch have to bug us, anyway?"

Ron shrugged. "You know hookers. Gotta give a guy grief. Even if we'd told her what we were gonna do, she woulda done the same damn thing."

Rich glanced at the dead woman and frowned.

She lay on the floor, wrists taped behind her back, ankles taped together. The plastic bag they'd pulled over her head and taped tightly around her neck was still in place. Inside the plastic, the hooker's taped mouth was visible, glinting in the haze of the streetlamp across the street. Her heavy makeup was splotched and streaked, creating a grotesque pattern on her blue skin.

"There's a crick about two hundred yards off the road." Ron pointed. "Saw it when we came out here before. I don't think you'd seen it; you were checkin' out that dirt path on the other side of State Road Twenty-Seven."

"Wanna toss her in the crick?"

"Yeah. It's low down there, and I didn't see any signs of life. We'll just stick her in the mud, then stand on her to push her down. She'll stay down, and we won't have to worry about some asshole diggin' her up. Doesn't look like there's fishin' down there, or a good spot for kids to be fuckin' around."

"What's gonna happen when the ol' man finds out about this?"

Ron shot him a look. "*You* gonna tell him?"

Rich shrugged. "Hell, *I* won't. But he's bound to hear about it — "

"How's he gonna find out if we don't tell him?"

"Guess I'm just nervous."

"Don't be." Ron hated it when his brother got the shakes.

Rich said nothing.

Ron grabbed a flashlight from the glove box. He pulled the stainless Smith & Wesson .357 Magnum from underneath the seat, stuck it in his waistband, and checked the deserted highway. "C'mon," he said, opening the driver's door.

Rich opened his own door, jumped down, opened the back door, and began pulling the dead woman out by her ankles.

***

"There had been an escalation earlier that year." John sipped his drink and avoided the unsettling stare of his friend. "The snipers were called in and told there were bounties on all of us, and that the biggest bounties were on Bill and myself."

"Why?" Buster asked.

"The insurgents knew about our hits and took up a collection. I'd pegged one of their best IED planters at slightly more than a thousand yards. He was crawling under one of our IFVs and rigging it, and when he was finished, he got back up and provided the perfect target. It was a head shot at high wind.

"This bastard had led a group that overran one of our key sniper positions, which killed four Marines out of a team of six and then videotaped the bodies, which were stripped and covered with anti-American graffiti, then distributed all over the Internet and Al Jazeera. These people were rigging just about everything—broken down jeeps, IFVs, CFVs, armored cars, mortal carriers, animal carcasses, dead American GIs—and a lot of people were being killed in the process, including Iraqi kids and women.

"Just before I made my big hit, an eight-man Marine sniper element was blasted by a remote-control bomb, killing two and disabling the rest of the team. At basically the same time, that Haditha massacre made world news, and everyone walked on eggshells for a while. Except the insurgents, of course. Right after the massacre, two Marine sniper teams just a few miles from Haditha were ambushed and killed, and video footage was once again provided and distributed to Al Jazeera TV."

"I'd heard about that massacre from TV," Buster said. "It was really bad."

"Third Infantry Division was losing a lot of men. Our Shadow Team detachment was sent to Ramadi to stop the IED planters. Every one of us had a special place to hide, and we were eventually able to clear it out and eliminate a good portion of the IEDs as well as the planters."

"Tell me…what about Bill? What happened, Johnny?"

John finished his drink and splashed more in his glass with a shaky hand.

"One morning not long after we'd eliminated the batch of planters, I did a little investigating with another guy in a jeep. We had just been ordered to clear out and meet somewhere else for another thorough cleaning. Everything was escalating again, and we were getting hit really bad."

John suddenly stopped talking. He sat in silence, studying the whiskey in his glass. With one shaky hand, he reached up and unbuttoned another shirt button. His skin gleamed beneath the harsh kitchen lighting.

Desert…

Hot. Muggy. Dry. Steamy.

You began to sweat. You sweated during the day, and you shivered during the night. Dust storms. The weather changed so drastically, half the time you didn't know if your shivering was from the intense heat or the intense cold. Your throat stayed sore. Your sinuses drained constantly. You ate, but lost weight because nothing stayed with you.

You bled through every pore.

The life oozed out of you.

You were afraid that you were dying by the second.

You lay on the ground for hours on end and made no sound.

Because your life depended on it.

Not a grunt. Or groan. Or sigh. Or fart.

You were a living dead man.

And you killed.

No matter what it was, you killed it.

You killed anything that moved.

And if something didn't move, you jabbed it with your bayonet and twisted it around to make sure.

They were dispatched in a remote section not far from where the enemy had constructed a network of sophisticated booby traps. John and the others were deep inside enemy lines and were taken there in the middle of the night and dropped off two miles out. There were six of them left from the Shadow Team: Bill, John, and four other guys. They were called 'gray phantoms of the Infidel' by the Iraqis, because they always arrived at night, then disappeared in the wee hours of the morning, before the fog burned off.

They spread out and made their way into the area. They were given seventy-two hours to make their hits, and coordinates where to regroup afterwards, where they were to be picked up.

Left...

Abandoned...

John took a long swallow of whiskey and placed the empty glass carefully on the oilskin tablecloth. The anger had come back in all its glory. The anger, the fear, and the intense trembling that accompanied the anger every single time the memories came thrashing back.

"What happened then?" whispered Buster. "How did Bill get it?"

"The asshole masterminding this operation, Captain Lou Shank, had somehow neglected to share his plans with anyone else. We were supposed to be given air support. Choppers. Just one or two, but enough of a distraction to avert the enemy and draw their fire. But there was nothing. No one knew we were there in the first place. Shank hadn't bothered keeping up with the news and didn't know what was being set up in that area."

The rage had come back as if it had never left. He could feel the insanity edging back as well, since it, too, had never really abandoned him in the first place.

"Shank had this drinking problem, and the nasty habit of experiencing blackouts whenever he went on a bender. According to the grapevine, he'd just received a Dear John from his third wife and wasn't worth the energy it would take to put a hole in his head."

Buster's face had turned pale.

"What was being set up, without our knowledge, was a team of suicide enemy guerrillas. There were three separate teams, each with more than a dozen insurgents, and they were dispatched on a suicide mission where they were dispatching IEDs as well as remote control bombs on every path imaginable. And when we found out we were trapped inside an elaborate network of lethal booby traps, we knew we wouldn't make it back out. There were only six of us, and we were facing more than three dozen insurgents, and no one other than Shank and our driver knew we were even out there."

John began seeing red all over again. With the memories came the anger of being set up; and with this anger came a scorching ball of heat filling up his gut.

The insurgents were everywhere. It wasn't long before they spotted John and the others. Harris was the first to be blown up. Then Madeira. Then Michaels. Only hours later, Carstairs was blown up when he stepped on a tripwire that set off a string of IEDs.

The brightness of the following morning awakened him; he opened his eyes in the makeshift bunker.

John had barely slept. The heat was thick and stale, filled with the sour stench of cordite and charred flesh from the previous evening, when four of his comrades were shot, their bloody remains hanged unceremoniously over a fire of bamboo, coals, and dried kindling.

He squirmed carefully out of his sand-covered bed, mindful of where he was, of what lurked so dangerously close. He raised his head a few inches, his senses pricked, his consciousness in overdrive.

After listening for more than half an hour, he slowly crawled out of his sandy, makeshift bunker. Then he began looking for Bill Sebastian. They'd split up only hours ago, promising one another they'd regroup three miles north, after they'd determined what part of their mission could be salvaged.

For the next half-hour he low-crawled on the hard, scorched ground, moving one knee, then the other, then an elbow, before sliding his belly six more inches on the hot sand. Listening. Low-crawling some more. Then carefully lifting his head an inch at a time to see what there was to see.

Although he'd seen nothing, he knew they were close, hiding in the barren terrain just thirty or forty feet above him, their trained eyes eagerly searching for him.

But what weighed heavily in his mind hadn't been dark-skinned maniacs lurking in the blazing darkness, nor the abrupt, nauseating sounds of explosion or enemy gunfire.

Foremost in his head was getting out of this hellhole alive, then returning to his unit and squeezing off a .50 round into the drunken, sneering face of Captain Louis Allan Shank, who'd been stupid enough to dispatch six of his best men into enemy suicide maneuvers.

John continued crawling, and when he finally reached the portion of the area facing the enemy's outpost, he found the perfect place to set up.

Then he heard the screaming.

It was Bill Sebastian.

The bastards had found him. They'd recognized him, sent word to their cohorts, and were eagerly waiting for what would become a public execution.

Bill was spreadeagled naked to the hard ground approximately five hundred yards from John's location. The insurgents were circling him and poking him with the tips of what looked like homemade sticks and machetes.

Using his scope, John could see that his friend's wrists and ankles were punctured with large skewers pounded deep into the ground. Bill's hands extended straight out, crucifixion style. Blood oozed thickly from them; a deep gash on his right side provided a large pool of spilled blood, which was readily lapped up by a mongrel dog.

Children also circled him. Some laughed hysterically while others shouted what sounded some sort of chant. One of them splashed his face and chest with a brownish liquid from a tin bucket. Even at that distance, John could smell the stench of urine and feces as the hot wind drifted his way.

"Bastards were going crazy," John said, the rage filling his being once again. "It was like they'd captured Satan and were making a religious service out of it."

"How long…how long did they…do that?"

"Until three insurgents showed up."

The one in charge faced Bill. He stood between Bill's spread legs and began laughing. The crowd laughed with him. Many in the crowd continued poking him and tossing flasks of urine in Bill's face.

Then, without earning, the insurgent kicked Bill squarely in the groin. Bill screamed. The crowd cheered. More of the crowd began poking him again, until Bill's entire body gleamed red as his blood splashed wildly.

A moment later, the insurgent removed a large, glistening knife from his belt and held it proudly in his right hand. He turned and held up the knife for everyone to see. Then, after much applause and yelling, he turned back to Bill, bent, then calmly sliced off one of Bill's ears in an unhurried, see-saw motion.

"The bastard stood there more than five minutes, smiling and taking bows." John groaned and went silent. He stared at his fists, which had turned white at the knuckles.

It took nearly a minute before he could continue.

"When the crowd grew quiet, the bastard tossed Bill's ear to one of the village dogs."

"My God..."

"He repeated this same procedure with the other ear," John added, his fists trembling. "He saved his balls for last. As you may well imagine, he took his good old time getting down on his knees to do the deed properly. I guess he wanted to build the suspense slowly for his eager audience."

Buster couldn't speak.

As soon as the insurgent assumed the proper position, he held up his arms for more frantic applause. In that same moment, John's rifle, deadly calm and carefully aimed, put a massive .50 slug directly into the center of Bill Sebastian's head.

The roar of the crowd instantly ebbed. The man kneeling before Bill remained deadly still for more than ten seconds, providing the perfect target. John's rifle roared again, this round tearing into the insurgent's forehead and punching out most of his skull and brain matter through a fist-sized hole in the back of his head.

Another insurgent jumped up as his comrade dropped to the ground. He opened his mouth and took a round in the jaw that forced his head back so viciously, his neck snapped like a toothpick just as his severed jaw sailed into the panicking crowd.

"By this time, everyone was running around and screaming like a bunch of crazies escaping an asylum. But I was still shooting. I had time to reload and just kept pulling the trigger. I was so enraged, I wanted to kill them all."

"How many...did you get, Johnny?" Buster asked in a tense whisper.

His mind a white core of blinding heat, he jumped up from his nest. He had his knife out and was ready to stab anyone within reach. But by this time, the enemy discovered what was happening, and had taken shelter.

"I...don't know," he told Buster, shaking his thoughts from the death scene. "I was crazy by that time and didn't know what the fuck I was doing. All I could see was Bill's body parts flying all over the place. All I could hear was his screaming. I even remembered the joke he'd told me two nights earlier, when we were coming out of the shower. I remembered some things he told me the week before, about his plans when he got out. I thought of you getting blown up, and Carstairs, and

Madeira, and Michaels, and Harris…and all I could see was death and bodies flying all over the place. I knew I would also be killed, so I decided to kill as many as I could before they got me. I began running, and knew that every time I saw someone, I had to kill them."

"How many did the Army say you killed?"

John had begun shaking again. There were tears in his eyes when he said, "The official count…I think…I recall them saying seventeen."

Buster didn't reply.

"Seventeen," John repeated, mostly to himself.

Buster swallowed. "Is that accurate?" he asked, finding his voice.

John gave a slight nod. "I emptied almost all I had on my belt. It might have been more, I don't know. I wasn't counting. Everything had turned a deep shade of black."

Buster didn't speak.

John sighed brokenly. "I had this really strong feeling that my spirit also turned black that day."

***

After burying the dead hooker in the creek, the Murphy twins got back in their truck and found a cheap motel room on the other end of town.

They checked in, then got out of their muddy clothes. After showering, they changed into clean duds, tossed their dirties in a dumpster, and left the motel.

Half an hour later, they were right where they were supposed to be.

For the rest of the night, they remained in the deserted parking lot of the Burger King on East Main, watching the street from the truck.

"That's it," Ron said. "The two-story."

Rich nodded. "The one with the lights on."

"Yeah."

"He's up kinda late."

Ron shrugged. "Maybe the lights are on in case he needs to get up to take a leak. Maybe he doesn't wanna run the risk of fallin' down the stairs."

Rich said, "What's that Lincoln doin' in the drive?"

"Dunno. But I don't like it."

"Want me to check it out?"

"Make your rounds. But be careful. We're s'posed to do it in the mornin', while he's gettin' ready for work, so we need to check out everything. He better not have company when we're s'posed to be doin' him."

Rich got out of the truck and hurried across the street.

***

Shoulders slumped, Buster stood in the kitchen doorway, gazing at the linoleum floor.

He looked very tired; and, as John observed, much older than he'd appeared before John had told him what happened in Iraq.

"I've gotta get up for work," he said in a soft voice. "But I'm gonna take off half the day, so I'll be back to fix us lunch, if you like."

John looked surprised. "You don't want me to leave?"

"What for?"

"I thought, maybe you wouldn't want me around after—"

"You did what you had to." There was a cold, dark look on Buster's face. "In my mind, you got our friend out of a shitload of misery. What you did was help a friend the only way you could."

John didn't reply. Since he could never forgive himself, he didn't think he could expect forgiveness from anyone else.

"What happened after you got back?"

"At first, they wanted to give me a medal. But when they saw that there were kids among the dead, they got scared and did whatever they could to keep as much from the media as they possibly could."

"What about you?"

"Let's just say I left Iraq in the middle of the night."

"They smuggled you out?"

"Got my own plane, too. Chartered flight. And my own personal escorts. MP's. Four of them, but they were on my side. I don't know what happened to Shank. I wanted to frag the bastard for setting us up, but he disappeared. One of the MP's told me he heard someone else might have fragged Shank, but he thought it was probably just bullshit."

"From what I heard, that happened a lot."

"So they say."

"Did you know that the IED I stepped on was one of ours?"

John nodded. "But we'll never know who planted it."

"I don't *wanna* know."

"Don't blame you."

Buster was silent. After a while he shrugged. "Can you occupy yourself while I'm at work?"

"I thought maybe I'd waste a little time doing some shopping. Anywhere I can buy some DVDs?"

Buster laughed. "The same old movie buff, eh?"

"It's always been my own special way of escaping reality for a couple of hours at a time."

"I hear ya, believe me."

"Does your drugstore have much of a variety?"

"They've always got a few bargain bins. There's also a new place at the corner of Main and Sixth. Just opened three, maybe four weeks ago. Vinnie's Videos. Guy's a movie fanatic — almost as bad as you."

"Guess I'll be spending some money this morning."

"He's got some real bargains. I've been told he specializes in old comedies, and I'm talking *old*. Harold Lloyd. Chaplin. Keaton. Go on over there and see what you can find, then c'mon over to the Post Office. It's just up the street from the intersection. I'll show you around. Letcha see the assholes I've had to put up with all these years."

"Sounds good."

A sudden tense silence.

Moments later, Buster sighed. "You did right, my friend. Don't ever forget that."

John didn't reply.

"I'm sure Bill would've thanked you, if he could have."

A wave of sadness swept through John. "The only gratification I have is that I got him quick. He didn't feel a thing."

Buster said nothing. He seemed to be contemplating the floor again.

Without another word, he limped out of the room.

***

John leaned against the sink, gazing at the streetlamps.

There was an inch of whiskey in his glass, but he didn't want it. He was thinking of Bill Sebastian and wondering what their friend was thinking the moment before John's .50 slug had ended his life.

The look on Bill's face was clear in his head, and for a moment he thought he actually saw his old friend sneaking around in the dark. But he shook himself out of the past, regarded the drink in his hand, and spilled the brown liquid down the sink. The past three swallows had been bitter. He'd learned long ago that it was time to stop when the whiskey started tasting nasty.

Anyway, he'd had enough. He'd finally told his story. And the important thing was that Buster believed him and forgave him.

John moved to the doorway, flicked off the kitchen light, and went down the hall that led to the staircase.

***

Rich Murphy ducked into some shrubbery when he saw the strange face in the kitchen window.

Not Norton, he reflected, his pulse quickening. The face didn't belong to anyone they'd seen in town.

This could change everything. It could also fuck up the plan. If Norton had a guest staying with him, the twins wouldn't be able to do their job.

"Gotta tell Ronnie," he whispered to himself, watching as the stranger moved away from the kitchen window.

Rich disappeared in the darkness.

Chapter 2 - Monday

Buster was fixing breakfast when John came into the kitchen.

"Sleep any?" He poured coffee and slid a cup in John's direction.

John sat and sugared the coffee. "Not very well. It took me forever to get there. Then I kept waking up."

"Know what you mean." Buster set a plate topped with scrambled eggs and bacon on the table between them. He sat awkwardly, bumping the table with his artificial knee. He poured more coffee for himself. "It was my fault. If I hadn't brought up the damned past…" He shrugged a shoulder.

John spooned some eggs onto his plate and picked up two strips of bacon. "You had a right to know."

Buster nibbled thoughtfully on a piece of toast. "Funny thing, though. I could've tried getting in touch with his folks, but there was always some reason to put it off. It was like part of me knew Bill was dead. You were the only one I ever corresponded with." Buster smiled thinly. "Now I know why you were always so vague. Especially when I asked specific questions."

"I guess I stopped writing not long after because I didn't want to tell you about it."

"The more I think of it, the more I wonder if I really wanted to know anything at all. I mean, he was our friend, and I never once tried getting in

76

touch. He was from Cleveland, dammit. I could've easily gotten a number online or from somewhere else. But I'd been going through some shit of my own and was feeling so sorry for myself, I guess there was no room for me to share my own personal hell with anyone else. Or maybe I didn't want to be reminded of what happened over there. I guess it was enough, those two or three letters you and I exchanged."

"We all had too much to forget."

"We'll never do it." Buster sighed and adjusted the open collar of his uniform.

"I know. If I live a thousand years, that day will be just as fresh and as clear in my head as if it had happened yesterday."

***

The Murphy twins waited tensely in the truck.

After Rich had returned with news about Norton's visitor, the boys had spent the night quietly, one watching the house while the other tried to relax in back.

They decided to start their workday at six, Ron at the binoculars, his mind busy with some sort of plan involving Norton's house guest.

"See anything?" asked Rich.

Ron put down the binoculars. "Just that damn Town Car. The one thing we didn't expect was a crowd. Norton was always a loner, dammit. What the hell changed?"

Rich's sour expression showed clearly. "The ol' man — "

"Lemme worry about the ol' man. Like I said before, he only knows what we tell him."

"But won't he call somebody in town?"

"I don't think he knows anyone here. He's not exactly what you could call a social butterfly. Besides, I think he's more concerned about gettin' it done, rather than when or how. Long as we do it, and don't give the cops somethin' to worry about, I don't think he'll give a shit."

"Hope you're right."

"Like I said, lemme worry about it."

Rich watched the house for a while. "I don't guess we oughta take out the other dude."

"Don't know anything about him. Where he's from. If he's got kin here. If he's got kin, and we do him, this'll turn messy. The kin start askin' questions, the pigs get all hot and bothered, and then it's on the news. The ol' man hears about it, finds out that we sparked this dude on the sly, and he gets his panties in a wad. Starts talkin', and we're the ones get fucked in the end. Next thing ya know, we gotta pull up stakes and move to a place where nobody knows us. And we can't use any contacts back here cause of the ol' man, who's fucked us because we did somethin' stupid."

Rich nodded. "Shame, though. Dude looks easy. Not very big. Be a cinch, poppin' him with the gimp."

"We'll do it the way we planned. Be better for everyone. Especially us." Ron picked up the binoculars and stiffened. "Uh-oh."

"What's up?"

"That other dude. He's gettin' in the Town Car."

The Lincoln pulled out and moved down the street. It stopped at the intersection, then made a left.

"Now what?"

Ron put down the binoculars. A disturbed look had covered his face. "My guess is, we'd better be doin' this right about now."

"Why?"

"Dude made a left."

"So?"

Ron looked at his brother. "Where would a left take him?"

Rich shrugged. "To town."

"That tell you anything?"

"Not really."

"Don't that tell you he might be gone a little while?"

"How d'ya figure? He might only be headed to the drugstore."

"Even so, he might be gone fifteen, maybe twenty minutes. Even if he's headed for the newsstand for a paper, he might bullshit with the clerk, then come back in half an hour. Either way, we got enough time. When ya know exactly what you gotta do, you can do it in a snap."

Rich was silent.

"We got maybe five minutes for the dude to get to town and park that Lincoln. Another five or so for him to get whatever he's gonna get, then five more to come back. That's fifteen, maybe twenty minutes. Take us two minutes to sneak over, do Norton, coupla seconds to take the package, then two minutes to get back. No one'll see us 'cause the Burger King don't open till eleven. There won't be anyone around here, and we'll be all done by the time it gets busy. Think we oughta count on the other dude comin' right back in twenty minutes, just to be safe. I'm pretty sure we can do it in way less than twenty minutes." He grinned. "Ready for some fast movin'?"

Rich grinned nervously. "I'm with ya."

***

John spent the next hour in downtown Bern, trying to take his mind off Bill Sebastian.

He drove to the 7-Eleven at the other end of town, filled up the tank, bought a paper and a software magazine, and tried focusing solely on Buster and the cute little town of Bern, which served as a pleasant contrast to the congestion, mayhem, and other major problems associated with his home in Central Florida.

Later, John slipped into the East Main Drugstore and moved slowly down the aisles, glancing at the racks of DVDs. Although several 40's classics were offered for a good price, he quickly discovered that movies had become extremely unimportant—at least for now. He found that he could not think of anything but Bill Sebastian.

Though Bill and Iraq were ancient history, that aspect of his life was still very much alive. Perhaps more than ever before. And the fact that John had savagely murdered seventeen people in a brief span of three or four minutes made everything even more etched in his memory.

He'd spent seven long months in the hospital, sitting in the darkness, tended to by faceless figures in white whispering things while trying to sound kind and understanding. People who couldn't possibly understand what had happened, who hadn't a clue how to deal with someone who had butchered a crowd of people in a small village halfway around the world.

More than a dozen doctors had spent time with him, going over his files, consulting with others, examining him, analyzing him. They'd told him things they thought he should know, given him medication to help him sleep, even suggested things he could do that might possibly help bury his monsters.

They released him without fanfare, gave him a clean bill of health without bothering to interpret what had actually happened to him, then closed his file without taking the time to find out if they'd done anything to make a difference.

John knew they were merely babysitting him. He even suspected they were keeping him there to make sure he wouldn't lose his sanity and turn crazy again. The Military had rooms filled with kids who had gone over there young and healthy and come back physically damaged and clinically insane.

John realized that, even though Buster hadn't been through what he himself had been through, Buster's hell had been just as real. And as painful.

Like nearly all the young men and women who had served in combat situations, Buster had left a part of himself in the land of the enemy.

John had also left something.

Something just as tangible as Buster's leg.

As he left the drugstore and got back in the Town Car, he knew that what he'd left amongst the blistering sand and the charred bodies was something much more precious than what Buster had left behind.

***

Erika sat in front of her living room window, sipping coffee.

It was nearly eleven. She'd called the bank earlier, told them she wasn't feeling well, and wouldn't be coming in.

She picked at the small wedge of cinnamon toast and watched the light traffic cruising lazily down the street on that cloudy morning. She thought about Paul's phone call an hour ago and caught herself clenching her jaw until her teeth hurt.

"I won't be back until after the court settlement," he said after she had picked up the receiver.

"Fine," she'd replied, experiencing a warm wave of nausea. It felt like she was talking to a stranger.

"Kenny's handling this for me. We've already talked."

"He knows?" She was shocked to hear that he had already started up the machinery.

"I figured it was best to get this thing hashed out as quickly as possible."

"Perhaps you're right."

"Have anyone in mind?"

This made her wonder if he actually cared. She guessed he was just in a hurry to get it over with.

"To be honest, no. I guess I'm not in as much of a hurry as you are."

"This has to be worked out. Better find yourself a lawyer. Kenny says he might be able to squeeze us in within the next two weeks."

Now, as she sat looking out the window, she found herself shaking again.

The man I once loved and cherished so much... He ruins my life, then calls to tell me I need to find a lawyer so we can get this nasty business over with.

Seven years of marriage, and all he cares about is how quickly we can get the divorce worked out.

She tried thinking of other things but failed miserably.

A light-blue Town Car passed, slowing at the corner. It stopped in front of the old two-story before pulling up the drive.

The house belonged to the man who worked at the Post Office in town. He was a disabled Army vet and had an artificial leg. She always felt so sorry for him—the way he moved, the pronounced limp. His name was Larry Norton, and he was always friendly, cracking jokes, making her laugh. She had heard something about his family being from

Wheeling. Other than that, she knew nothing about the man.

A man got out of the Town Car, turned, and moved briskly up the walk. He was dressed in slacks and a polo shirt. He looked vaguely familiar.

Erika watched as the man quickly ascended the steps, crossed the front porch, and disappeared inside. Then she turned back to her toast and coffee.

She began thinking of Lizzie Peterson, an old high school chum who lived in St. Clairsville and worked at the courthouse. She'd been Lizzie Maxwell in high school and married Al Peterson a year or two after graduation. Al had been studying law and had done well the last few years. Al's forte was taxes but, according to Lizzie, he occasionally handled divorce cases.

She decided that she should see if he would work her case. Since she actually knew him, she figured it might possibly make the situation a little less traumatic. If she was forced to do go through something like this, she assumed it might as well be handled by a friend.

Erika finished her toast, got up, and went to the kitchen to make her phone call.

***

John opened the front door and gasped.

He stood quite still, trying to evaluate, to rationalize. But his mind just wouldn't cooperate.

He knew something was wrong when he'd driven to the Post Office just ten minutes ago and was told by the short blonde-haired clerk that Buster hadn't shown up and wasn't answering his cellphone.

At first, John had thought Buster had second thoughts about going in. Maybe the talk about Bill had upset him more than he'd let on. Maybe he'd wanted to spend a little more time with John.

But whatever the case, when the little blond lady had given him the message, John's first reaction was to rush back to the house and see for himself that his friend was all right. And when he saw Buster's car in the drive, in the same place it had been since the night before, John felt a sudden tingling he hadn't felt in years.

There was something about the car. The way it sat in the drive. The way it looked. It told him something was very wrong.

Buster lay on the floor at the foot of the stairs. He lay on his stomach, his head twisted at a sharp angle. An ugly purple bruise bulged on his forehead, just above the left eye. A puddle of dark blood stained the carpeting beneath his smashed nose. His artificial leg had been wrenched loose, forming a six-inch gap beneath his trousers. His left foot rested on the bottom step of the staircase. His left arm was wedged beneath him; his right, behind his back.

Buster had obviously fallen down the stairs.

My God...

John stood there, trembling.

Buster?

This couldn't have...it just didn't...I'm not seeing...this is a fucking dream!

85

Pull yourself out of this!

Think, *for God's sake!*

Find out if the man's unconscious. Try to help. Then—and only *then—you can let your mind switch off.*

John lowered himself slowly to the floor. Bent forward. His arm felt like it weighed a ton as he reached out and felt for a pulse.

There was none.

Buster was dead.

John stood up. A wave of nausea hit him, and for a moment he felt like he might faint. Bright colors raced across his vision. The room began jumping around, like a bad TV channel. He closed his eyes and kept them closed. When he opened them, he took a deep breath. The nausea passed.

Phone. Call someone.

John's mind went blank again.

Where's the damned phone?

John looked around. For a moment he couldn't remember whose house this was. Or why he was here. Everything seemed so unfamiliar, so strange.

Another wave of nausea made him tighten his hands into fists. Then he looked down. And saw the body.

Buster. My friend.

Dead.

Fell down the stairs, remember?

The phone. Use it.

There it was, sitting all comfy and warm in his jacket pocket.

Grab it, pull it out, and call someone!

John fumbled for the phone and managed to pull it out without dropping it. *Baby steps. Now try using your brain for a change.*

The cell was cold and heavy in his palm. He moved his index finger toward the numbers but couldn't remember who to call.

Nine-one-one, you idiot.

Buster. Dead. Emergency.

Try getting someone here...think you can manage that?

Maybe someone with medical equipment?

You think they might find out if Buster's really dead?

Maybe try getting this done quickly?

Like right now!

John managed, after tense, agonizing moments, to get his hand to stop shaking long enough to dial the number.

***

The big cop appeared from nowhere.

He stood tall and proud, looking down at John, who sat on a curved plastic chair in the hospital corridor.

With one hand, the cop reached up and pushed the shiny brim of his service cap up an inch, exposing jagged wrinkles on his leathery forehead. With the other, he removed a thick black notepad from his shirt pocket.

"You Callen?" he asked in a gruff, low-pitched voice.

"Yeah." John looked down at his hands, which were dangling loosely between his legs. They'd stopped shaking but now felt clammy and cold. He rubbed them together, then wiped them on his slacks.

"You're the one, called it in." It was a question that sounded like a statement.

"Yeah. I called it in."

The cop frowned. It was obvious that he hadn't liked John's tone. "State your name," he said, getting his ballpoint ready to hit the notepad. "And your address."

John stared at the man. The name *GRUBB* was printed in bold, square letters on a shiny piece of fabric stitched carefully over the tan shirt pocket. John pegged him at around six-four and maybe two-forty. His arms were long and gnarly, but his torso was thick, and appeared rock-hard. He looked like he'd played football years earlier, and seemed to be about fifty, maybe fifty-five.

John gave him what he wanted.

The cop wrote busily, occasionally glancing at John. "What're you doin' here?"

John shrugged. "I wanted to follow the ambulance in, find out if I could be of any — "

"I meant, whatcha doin' *here*? In *town*?"

"Visiting an old friend."

"Norton was your friend?"

John nodded and looked down at his hands again.

"Where'd ya know him from?"

"We both served in Iraq."

88

The cop pushed the brim of his cap up two more inches, exposing more lined forehead. "You and Norton?"

"Till he got his leg blown away when he stepped on that damned IED." John rubbed his eyes.

The cop's manner had suddenly changed. "What did ya do over there? Same outfit as Norton?"

John nodded. "Third Infantry Division. I was a sniper."

The cop had pocketed his notepad. He sat beside John and crossed his long legs at the ankles. "Sorry about the attitude. But I didn't know ya, and we're suspicious of strangers."

"No problem."

"We all knew Buster. I was just makin' sure I knew what was happenin'."

"What *is* happening?"

A shrug. "Buster's dead. We checked the house, didn't find nothin' special. Looks like he just fell down those fuckin' steps again."

John blinked. "Again?"

"When Buster first moved in, he started havin' problems. This was *way* long ago, and he wasn't used to that damn leg. He's got a sister in Wheeling. She and her old man came over, helped him move in. Then she started givin' him grief about those steps. Told him he didn't need steps, and he should only use the second floor for storage. She was afraid his leg would give out on him one day."

"He seemed pretty good on that leg."

"He was—after he got used to it. Took him coupla years, gettin' it right. He fell down those steps twice that I remember."

"Twice?"

"First time, he was movin' in, like I said. He was about halfway down, totin' a box, and lost his balance." Grubb shrugged. "Didn't hurt himself much, just banged his shoulder on the banister."

"What about the second time?"

"Tripped goin' up. Only fell the first three or four steps but managed to scrape the shit out of his elbow when he landed."

An orderly pushed a gurney down the corridor past them.

Grubb sighed. "Looks like this one was from the top, don't it?"

John didn't speak. He was wondering why Buster didn't use the room just off the dining room for a bedroom.

The cop had a sour look on his face. "Too late to say it now, but Buster's sister shouldn'ta let him live alone in that house."

***

The Murphy twins sat in their truck, munching on cheeseburgers while watching the last of the cop cars scurrying back to headquarters.

It was twelve-thirty. The afternoon sun was hiding behind a heavy cloud. The lunch hour business was booming. The Burger King lot was filled. High school kids in restored convertibles and beat-up El Caminos screamed at one another and acted like total idiots.

"Whatcha think, Ronnie?" Rich sipped Pepsi.

"I think we're gonna be just fine. They'll think Norton just fell down the steps."

"Think the dude in the Lincoln suspects anything?"

"Why should he?"

"Dunno. He found the body."

"Think he's smarter than the cops?"

Rich glanced at the square bundle lying on the floor behind the seat. "One thing bothers me."

"What's that?"

"If we're gettin' paid ten grand for this thing, what's it really worth?"

Ron shrugged. "What's it matter?"

Rich finished his burger and crammed the wrappings into the wrinkled bag. He washed down his last mouthful with another slug of Pepsi. "If it's worth that much, why don't we —- "

"Hold out?"

"What's wrong with that?"

"We hold out, it means we spend a bunch of time, energy, and money gettin' with other dudes who'd like to get their mitts on that thing. We'll be S.O.L. before you know it. The ol' man'll put out the word. Hell, he might be so pissed, he'll call in the law, tell them what we did. That happens, all we gotta do is cross the state line and the Feds'll be after us, tryin' to nail our hides." He raised his brows. "Get the picture?"

***

The slender, white-haired doctor looked solemn.

"The man's neck was badly broken. So was the nose, which was smashed upwards, sending splinters of bone and cartilage into the brain tissue. Mister Norton's nose was obviously broken on a step during his fall. This might very well have twisted his neck at the excessive angle. There was massive hemorrhaging, of course, plus several broken bones and cracked ribs. But I really don't think the man suffered much, since — "

"What do you think made him fall?" John asked.

The doctor shrugged. "Might have been the prosthetic. I wasn't Mister Norton's doctor, but I've seen prosthetics fail. Mister Norton's leg was of good quality, of course, but prosthetics are, at best, only as reliable as their wearer. I've seen too many wearers move the wrong way and fall. They expect the prosthetic to do things it just wasn't designed to do. A prosthetic has its limitations and will move only as it was designed to. Some wearers are injured when they demand the impossible. Mr. Norton's prosthetic device was fairly old, but — "

"What's the life expectancy of one of those?" John asked.

"Depends on the material. And, of course, how it is used." The doctor pushed his glasses upward. "As I was saying, the prosthesis was designed more than a decade ago but was equipped with the same sophisticated electronic circuitry that has been developed in more recent years. The circuitry in Mr. Norton's prosthesis picks up nerve, muscle, and tissue impulses reaching the stump from the spinal cord, just as our newer models do. With electronics, the prosthesis becomes an actual limb, allowing for extreme movements and sudden awkwardness."

"Are you saying Buster's leg should not have failed at all?" John asked.

The doctor smiled thinly. "What I'm trying to say is that your friend's prosthesis could possibly have malfunctioned in *some* way, and this might have contributed to his fall. Mister Norton's prosthesis consisted of three extensions. The foot, lower leg, and upper leg. Each extension consists of an inner strut made of various materials. His prosthesis had an ankle mechanism, shin extension, knee mechanism, and thigh extension. There was a strap for the stump, which was made from very strong, durable leather, much like a high-grade leather belt."

"And?"

"Your friend's prosthesis might have shifted very slightly at a key moment."

"Does anything about any of this look wrong to you?" John asked.

"Wrong?" The doctor tilted his head.

Sheriff Grubb was leaning against the door frame, listening intently. He pushed himself forward and approached them. "What're you gettin' at?"

John shrugged. "Just that my friend's dead and I'd like to know exactly what happened."

"We've been examining the prosthesis," replied the doctor. "However, it was damaged in the accident, compromising things a little."

"How bad was the damage?" John asked.

"The ankle and knee mechanisms were both badly twisted. We can't tell if they were instrumental in the fall or twisted as the result *of* the fall."

"In other words, you're saying you don't know *why* Buster fell."

"Unfortunately, that's exactly what I'm saying."

***

Erika and Lizzie Peterson sat facing one another in Dolby's Coffee Shoppe in St. Clairsville, having coffee and sharing a small plate of freshly baked sugar doughnuts.

It was three o'clock. School buses stopped at the intersection, letting off hordes of loud, unruly kids.

"Then it's mostly Paul's decision?" Lizzie drank some coffee.

"Let's just say it's very mutual right now." Erika finished her doughnut and wiped her fingers with a napkin. "It's been leading up to this the last few months, but I kept thinking it was Paul's business keeping him away. I had every intention of trying to bring everything together. But last night I found out that Paul hasn't been too wild about sticking around."

"What's his problem?"

"He's having an affair."

"Really? With who?"

"Her name's Stacy Hutchinson. He calls her his 'associate.'"

"Is *that* what they're calling them now?"

94

The short, skinny waitress appeared, waited until Erika put her mug down, splashed it and Lizzie's mug with hot coffee, then hurried back to the kitchen.

"What's this Stacy look like?"

"Blond, beautiful, intelligent. And, of course, ten years younger than I am. The average housewife's basic nightmare." Erika lowered her voice. "He also threw in that she's a good lay and, well, you know..."

Lizzie's lips twisted down. "Bastard. Did you thank him for sharing?"

Erika stirred her coffee. "Could you ask Al if he'll represent me? Or would it be better if I asked him myself?"

"I'll be glad to. He'll take you on."

"How expensive is he?"

Lizzie laughed. "Very." She held up a pudgy right arm, which was decorated with an ornate golden bracelet. "Do you honestly think I can afford something like this on *my* salary, working at Probate?"

Erika smiled sheepishly. "I don't think I can afford him, then."

"Don't worry. It's for an old friend. He'll just soak someone else later on to make up for it."

***

At four-thirty, John sat at Buster's kitchen table, his head filled with dark thoughts.

Grubb told him he could stay there and wait for Buster's sister to show up from Wheeling.

"Buster would want that," the cop said. "You two were buddies. He'd want you to watch his stuff."

John felt guilty for not being close when Buster had fallen. An inner voice kept telling him Buster might still be alive if John had been with him.

*If I'd been here, instead of wasting time in town, I would've been talking to him. I might not have been able to prevent the fall, but I sure as hell could have done some*thing...

I might have even been able to break *the fall.*

Buster might have been more careful.

John poured a cup of fresh coffee and took it into the living room. He couldn't help wondering why Buster had gone upstairs in the first place. His friend was wearing his postal uniform when John found him. Which meant Buster, for some strange reason, had gone upstairs after John left the house.

Something just wasn't right about this.

Buster lived in a two-story house. He was a hard-working, active man with a prosthetic leg, who used the upstairs bedroom and bathroom.

But would he go upstairs if he didn't have to? Especially if he was already dressed in his uniform and about to leave for work?

John went back to the moment he'd walked into the kitchen. Surprisingly, the scene was quite clear.

Buster at the stove, cooking breakfast.

John remembered bits and pieces of their conversation, but the memories quickly began fading, and the more he thought about it, the less sense it made, Buster hobbling back upstairs when he was already dressed and ready for work.

There was no reason for a man with a prosthetic leg to brave fourteen stairs when he was ready to leave the house.

No reason at all.

***

At five o'clock, Ron Murphy waited patiently outside the Burger King for his employer to answer the phone.

After four rings, he heard the familiar raspy voice. "Yes?"

"We got it."

"Your call is late."

"Somethin' came up."

A pause. "Anything…serious?"

"Nothin' we couldn't handle."

Another pause. "All right."

Ron waited.

"Tonight, as planned."

"Tonight, it is."

"Eleven o'clock."

Click.

***

At five-thirty, John wandered into Bern's Homestyle Family Restaurant on Main and chose a window booth overlooking the hardware store and Hallmark shop across the street.

Her dull black hair pulled back and fastened with white plastic clips, the short, stocky waitress handed him a menu before hurrying back to the kitchen.

97

John gazed at the menu but could not stop thinking of Buster.

It was painfully difficult, accepting the fact that his old friend was dead. Only a few hours ago, they were having breakfast. Less than twenty-four hours earlier, John had pulled up the drive to see the man after nearly sixteen years.

Now Buster was dead, and John, once again, blamed himself.

But why blame himself for the accident? People fell down staircases, tripped in the shower, and suffered mishaps all the time. Why should Buster's mishap be any different?

John tried to remember what the doctor had said. Buster's prosthesis might have failed him at the wrong moment and sent him plummeting to his death.

But whatever had happened didn't matter. Buster was dead, and John just couldn't believe that his friend had died because his artificial leg hadn't bent—or turned—the way it was supposed to, when it was supposed to.

The Army managed, after all these years, to kill him. It took them a decade and a half, but they did it.

The poor guy stepped on an IED manufactured by the United States Army. And now, years later, the same organization that had tried to kill him before completed the deed by manufacturing a prosthetic device that ultimately failed at the wrong moment.

John recalled what Buster had told him the day before. The incident at the hospital, with the multiple amputee.

"Boy was really chipper. They'd told him his new arm was in. Getting it attached within the week. Had a real appendage. Looked like a genuine hand. Connected to your nerves. Could soon light his own cigarettes, wash and dress himself. Even wipe his own ass, all by himself."

The thought
(real appendage)
tore into his head
(connected to your nerves)
like a cyclone.

It *wasn't* the prosthetic after all...

So then, what the hell *was* it?

The waitress was standing at his table. He struggled to remember why he was here when he had no appetite. A waitress was standing right there, waiting for him to say something, so he should snap out of this fog right now and not make her angry for wasting her time. "What's on special?"

"Oven-baked pork roast. Comes with mashed potatoes, carrots, and salad. And a hot, buttered roll."

He looked past her and eyed the bar. "Bring me a Jack's on ice," he said, handing her the menu. "Make it a double."

***

Erika slipped into the family restaurant and sat down at a table in the center of the half-filled room.

After talking to Lizzie in St. Clairsville, Erika drove back to Bern. She decided to stop for a drink before going home. Being in the house all alone would depress her, and she was miserable enough. She knew she shouldn't be sitting in the dark, sulking over her failed marriage.

She ordered a Tom Collins. While the waitress went to fill the order, Erika sat back and glanced around the room.

And saw him.

It was the guy who helped her last night at the Holiday Inn. The man she had seen getting out of a Town Car in the Norton driveway down the street.

Just then, he turned and smiled. She couldn't help noticing that he looked very tired.

Slightly embarrassed, Erika waved. Just then, she thought of her husband. And when she visualized a willowy blond with perky breasts and eager lips, her embarrassment quickly vanished. "Would you like to join me?"

He got up, walked over, and sat down facing her. "John Callen." He held out his hand.

"Erika Larson." The warmth of his hand somehow relaxed her. For some reason, she didn't feel guilty for asking him over. It wasn't exactly a pickup, was it? She was alone; he was alone. In her view, it seemed quite innocent.

"Any more problems with drunks?"

She smiled. "Actually, he was my first."

"Really?"

"You seem, well, surprised."

"I take it you don't usually go to bars alone…"

"I guess you could say last night was sort of a fluke."

"Well, I'm sure you'll be safe in this place. Drunks usually don't like making asses of themselves at family restaurants."

She laughed. "Hope you're right."

"So am I."

"New in town?" She suddenly wanted to know more about this man.

"I came to visit an old friend." A dark shadow suddenly crossed his face.

The waitress brought her drink. She glanced at John, studied him, and scratched the back of her head. Realization hit. She turned to the other table. "Oh! You're *here*, now!"

He winked. "You're good. And I'll bet you were about to bring me a refill."

"No problem," she said, whisking away.

Erika said, "You're a friend of the man who works at the Post Office?"

"How'd you know?"

"My husband and I…we live just down the street." Funny, how odd that sounded. She suddenly felt as if she were talking about some other couple. "I saw you today. The light-blue Lincoln?"

"That was me…"

"I wasn't being a snoop or anything," she said quickly. "I was sitting at the window when you were pulling up the drive. Everyone likes Mr. Norton. He's such a nice man."

He gave her a strange look.

"Did I…did I say something wrong?"

"You haven't heard?"

The waitress brought his drink and quickly disappeared.

Erika sensed something terrible had happened. "I guess not."

John studied his drink for long moments. Then he sighed. "Buster's dead."

"*What*?"

He picked up his drink and drank nearly half of it. "When you were watching me, you saw me go inside. That's when I...when I found him."

"What on earth happened?"

"He fell down the stairs." John drank more of his drink and looked around for the waitress. "The Sheriff met me at the hospital. They said Buster's artificial leg made him lose his balance."

The waitress appeared. John pointed to his glass, then Erika's.

"I'm so *very* sorry," Erika said. Inwardly she was remembering the times the man had joked with her when she'd gone to pick up something at the Post Office. The times he'd delivered postal worker jokes at lightning speed. She remembered him sitting on his front porch in the evenings as well as the times he'd tended his vegetable garden on weekends.

"He was a good friend," John said quietly. "We knew each other in Iraq. We hadn't seen one another since...since he got blown up. They shipped him home when that happened. We corresponded for a while, but you know how that goes. You try to continue where you'd left off. Then you start a new business, get married, and before you know it, years have flown by."

"I understand." Erika sipped her drink. "I never knew your friend other than talking briefly with him. I work at the bank, but he only came in once or twice. I assume he had an account with the other bank." She tilted her head. "I was always curious about his leg. What happened? I mean, how did he—"

"Buster stepped on an IED."

"My God. How horrible!"

"The really awful thing was that it was one of our own. But Buster was lucky. Most guys who trip those things end up dead. The way I heard it, Buster was running at the time and had just cleared the wire that set off the damned thing. It trashed his leg up past the knee, but the rest of him managed to get out of the way without being torn up."

"What's going to happen now? I mean, with Buster's house and everything. Did he have relatives? I don't recall seeing him having much company — "

"His sister's coming over from Wheeling to settle things. They told me she'll be arriving tomorrow morning. I'm gonna stay in the house till then. You never know. Someone might get the idea that since the house is vacant, it's perfectly okay to walk right on in and take whatever the man had. You know how people are."

Erika began thinking of her husband and the young woman who had just become the new love in his life. "People don't seem to care about anything anymore."

"I'm going to stick around for another day or so. From what I've seen, Buster wasn't much of a collector. There's a shotgun over the mantelpiece, but it doesn't look like it's worth much. We didn't discuss it, but I'll bet it was left by a relative. Aside from that, I didn't see much a thief would be interested in."

"Was he ever married?"

"He told me in one of his few letters that he married someone right after he'd started working at the post office. It only lasted a year or so, and he didn't mention it again. I don't think it was very pleasant for him."

"A shame. He was such a nice man."

John went silent. Darkness clouded his face. "Iraq didn't do much for us as far as relationships went. We all came back different."

She watched him, noting the clenched jaw, the wrinkles around his brown eyes, the twitch near the outer edge of his lower lip. It was obvious the man was hurting and that he'd probably been hurting long before his friend had died.

We're all hurting, she wanted to tell him. *Every last one of us.*

"I'm really sorry," she heard herself saying. "I'll bet the same thing happened to you."

"With me, it was different. I came back worse."

"Worse?"

He didn't speak. Erika guessed that he was thinking of a polite way of expressing himself, of telling her what had happened without shocking her.

"Buster came back long before they'd taught him to kill. I was there much longer. I was taught. They taught well, and I learned well. They sent me home after I'd done all the killing they wanted me to do."

"But wasn't it kind of, well, necessary? I mean, wasn't it a kill-or-be-killed type of thing?"

"It's something they expect you to do quite naturally over there, something you're supposed to instantly forget when you come home. Sort of like turning a light switch on and off. But it doesn't work that way. They know it but won't admit it."

Erika realized at that moment that he was telling her he was still a killer but didn't want to be.

"Enough of that," he said, forcing himself out of his darkness. "Tell me about yourself. You said you're married."

She was about to ask how he knew when she remembered that she'd mentioned her husband earlier. Then she felt the wedding ring on her finger. She suddenly realized that she'd been unconsciously covering it with her right hand. "Paul and I have been married seven years."

"What's he do?"

For a moment she couldn't exactly remember. Then she began wondering why she didn't want to talk about the man. It took her only a moment to realize her mindset. "He owns a software business in Wheeling. Larson & Associates."

"I think I might have heard of them. I buy and sell software myself. Independently."

"Where?"

"Orlando, Florida. I live there, but come to the Tristate area once, sometimes twice, a year."

"That's why you're here?"

"My uncle passed away. I flew to Pittsburgh for the funeral, then decided to come here and see Buster. It had been too long. I knew it was time."

"You've had such a very sad visit." She wanted to reach across the table and cover his hand but knew that would be inappropriate. "I'm very sorry about your uncle. *And* your friend."

"Thank you." He drained his drink and pushed back his chair. "And thanks for the company. I think I ought to go back to the house now. I hate to leave you, but —"

"I understand." She picked up her purse, but he waved her down.

"It's really my pleasure."

"Thank you." She watched as he dropped two twenties on the table and stood. He was smiling. The darkness that had covered his face just moments ago had passed. He was handsome all over again.

Outside, they watched the remnants of the rush-hour traffic gathering at the intersection. Erika suddenly felt nervous in his presence. She didn't know why, but something inside her told her why it might be.

This man's a doll, and you're extremely vulnerable right now.

106

"Maybe we'll see one another again," she heard herself saying.

"Maybe you and your husband could— "

"We're getting divorced," she blurted out, and felt herself flushing again.

He blinked. "I'm…really sorry to hear that."

She shrugged. Inwardly she was angry. At herself, for feeling the need to tell this stranger. At Paul, for making it all happen. And at a beautiful gold-digger named Stacy, for instigating it.

And especially at this man for entering her life and unknowingly stirring things up.

"It happens," she said, hating herself for such a lame statement.

"I guess that would explain why you went to the Holiday Inn by yourself and wanted to be left alone."

"Yes. It really would."

He went silent and watched her, and she could tell he wanted to say something that would make her feel better. She knew she couldn't really be certain, but she saw something in his eyes she liked very much. Something soft. Something warm.

Something that made her sadness not quite so intense.

"Where's your car?" he finally asked, breaking the silence.

She pointed.

He looked at her.

"Something wrong?"

He was smiling. "Didn't we do this before?"

She laughed. "We sure did."

"Another time, then." Still smiling, he waved and started walking away.

As she watched him get in his car, she thought, *I sincerely hope so.* Then she went over to her own car and got in.

***

The kitchen wall phone was ringing when John got back to Buster's house.

He hurried over and scooped up the receiver. "Hello?"

"Is this John Callen?" asked a husky female voice.

"Yes."

"I'm Julie. Julie Simpson. Larry's sister."

"Larry?"

"Buster. Sorry, I forgot." A chuckle. "I'm practically the only one who still called him that."

"I never used his real name. And I'm sorry for your loss, Julie."

"Thanks. And thanks for being there." She sighed. "We hadn't been close — that is, not as close as brothers and sisters should be. Larry was five years younger than me. I was married and already had a kid when he went in. We never really knew one another, though we had been getting together more frequently the last year or so."

"Buster mentioned you, but he wasn't much for talking about his family. In fact, he only said a couple of things about his marriage. Just that it didn't last very long, and that she walked out."

"Yeah, she was the one did the walking. But Larry was much better off."

108

John didn't reply.

"The police called a few hours ago, told me you took care of everything. Where is he now?"

"I was told there's only one funeral parlor in town, so I quite naturally let them take him. I hope that was all right."

"It's fine. Thanks. We've got a family plot out here, so we'll have him brought back for the services and burial. I'll be coming over tomorrow morning. If you can stick around for a while, I'd be grateful."

"No problem. I'll be at the funeral, so I might as well stay somewhere."

"You're welcome to stay at the house as long as you wish."

"Thanks. I'll be watching for you tomorrow morning."

***

As Erika heated up a small portion of the roast she'd prepared for Paul and herself, she began thinking about John Callen. And how this handsome, personable guy was sent with Buster and countless other young men to a violent country on a mission of mercy, to come back broken, disillusioned, and scarred for life.

And now, after fifteen years, John comes here to see his old friend and is forced to live through yet another nightmare, this one just as horrible as what he'd gone through in Iraq.

It just wasn't fair.

The phone rang.

It was Lizzie Peterson's husband, Al.

"Lizzie told me you and Paul are starting divorce proceedings."

It took her several moments to stop thinking about John and focus instead on Paul and her own personal nightmare, which, for some strange reason, seemed much less devastating than what John was going through.

"I hope it was all right for her to volunteer you without checking first..."

His laugh was loud and spontaneous. "No need to worry about that. That wife of mine is always volunteering me for something, so I'm used to it. You get used to anything in twelve years."

"I guess so."

"When can you stop by? We'll have to go over the particulars as soon as possible. Who's representing your husband?"

"Ken Abrams. He's Paul's friend and works for Larson & Associates."

"I know Abrams. He's got an office in Wheeling. How do you want this handled?"

"What do you mean?"

"Would you like to hash out everything with your husband and leave the legal stuff to Ken and me? Or would you like to stay out of it as much as possible and have Abrams and myself work out something mutually suitable?"

"That way would be fine. This isn't my idea, and I'm really not up to fighting with Paul anymore."

"I understand. Lizzie told me about your conversation. What I'd like to do is get together with you tomorrow afternoon. Then we'll discuss what you'd accept as a settlement. I'll get together with Abrams after we talk and let him see what we've got on the table. Fair?"

"Fair. What would you like as a retainer?"

"We'll discuss that tomorrow."

"Thanks, Al."

***

John relaxed on the living room couch and tried to decide what was bothering him.

He picked up the glass, frowned at the two inches of whiskey left in it, then tilted it against his lips. It went down smoothly, sending a warm tingling through his limbs.

Buster's dead, but I won't accept it. For some reason, I feel that it's my fault.

The man survived an IED and came home in pieces. He survived the loss of a leg, the demise of a marriage, and managed more than a decade and a half without too much fuss.

Then I come along and in just twelve hours, the man is dead.

John drained his drink, put down the glass, picked up the bottle, and dropped another healthy splash into the glass.

He began wondering if Julie also blamed him for Buster's death. It didn't seem so. At least, she hadn't sounded edgy when they'd talked.

It was enough that he blamed himself and just couldn't help thinking Buster's death didn't make any sense.

His thoughts suddenly shifted, and he found himself thinking about Erika Larson. He fondly remembered the incident at the Holiday Inn, then their conversation at the restaurant.

Images of her thick black hair flashed in his head. The way it hung over her shoulders. Her large almond eyes—how they held on to you when you were talking. Studying you. Watching you. Making you feel like you were the most important person in the world.

He couldn't stop wondering what kind of idiot would reject such a woman.

After finishing the bottle, John flicked off the living room light. Then, forcing himself to turn away from the dried blood spatter on the carpet, he quickly ascended the stairs.

In the spare room, he shrugged out of his shirt. After draping his trousers over the chair, he looked around the room as if he had no idea where he was.

Something felt wrong.

Or was it just that he was alone in a strange house?

Suddenly tired, he reached for the light.

Something nudged him again, but he ignored it, promising himself he'd consider it in the morning.

He flicked off the light and lay down. After turning on his side and closing his eyes, the nudging became unbearable.

John sat bolt upright. He lowered his feet to the floor, flicked on the light, and stared directly at the wall.

And gasped.

***

At a few minutes before eleven, the Murphy twins waited anxiously in their truck, their eyes firmly fixed on the gray metal door leading to the basement of the old four-story building.

"Can't stand this waitin' around shit." Rich squirmed uncomfortably in his seat.

Downtown Wheeling wasn't exactly their favorite place. To make matters worse, this wasn't what you would call the best area in town. Rich had double-checked beneath his seat to make sure the small Ruger .38 Special he always brought with him lay within easy reach.

"Patience," Ron reminded firmly.

"You sure that clock's right?" Rich stared at the clock on the dash, which said 10:57.

"Settle down." Ron shot him a look. He really hoped his brother wouldn't get the shakes. They were much too close to picking up their money to have something go wrong. "He'll show. He's prob'ly inside, waitin' for the right time."

At precisely 11:00, the gray door cracked open, exposing a white sliver of vertical light emanating from inside the building. The slim figure stood in the broadening crack, looking out. The gesture the figure made by raising his right hand was unmistakable.

"It's time," Ron said. "I'll follow you in." He reached under his seat, pulled out the .357 Magnum, and stuck the revolver in his waistband. He knew the old man didn't like guns, but Ron didn't trust the neighborhood. You couldn't see the gun beneath his loose sweatshirt, so there would be no problem to speak of.

Rich turned in his seat, grasped the bundle, picked it up carefully, and laid it in his lap. He smiled at his brother. "Time to pick up our paycheck," he said.

Without a word, Ron carefully opened the driver's door and climbed down.

***

John stared in disbelief at the grouping of winter scenes on the wall opposite the bed.

Four, he told himself, over and over.

There were four of them. Yesterday there were five, but now there were four. A grouping of four, rather than a grouping of five.

What the hell happened here?

For fifteen minutes he remained totally still, desperately trying to remember if there had actually been five. After several tense minutes, his brain began getting tired, and he sat down on the edge of the bed and rubbed his temples.

Were there actually five? Or was he trying to rationalize a bad situation? Putting things in his head so he didn't have to blame himself anymore?

He studied the grouping again.

Four winter scenes.

One pictured a log cabin with a cozy fire pushing blue smoke up the chimney, with the smoke disappearing in the darkness of the night.

The second showed a snow-covered barn, with three horses grouped together in a paddock,

114

watching the bundled-up little girl heading their way, lugging feed buckets.

The third displayed an aerial view of an old two-and-a-half story farmhouse, with a barn in the background, several outbuildings, stacks of cordwood, and paddocks of horses and cows outside the barn.

The fourth, a Rockwell-type village, featured a young couple skating on a glittering, ice-covered pond.

Then it dawned on him.

The one with the boy and girl, pulling the sled.

Gone.

Five. There had been *five.*

He got up and approached the wall. A small nail hole in the very center of the grouping gawked at him.

A disturbing heat rubbed his face. A picture had been hanging here but was now gone.

A picture that was here last night.

A picture that was now missing.

A heavy throbbing made him cover his ears.

Why would Buster come upstairs just before driving to work, pull a picture off the wall, then head back down the stairs?

And, more importantly, where was the picture?

His head pounding, John frantically checked the spare room. Under the bed. Behind the bed. The closet.

Nothing.

He flicked on the hall light and rushed into Buster's room. Checked the closet, under the bed—everywhere.

Again, nothing.

He raced downstairs.

If Buster had been carrying a picture when he'd fallen, chunks of frame and shards of paint would be all over the place.

Not to mention the picture itself, which shouldn't have been far from where he'd landed.

John flicked on every light in the living room and hall. He dropped to his knees and spent the next half-hour searching under the couch, chairs, coffee table, end tables. Beneath the throw rug in front of the couch. Behind the drapes. The drawers beneath the window seats. The entrance closet. Every dresser drawer in the dining room.

Nothing. No chips, nor paint shards.

He checked the hall closet, the kitchen, every drawer and shelf. Every square inch of space.

Nothing.

The cellar took only a few moments. It was obvious Buster seldom went down there. The state of deterioration of the dust-covered stairs prevented anyone from descending them safely. Using the flashlight he found in the kitchen cabinet and examining the area from the top step down to the bottom, John discovered that the cellar consisted of a single damp room heaped with garbage and rust-covered farm tools.

No sign of a frame or picture.

John closed the cellar door. His thoughts spinning, he trudged over to the sink and tried desperately to make some sort of sense of all this.

Once again, he thought of Buster's chat with the multiple amputee. And his talk with the doctor at the hospital.

Real appendage.

Genuine hand.

Connected to your nerves.

Not a damned thing wrong with his—

The sudden reality of it made him want to scream.

Someone came in the house, took the middle picture from the five-piece grouping, and now Buster's dead.

Damn it to hell, he thought wildly, his blood pulsating through his veins.

Someone murdered Buster!

***

The tall, slender old man placed the bundle gently on the table and smiled a wicked smile.

Mine, he thought, the excitement making his face and the back of his neck hot. *After all these years...*

The very last one, and no one is ever going to get it again...

He heard laughter downstairs and frowned.

Those animals...

He suddenly wanted to be rid of them.

He didn't like strangers in his home. Especially trash, like the Murphy's. He'd got what he wanted;

117

now he wanted them out of his life. They made him feel evil, and he knew he shouldn't feel this way.

He *wasn't* evil. He really and truly wasn't.

All he had done was pay good money to get back what was rightfully his. It wasn't his fault they'd escaped him, had found their way into other hands.

That damned auction...

The very thought of that unfortunate event once again brought back the taste of the same hot bile that had soured his throat almost constantly for so very, very long.

Never again, he promised himself.

It's all over now...

He opened a drawer and pulled out a thick envelope. Before he closed the cellar door, he wondered if he should ask his friend to watch the bundle for him. His friend would take the appropriate steps necessary, should an intruder threaten their privacy.

But no. The bundle was safe, lying there on the table. He would only be gone a moment.

He didn't want to bother his friend. He wanted to be alone with his prize and not share the treasured moment with anyone.

Not even his friend.

He turned, forced a smile onto his gaunt looks, and slowly descended the steps.

It would take only a moment to give those animals their due. Then they'd be out of his life. Forever.

Later, he and his friend would celebrate.

When they were alone.

The two of them.

And their treasure.

The two of them, their treasure, and an old bottle of Benedictine brandy.

It would be a celebration for the ages.

He couldn't wait.

Chapter 3 - Tuesday

Large and bulky, with masculine features and thick red hair, Julie Norton Simpson stormed through the front door.

After shaking hands with John, she went right over to the coffeepot, poured a mug for herself, and sat down heavily. "I wanna thank you again. It was nice that my brother finally got to see you. He mentioned you several times over the years."

"It was great, seeing him again. But we didn't have that much time together. If only I'd been here when Buster had fallen — "

"Please don't blame yourself. My brother and I had a lot of heated arguments about this place."

"Sergeant Grubb told me."

"Really?"

"He said you didn't want your brother living here."

She sipped coffee. The cracks between her heavy brows disappeared. "I didn't want Larry living in a place with so many damn stairs." She groaned. "My brother had it rough, that metal leg and all. I knew damn well he'd fall one day. It had nothing to do with him. It's just that I've seen people with two healthy legs fall, and I didn't want my brother suffering the same fate. I guess you know he'd fallen before. This house..." She shook her head. "I thought he could do better. A damn shame I had to be right."

"I still blame myself."

"Whatever for?"

"I don't know. Maybe because it happened in the first place. Or maybe because it happened while I was in town, when I should've been here, with him."

"Bullshit. I'm just glad you were here to take care of things. And I'm sure Larry was happy to see you after so many years."

"What do you plan to do?" he asked. "About the house, I mean."

"I'm afraid we're gonna have to sell. Can't see any other option." She finished her coffee, got up, and poured another cup. "My hubby thinks we should rent it out, but I don't like the idea."

"Why not?"

"It's total bullshit and too damn much heartache. You rent it to a bunch of slobs, they dirty up the place, get behind on the rent, and you end up throwing them out. The only way you can recoup your losses is by keeping their deposit, but then you gotta blow it all on the cleanup: replacing carpeting, painting walls, and so forth. You raise the rent to cover some of your expenses, then you go through the same damn thing if you wanna rent it out again."

"Why not go through an agency?"

She shook her head. "All those jerks do is make a phone call, get someone in, and take twenty percent right off the top. They don't screen people, don't check references, don't watch the place. All they do is take your money."

John was wondering if he should mention the missing painting. He knew he couldn't tell her he suspected her brother had been murdered. At least, not at this stage of the game. Especially since he wasn't one hundred percent certain he was right.

After all, what proof did he have?

After checking the place, he'd examined the doors and windows but saw no signs of jimmying, damage, nor anything else. As far as he could tell, everything looked normal.

But no matter what he thought, the fact remained: one of Buster's paintings was missing. And Buster was dead.

He just couldn't imagine Buster pulling the painting from the wall and laying it somewhere. Or hanging it in some other place.

Why would he take the center picture from a five-piece grouping and hide it? Buster hadn't the time—nor the ability—to climb into the attic and stash it. And there certainly hadn't been enough time to take it out of the house, come back inside, limp back upstairs, and have his deadly mishap.

It just didn't make sense.

If Buster hadn't touched the painting, what happened to it? And if someone else had taken it, did it have anything to do with Buster's fatal accident?

If it *was* an accident...

Had Buster surprised someone who managed to sneak into the house?

If this were the case, wouldn't there be some sign that someone else had been here?

He was certain *some*thing strange happened and determined to see it through. If he ended up with egg on his face, so be it. But Buster was dead, and if there was a chance in a million that it wasn't an accident, John had to find out. He owed Buster that.

He stood up. "I'd like you to see something."

"Something about the house?"

"About Buster."

A frown. "What are you talking about?"

"I'd rather show you."

***

Erika sat facing Al Peterson at the kitchen table, nervously watching as the broad-shouldered, slightly balding man scanned what she'd carefully written down in an itemized list.

"I don't know about the house, Erika." He laid down the paper and pulled off his reading glasses.

Erika sat up sharply. "I think I'm entitled. After all, I was the one who picked it out. I dealt with the realtors and handled nearly all the negotiating. I even came up with the down payment because, at the time, Paul's money was tied up in his business. As for cleaning out the house, getting it ready, then furnishing it, I was the one who — "

"That, unfortunately, doesn't matter." A grave expression had clouded Al's heavy-featured face. "During an ongoing divorce, things change, turn upside-down. Priorities get lost in the shuffle. Tempers fly. Things are said which change the natural course of events. The fact that your husband is having an affair will put things in your favor, of course, but we can't expect this to be our ace in the hole."

"Why not?" Sudden anger made her cheeks feel flushed. "I should think that a cheating husband —"

"I've handled dozens of divorce cases, Erika. I could tell you things that would curl your hair. People say and do things that would make you a non-believer in the human race. They turn nasty. Mean. Vengeful. The things you see and hear make you wonder how they even got along with one other in the first place. You begin to wonder what love really is. If it's all it's cracked up to be. Because, when it dies, it turns into something very unpleasant."

"I can understand that." Erika's thoughts immediately went back to their terrible argument the other night. What had been said, the savage way Paul had turned on her.

Even so, she had to move on. And if taking the first step meant walking out of her dream house, then this was what she had to do.

But she promised herself she wouldn't do it without one hell of a fight.

"Maybe the house can be sold, and Paul and I could split the amount. Minus your fees, Paul's attorney's fees, court costs and everything else, of course. I'm sure Paul will let me have most of the furniture, since I was the one who picked it out and put it on my card." She glanced at Al's expression and sighed. "But if he wants to be ugly, I guess we'll just have to split that up, too."

"Abrams and I will be meeting later today. If you like, I'll put everything on the table and see

124

what he plans to offer. I talked briefly with him after I talked with you yesterday, and he said he had already talked with your husband. Give me a chance to feel them out and I'll get back with you. Is that satisfactory with you?"

"I guess it'll have to be. It's all right if I stay in the house, then?"

"Until we get the courts in on this, it's still your house. How does your husband feel about it?"

"He already called and left a message saying he won't be coming back until the divorce is finalized. Anyway, I think he's much too preoccupied right now to worry about what I'm doing." She hoped she didn't sound like a scorned woman.

Al's expression suggested he understood. "Okay, then." He stood. "I'll give you a call later on. Will you be home? Or at the bank?"

"At the bank. I called in yesterday, and almost called in today. But I think I need to be doing something. I'm much too depressed, being at home by myself."

"Good idea. Work might be just the thing for you right now. And try not to worry. I'll get you through this as painlessly as possible."

***

The naked hooker lay on her back on the motel room bed, her blond hair covering one silicone breast, her right arm pulled back. The dull, steady hum of her snoring had quickly become revolting.

"Think we oughta dump her?" Rich Murphy shifted uneasily on the other bed. "She can identify us, ya know."

125

Ron sat in the chair, sipping coffee he'd picked up from the 7-Eleven across the street. He shook his head. "Hookers aren't exactly great witnesses. For one thing, they hate cops. Whenever they're brought in, they get pissed 'cause they end up sittin' in a police station all day and can't make any money. Then their pimp beats the shit out of 'em when they get back out on the street."

Rich regarded the hooker again. She sure was good, and really knew how to use her mouth. They'd just done a double whammy, forcing her on all fours while the two of them pounded her.

Pretty damn good for three hundred bucks.

However, if there was even one chance in a million she'd do a number on them, Rich thought they ought to bundle her up and dump her.

He knew it wouldn't be too hard to just roll her up in a sheet, wrap her with duct tape, then toss her in the truck. They could take her out in the woods, just like the other hooker, and stick her in the mud. Easy as pie.

But since Ron didn't think she'd be a problem, there was no need to work up a sweat, was there?

"What're we doin' today?" Rich asked.

Ron sipped more coffee. "Figure we'd lay low for a while, just relax. We'll have our lady friend finish us off a few more times, then put her back on the street. The ol' man mentioned givin' us a referral, so we might as well stick around for a few days. We might get another job pretty soon."

"Sounds great."

The hooker stirred.

Ron put down his coffee cup. "Wake 'er up. She's had enough shuteye."

***

"Where the hell's the one with the kids and the sled?"

Hands on hips, Julie glared at the grouping on the wall. "Hell, that was one of Larry's favorites!"

"Gone," John said.

"Whaddya mean, *gone*?"

He remained silent. He couldn't come right out and tell this woman he was almost one hundred percent certain her brother had been murdered.

At least, not without proof.

But as he thought it over, he grew more convinced than ever that Buster had indeed been murdered, although he hadn't the faintest notion why.

The paintings were all originals but hadn't been worth much. John had studied the signatures earlier. He had never been a collector but had taken art courses in college and knew a little about the masters. In this case, he hadn't heard of these artists and guessed they were most likely locals.

There were dates on three of them: 1959, 1978, 1991. The fourth wasn't dated, but it didn't look like a collectible, or antique. The names of the artists — G. Stephens, Pamela Withcoate, Dan Huggins, J.D. Purdy — didn't ring a bell. But *some*thing was very wrong, and he intended to find out what it was.

"Julie, I don't know what's happened here, but something obviously smells."

"Got any ideas?"

"Someone pulled a picture off that wall very recently."

"How recently?"

"You're not gonna like my answer."

"Tell me anyway, dammit."

"Five pictures were on that wall yesterday morning, when I went downstairs to have breakfast with Buster. Last night, when I got ready for bed, there were only four."

Julie lowered herself to the bed. The springs in the mattress groaned under her weight. She shifted her gaze from John to the picture wall. Then she turned back to John. "Do you know what you're saying?"

He nodded.

"Were you with Larry? All morning?"

"I left him right after breakfast. I wasted an hour or so in town, at the drugstore. I went to the Post Office later, to meet his friends, but they told me he never showed."

Julie listened in silence. The pale, rigid look on her face was disturbing.

"I knew something was wrong when they told me, especially when they said he never missed a day of work, so I hurried back here. I found him lying at the foot of the stairs."

Julie gazed at her hands in her lap. When she looked up at John, her eyes were moist. "Are you saying," she said in a soft voice, "some son of a bitch murdered my brother?"

He sat down beside her. "I think it's much too early to start thinking along those lines."

She suddenly looked angry. "But why would someone want that picture? Why would someone bother to steal a worthless painting? It just doesn't make any sense!"

"No. It doesn't."

"This is crazy, John. This is fucking crazy!"

"I know."

"My brother wasn't rich, you know. He had money coming in from the Army for his disability, and he made good money at the post office. Our folks weren't wealthy, so they couldn't leave us much. Larry collected winter scenes. He didn't care who did them, he bought them whenever he saw something he liked."

She gazed at the grouping. "I don't think my brother ever spent more than twenty-five bucks for a picture, including that big one downstairs, in the living room. Do you honestly think the one missing was worth his life?"

"Of course not."

Her eyes were still moist. "Talk to me, John. I have to know what you're thinking."

He stood and patted her shoulder. "Let's go back downstairs and have more coffee. Or maybe some whiskey. We need to hash this out."

***

His eyes moist, the tall, skeletal man sat in the corner nook of his basement, gazing at the bundled treasure.

He had spent most of the night looking at it, but he still couldn't get over the fact that it now belonged to him. It had taken him thirty years to acquire them all; nothing in this world was going to take them from him ever again.

He glanced at his watch. 10:00. He'd be opening up again very shortly and would have to be presentable: his usual courteous self. He couldn't betray himself or let anything jeopardize the future. Nothing he said or did could reveal his triumph.

After another twenty minutes of gawking at the package, he picked it up gingerly, walked over to the huge red safe, opened it, and slid it inside, on the bottom shelf, with the others. With a deep sigh, he closed the heavy metal door, waited for the loud *click*!, spun the wheel, and straightened.

Before leaving the room, he reminded himself to buy a new humidifier for the safe.

Couldn't have the elements contaminating his treasures, could he?

***

"How the hell can you expect me to remember anything like that, Johnny?"

John knew this wasn't going to be pleasant. He also knew he needed to ask Julie some irritating questions if he wanted to find out everything he could about Buster. "Sorry," he said. "I'm just trying to sort this out."

Julie was still frowning, but she seemed to be calming down somewhat. "I only saw my brother half a dozen times a year. How could I possibly remember what happened when I wasn't even there?"

"Do you have any idea where your brother bought his artwork?"

"Some he bought here, I guess. Other times in Wheeling, or Bridgeport. 'Buying back my childhood,' he called it. But he was cheap, and usually ended up just looking."

"What about auctions?"

She shook her head. "Naw, he didn't—*wait!*" She rubbed her temples. "Now that you mention it, I do remember him calling me one day. Just before Christmas, if my memory serves me. Last year. He'd come to town and was gonna stop by, but something came up and I had to tell him to come over another time. I don't remember why we had to beg off, but we didn't see him that day. As I recall, Larry had bought a painting and wanted me to see it."

"But you didn't?"

"Not that day. I don't remember when I did finally get to see it, but it was a good while."

"You remember which painting it was?"

"The one with the kids and the sled. The one that's missing."

"Are you sure?"

"Why else would it be stuck in my head? I mean, the picture itself was cute, but nothing special. Matter of fact, it looked like it was painted by a kid. Or someone with a shaky hand—maybe some elderly person. The brush strokes were jerky, but the scene itself was what Larry and I liked. Probably because we'd both enjoyed Christmas and sled riding—all that cool kiddy stuff you forget when you grow up. As a matter of fact, my brother's very first sled was just like the one in the painting. A Red Flyer. I remember, because the folks kept it stored in the garage for the longest time."

Julie went silent. Her eyes moistened again. "Maybe that's why my brother wanted the painting so bad."

"What did Buster tell you about the auction?"

Julie finished her coffee and got up for a refill. She brought the pot back to the table and poured some in John's cup. She suddenly looked angry. "If I'm not mistaken, that was the time Larry had a rough go with a buyer there."

"What kind of a buyer?"

"A dealer. Antiques, most likely. From what Larry told me, this guy showed up at the auction and tried to outbid him. Told the auctioneer he liked the frame and could recondition it and make a profit."

"So why didn't he outbid Buster? Surely a dealer has more resources than the average Joe who wants to pick up something for his home."

Julie sat down. "From what I've heard, dealers are too damn cheap to spend very much on one item. They're more interested in turning a profit. Because of that, they normally won't go very high. Unless, of course, the item's a collectible."

"Makes sense."

"Larry told me how everyone was watching the dealer when they were going at it. I don't remember what the final bid was, but Larry said the dealer abruptly dropped out and stomped out of the room."

"Strange."

132

"Makes you wonder why he suddenly stopped bidding, doesn't it?"

"It also makes me wonder why he was so upset that he left without buying the painting."

Julie nodded.

"Any idea who the dealer was?"

"I remember Larry saying the man had a shop just off Main Street, in downtown Wheeling."

***

At one-thirty, Al Peterson called Erika at the bank.

"Sorry I'm late, but it's been kind of hectic here."

"It's all right." She lowered her voice and swiveled her chair around. "What did you find out?"

"I'm afraid it's not good, Erika. From what Abrams said, it sounds like your husband is out to get as much as he can."

She felt her pulse quicken. "You mean, he wants the house?"

"Among other things. Seems to me that this is liable to turn into one of those bloody battles where everyone stands to get hurt. Your husband told Abrams that he intends to charge you with mental cruelty."

Erika's face flushed. She sat stiffly, taking deep breaths, trying to make sense out of what Al had just said. Two tellers passed her workstation, but she hardly noticed. Right now, she didn't even remember where she was.

The man cheats on me, then tries accusing me of something utterly ridiculous...

Suddenly, part of their last argument flashed by,

("then we'll see who gets the house")

and she knew exactly what this was all about.

Forget the miscarriages. And the fact that Paul was cheating.

It was all about spite.

What kind of man did I marry?

"Mental...*cruelty*?" she whispered, her voice barely in control. "Isn't that when one member withholds sex? Or abuses the other in private, so no one else has a clue what's going on?"

"In legal terms, mental cruelty is sort of a catch-all — or generic, if you will —that is used when nothing else seems to be tangible. Like irreconcilable differences. But what it really amounts to is that one member wants out of the contract and does not have quite enough grounds."

"Paul has absolutely *no* grounds to stand on."

"I believe you. But like I said, in this case, it'll be his word against yours. If you want my opinion, your husband has a little more clout than you do."

"How?"

"In a word? Money."

Erika felt herself flushing again. "You're saying that he's going to take my house away because his attorney makes more money than you do."

"I didn't say that."

"You're implying it."

134

Silence.

"What about that girlfriend of his?"

"That's another of those hearsay things."

She felt her jaw quivering. "He actually *admitted* that he's been having an affair – "

"Admitting it to you is one thing. Admitting the same thing in a court of law is something else. I doubt very much that your husband will even remotely suggest that there is another woman in his life. And if he has been careful about his indiscretions, he just might be able to pull it off—especially if there are no witnesses to prove otherwise."

Erika sat back in her chair and struggled to retain her composure. "Hearsay can be a bitch, huh?"

"Unfortunately."

"How about if we catch them in the act?"

"That would be much better, but will this be possible?"

"Whaddya mean?"

"Proving it. Hard evidence. Something other than hearsay, in other words."

"I don't know, Al. I'm just grasping at straws."

After a brief silence, he said, "I might know someone who can help us with something like this. An investigator I've known since college. He's good, he's thorough, and he's very discreet. He's expensive, but whatever he charges will be worth it—especially if he can produce pictures of your husband and his mistress together."

"How expensive?"

Al sighed. "For a job like this? Could be upwards of five thousand. More, if it takes longer to catch them."

"But it might help me win the house."

"That's a distinct possibility."

Erika thought it over quickly. "Get him, Al."

***

At two-thirty, John parked along the curb and crossed Main Street.

Wheeling traffic was heavy. Hordes of people crowded the sidewalks while flocking to and from the stores, banks, and shops.

An antique shop sat next to the bank building, with the sign, *EARLY AMERICAN ANTIQUES*, in bold black letters hanging over the ornate wooden door.

The store was small; its clutter made moving around difficult. Old, tired-looking furniture had been pushed into every available nook and cranny. A slender path about three feet wide enabled him to walk from one end of the store to the other.

Paintings hung from walls, leaned against dressers, and lay on tables. Most were large, with elaborate frames chipped and nicked from age or mishandling.

A stack leaned against an oak hutch in the corner. John sifted through them but couldn't find anything like the picture Buster kept in the spare room.

The more he thought about it, the more he realized how hopeless this visit was. If someone from this store had gone to Buster's house, killed his

136

friend, and stolen the picture, it would be stupid to display it in this store, where anyone could see it. Unless, of course, the picture had been stolen for its frame.

In which case, it would take a miracle to find it.

"Help you?"

A short, heavy man about fifty-five approached him from the rear of the store. The man sported a black walrus mustache flecked with gray. A big smile covered his round, cherubic face. He appeared genuinely pleased to greet a customer.

John kept a close eye on the man's expression. "I'm interested in winter scenes."

The man rubbed his chin and turned. "Any particular artist?" he asked, moving to a stack against the wall. "Or will this be strictly for decoration purposes?"

"The one I'm looking for has a couple of kids pulling a sled with a Christmas tree on it. I remember seeing it at an auction last year, here in town."

The salesman scanned the pile. He scratched his jaw. "Doesn't ring a bell. Any idea who painted it?"

"Nope." John continued watching the man's expression, which told him nothing. "A very good friend of mine bought the picture at that auction. It was stolen the other day."

"Really? That's a shame." The salesman shook his head and frowned. He seemed genuinely upset. "A lot of vultures around. Too many, actually. Can't have anything nice, can you? Someone'll wanna take it. Did your friend have the work insured?"

John shrugged.

"It would be much easier and less painful if it had been insured. The insurance companies would keep their eye out. Fencing something like that can be difficult—especially if it's an original. You know, a one-of-a-kind. Whoever's stupid enough to buy it when it's on a hot list would find out quickly how badly they messed up. Ask your friend if he's got it insured."

"I'll do that. Thanks."

"Any other way I can help you?"

"How long has your store been here?"

"Opened up this March. Been in the business almost thirty years, but I just moved from Columbus. Family problems."

John smiled. "Thanks."

"Come back anytime."

***

After leaving the antique store, John walked into a place in the middle of the next block called *Cobb's Collectibles*.

A professionally painted wooden sign hung by two silver chains over the front door. It said:

Nathaniel Cobb, Esq.
Proprietor

A sleigh bell jingled when John pushed the door open.

The store looked like it had been decorated by a professional. Ornate dining room suites embellished both front windows. Living room sets placed in strategic places highlighted imported rugs. Ancient bookcases stood proudly in straight columns against the rear wall. Carefully arranged Early American conversation pieces accented various sections of the room between furniture.

One wall was covered with paintings of all shapes and sizes. Winter scenes, battle scenes, landscapes, and portraits, all done in every conceivable era, added remarkable color to the drab paneled walls.

John sensed that he was being watched.

He turned around.

A tall, anorexic-looking man stood about ten feet away, gazing at him. He had appeared silently; John hadn't heard a sound. The man seemed to be in his mid- to late sixties, with a smooth, unlined face and large black eyes. He was nearly bald, with wisps of yellowish-white hair encircling his large skull like limp feathers.

The man was smiling, but John strongly sensed that he wasn't the jovial sort. The eyes gave him away. They were a dull black, without eyelids. And as John watched, he discovered that the man hardly blinked.

"Might I help you?" he asked in a raspy, high-pitched voice.

"I'm interested in winter scenes."

The man's smile did not change. "Can you be more specific?"

John didn't take his eyes off the man's cold gaze. "Two kids pulling a sled, with a Christmas tree tied to it."

The large black eyes suddenly blinked.

John knew right then to keep up the pressure. "Oh, and now that I'm thinking about it, I believe there was also a dog."

The man continued smiling, but John was certain he saw a slight quiver near the sharply drawn jaw.

"Sound familiar?"

The smile remained, but it seemed to have been painted on. "No." The word came out flatly.

John didn't take his eyes off the man's face. "A friend of mine bought this painting about a year ago. He collected winter scenes. They were, as far as I know, his only vise."

"Were?"

John caught another twitch on the man's face. "He's dead now."

A slight pause. "How most unfortunate."

A thick billow of heat moved slowly up John's limbs. It was difficult, keeping his hands at his sides. "Yes. It really was."

An awkward silence.

John had the feeling he was no longer welcome in the store. The old man glanced at the front door several times.

John decided to make things a little more unpleasant.

"My friend bought the painting at an auction here in town. Funny thing, though. When he was bidding, a dealer also began to bid on the painting. Odd, don't you think?"

The old man shrugged. "Not if the piece was worth money."

"But it wasn't."

"Why was this dealer bidding, then?"

"The only reason I can think of is that the frame might be collectible."

The old man suddenly brought his hands from behind his back and spread them wide. They appeared long and slender, the fingers bony, the nails shiny and beautifully manicured. They looked like they belonged on the hands of a very rich old woman.

"There you have it then," the old man said, showing a mouthful of perfect white teeth. "Sometimes the frame is worth more than the picture."

"On the other hand," John said, "the picture could be worth more than what everyone thought."

"This would depend on the artist."

"I guess so."

The old man tilted his head. "Anything else?"

"I don't know. But I intend to find out."

"If it is important to you."

"It is." John struggled to keep from losing his composure. "You see, my friend was killed for the picture, and I'm going to find out why."

The old man didn't speak, but the smile on his face remained. John could tell it was held there by sheer will power.

After a few tense moments, the old man said, "If there is no other way I can be of help..."

"One other thing."

A deep sigh. "Yes?"

"How long has your store been here?"

Silence.

The smile loosened. John was certain he'd twanged another nerve.

"May I ask why you wish to know?"

"Just curious."

The smile returned awkwardly. "I've been in business many years."

"Is that how long this store's been here?"

Another sigh. "If I can be of further help, please let me know."

The anger growing within him, John watched as the bastard clasped his manicured hands behind his back and turned.

"Good day." Without another word, the lanky figure disappeared.

John yanked open the front door and made the sleigh bell jingle erratically. He managed to make it back out in the street without screaming or pulling out his hair.

That was him. He was sure of it.

That was the bastard that killed Buster.

***

Sergeant Grubb was sitting in Buster's rocker on the front porch when John pulled up the drive.

Climbing the porch steps, John tried to read the man's expression but couldn't see anything past the usual blank expression. "What brings you here?"

"Need to talk." The big man began working on his nails with a shiny metal clipper.

"About what?"

Grubb looked up; a sour expression covered his lined face. "For starters, you can tell me why Norton's sister bulled her way to the station and did helluva job, bustin' my chops."

John leaned on the porch ledge and suddenly felt stupid. He'd suspected Julie was the confrontational type; he just didn't think she'd become much of a problem. "What's she been saying?"

Grubb looked like he'd just swallowed something bitter. "Ya think Norton was murdered, and the asshole responsible is the same guy swiped a pitcher Buster had hangin' in the house."

John shook his head. Inwardly he was cursing Julie for not keeping her big mouth shut, then at himself for sharing his opinions with her in the first place. But he understood her motivations. She was, after all, Buster's sister. She deserved to be upset, and she certainly needed to know what happened.

But, going by the expression on Grubb's face, John knew he had to downplay this one. "Just a notion I had."

Grubb shook his head. "Nope. Won't do. Woman stomps into the station with her damn loud mouth and her weird accusations, then disrupts the works by pushin' folks around. You said this. You said that. Here's what happened. What're you boys gonna do about it? And now you're tryin' to tell me she did all that 'cause of some screwy notion you had?"

John flushed. He knew he'd have to treat this with utmost care.

"I'm really sorry, Sergeant. I guess I was just upset over Buster's death." He sighed. "Buster and I were good friends, and I just felt so guilty about all this that I wanted to think something else had happened."

"So you decided to toss his big-mouthed sister our way?"

"Not intentionally. I was just telling her my opinions. I assumed she'd wait until I had more facts. I had no idea she'd run with it so fast. I guess she's even more upset than I am, but I really can't blame her."

Grubb nodded. "Any truth about that pitcher she was blubberin' about?"

"I think so."

Grubb pocketed his file and uncrossed his legs. He seemed slightly calmer. "Tell me what happened. I mean, whatcha *think* happened."

John told him.

Grubb was silent for quite a while, thinking it over. "You realize what a long shot that yarn is?"

"I also know you can't do a damned thing about it."

"No evidence. I mean, we weren't lookin' for foul play when we went in. A man pushin' forty with a dummy leg fell down the damn steps. For Chrissakes, he was busted up in all the right ways." He pulled off his hat and scratched the crown of his

144

head, then replaced the hat quickly—as if he was afraid someone might see him without it. "Where the hell would we start lookin'? I mean, if that notion of yours is on track."

"I already went to Wheeling and checked out some antique places — "

Grubb waved him down. He stood up and groaned. "I don't wanna know *anything* about this. Far as I'm concerned, what you're tellin' me stays right here, on this damn porch. You could be feedin' me a fish story, for all I know. You might be a registered fruitcake. Matter of fact, lotsa guys I knew came back from Iraq so fuckin' crazy, they woulda been better off eatin' a slug. I don't know you from Adam, so I'm not gonna put my career on the line for ya."

"I don't expect you to."

"But lemme say this. You *find* somethin'? I'll get on it like a hound dog on a fuckin' marrow bone, and I don't let up once I'm goin' at it." His index finger quickly came into view, pointing at John's chest. "But don't get outa line. Understand?"

"Tell me something."

"Whazzat?"

"How'd you handle Julie?"

Grubb grinned as he slowly descended the steps. "Told her to go home, forget about it."

John cocked his head. "And she *took* that?"

"What else *could* she do? Station's *my* turf. She knew her place."

John nodded.

"Now you tell *me* somethin'."

"All right..."

"You got somewhere to go from here?"

"I think so."

"You gonna step on somebody's toes?"

"Already have."

Grubb moved toward the squad car in the drive, then stopped and turned. His grin was back. "*Knew* there was somethin' about ya I liked."

John smiled.

"But like I said before, don't get outa line. I'm too damn close to retirement to stick my neck out."

"I get it."

Grubb got in his car, fired it up, and backed down the drive.

***

The Murphy twins were having sex with the hooker when their cellphone buzzed.

"Wh-What's *that*?" she asked, freeing her mouth.

"Fuckin' cell phone," Ron said testily. "You know what those are, don'tcha?"

"Yeah, but they don't usually go off until after *I* do." She grinned and wiped her mouth. Then she got off the bed and hurried into the bathroom.

Ron jumped off the bed. He picked up the cell from the pile of clothing on the motel room chair.

The display on the tiny gray screen made him grin.

It told him there would be another high-paying job waiting for them.

"It's the ol' man." Ron kept his voice just above a whisper.

Rich sat up and waited until his breathing had returned to normal. "Another job?"

"Could be."

The hooker came out of the bathroom, blotting her face with a washcloth.

The two men regarded her nakedness in silence.

"Somethin' wrong?" she asked, dabbing at her mouth.

"Time to split." Ron picked up his trousers. He removed his wallet, pulled out a thick wad of bills, counted out four fifties, and held them out.

She grabbed it, counted, and frowned. "*Two* hundred? I thought you wanted me for two days."

"Change of plans." Ron pulled up his pants. A dark look had taken over his face. "Go find yourself another john."

The hooker looked hurt. "I thought you guys liked me. What's wrong? I piss you off?"

"No, but you're doin' it now. Like I said, there's been a change, so shut up and get out."

With a shrug, she snatched her clothes up from the floor and shuffled back to the bathroom.

***

At six-thirty, John sat in Buster's kitchen, sipping whiskey while thinking of a plan to trap the antique dealer.

The contempt he felt for the man made his gut tighten. The only thing that seemed to quash the flames building up inside him was the image of how the dealer's composure crumbled when John had mentioned Buster.

Once again, he struggled for some sort of rationalization that would help him understand why the terrible deed was done.

Buster had apparently bought a painting that was obviously more valuable than it looked. At least, more valuable to the dealer who had bid against him. Why the dealer had backed off during the bidding remained the mystery.

A sudden wash of warmth enveloped him. He finished his drink and poured more from the bottle. He began experiencing the same sort of heat he'd felt in Iraq while hiding amongst the smoldering rubble of bombed buildings.

Understandably, this feeling scared him.

My two best friends are dead. Bill, at the hands of the Iraqis. Buster, at the hands of...

Who in heaven's name would kill someone for the sake of recovering a print that wasn't worth much more than a couple of hundred bucks?

Was it worth just a couple of hundred bucks?

Or was it worth more?

The phone rang.

"John? Julie."

"We need to talk."

Her loud cackle hurt his ears. "I'll bet that cop was there, bendin' your ear about my visit to the station."

"I need you to do a big favor for me."

"Depends on what it is."

"I want you to forget everything I told you."

"What the hell?"

148

"Forget whatever I told you about the missing painting. I've got to — "

"Whaddya talkin' about?" The volume of her strong voice made him pull the receiver away. "You know damn well there's a missing picture!"

"I know."

"Then why—"

"The only way we can investigate this is on our own."

A long pause.

He could hear her sighing. "Those damn cops aren't gonna do anything, are they?"

"There's no proof. It's only our word that there's a missing painting."

"Are you tellin' me you just *imagined* Buster was—"

"I didn't imagine anything. Our theory happens to be right on the mark. What I'm saying is, we can't expect the police to help us out."

"Now that sucks."

"You're definitely right about that."

"Do we have any options?"

"Just one."

"Which is?"

"Doing this on our own."

"That sucks, too. Unless you've got a plan."

John didn't reply.

"*Do* you?"

Although he didn't want to tell her too much, he knew that he had to give her something. After all, she *was* his friend's sister.

"I…*think* so…"

"Tell me."

"Can't."

"Why the hell not?"

"It's only a fragment of an idea. I haven't given it enough thought to even consider it as something I can actually work on."

"You bullshittin' me?"

"No," he lied.

"You sure?"

"Yes."

"I can help, you know."

"The only thing I'd like you to do is stay away from the cops. At least, for right now."

She sighed heavily. "That's askin' a lot."

"All you'll do is piss them off and get them to come after me again. And when they're questioning me, I can't do what I need to do."

"All right. You got it. On one condition."

"What's that?"

"You tell me what's goin' on."

"I sure will."

"When will that be?"

"When I know myself."

A groan. "I guess that'll have to be good enough."

John hung up. He knew what he had to do, and he had to do it soon. The dealer already knew that John suspected something. This could force the old man to make an unexpected move.

John had learned one extremely important lesson as a sniper. It was something that had never failed him. Something that had saved his life on more than one occasion.

When you want to know exactly what your enemy is doing, there's one foolproof method that makes sense.

Make sure you're close enough to see him doing it...

***

Two rings.

"Ron Murphy."

"You gave me the impression no one else was involved in this matter." The old man's voice sounded even more raspy than normal.

Ron frowned. *What the fuck?*

"Whaddya mean?" he asked. "We pulled it off without anyone knowin' anything. It was perfect. The way you wanted it done. Just like an accident. The cops were only in the house half an hour, forty-five minutes, tops. They took the dude away in an ambulance, and – "

"Why was someone *here*, then?" The old man was barely keeping it together. His breathing quickened, then grew louder. "In my *store*! Asking me *questions*!"

Ron swallowed. *This doesn't sound right.*

"What happened? Who was in your store?"

"I *don't know*!" Cobb's breath came out in short, wheezy pants, like an exhausted old dog. "He came into my *store*. I thought he was a *customer*."

"How d'ya know he wasn't?"

"By the questions he was asking, you idiot!"

151

Ron gritted his teeth. The man's tone grated on his nerves. He wasn't too wild about being called names. That kind of shit took him back, and he didn't *want* to go back. It was dark back there, and cold. Terrible things had happened. Things that needed to be forgotten.

He had to proceed with caution here. He and Rich had their reputations to think of, and this ancient asshole was just the type to open his big mouth and fuck it all up.

"What'd this guy look like?"

"About five-feet-eleven, maybe one-seventy-five. Curly, dark-brown hair cut fairly short and professionally. Handsome, with intelligent brown eyes. Thirty-five, maybe thirty-eight. Alert and very determined."

Ron immediately thought of the guy staying at the house with Norton. The guy Rich hadn't liked. Their conversation came right back and made him wonder if his brother had been on the right track when he thought they should have dropped the other guy when they'd dropped Norton.

"I know who you mean. We saw him at Norton's house. We think he was a friend, and—"

"Why the hell didn't you handle them together?"

Ron took a deep breath. He knew it wasn't smart to waste your employer, but this old fuck was jerking the wrong nerve. "You didn't give us the okay to do it. You didn't tell us someone else might be around. And if you had, it woulda cost you extra — "

"I don't care! I don't want this…this *person*…walking around, asking questions, getting people upset—"

"Are you sure?"

"*Yes*, I'm *sure*!"

"This'll cost ya extra—"

Click!

Ron glared at the phone and growled. He wanted to slam it to the concrete walk and smash it with his boot.

Well, at least he knew what the game plan was.

By the man's tone, he knew he and his brother were about to become even richer.

***

At eight o'clock, John observed the street activity from the Town Car across the street behind Cobb's Collectibles.

So far, things had been quiet. Aside from light traffic, he saw very little movement.

His plan was simple. He decided to wait in the car for a while, then step outside and take a leisurely walk. He suspected he wouldn't be lucky enough to spot anything at first, but he wanted to have a look around. It was already getting dark, but the yellow haze from the streetlamps at each corner was more than enough to highlight points of interest.

He sat back and watched the drab gray block building. A shiny black BMW sat in the small gravel lot to the right of the rear door. A green dumpster with a large blue swastika spray-painted sloppily on its dented face sat at the corner, off the curb. John wondered for a moment if he should

153

walk on over and have a look but decided it was unnecessary. The information he needed remained somewhere in the store. The contents of a filthy dumpster would be of no help to him.

The dealer posed the key to all this. His reaction to John brought about the strong suspicion of direct involvement in Buster's mysterious demise.

The foxlike expression covering the man's unlined face also suggested something not quite right about him. The large, disapproving eyes and the defiant way he stood conveyed red flags. His inner tension betrayed him as well. Also, the way he struggled to keep his composure. His rigidity—arms at his sides, hands behind his back—spoke volumes.

The heat emanating from him.

The hatred in his eyes.

The sharpness of his tongue.

A totally different picture crept into John's head, making him queasy.

Buster, lying at the bottom of the staircase, head twisted, nose smashed, artificial leg pulled loose. The glazed look in his eyes.

Cobb's voice: "how most unfortunate..."

A wave of dizziness slammed into John. He closed his eyes and, gritting his teeth, rode it out.

That pathetic fucker killed Buster.

He killed him or had him killed.

And I'm going to nail him for it.

154

Fired up once again, John got out of the Town Car and began walking quickly down the dark street.

**

"Told ya we shoulda popped his ass."

Rich sucked down Pepsi and frowned. "I knew there'd be trouble when I first saw 'im."

"I know, dammit." Ron was growing more irritated by the minute. "But like I said, we didn't have a contract. Woulda been stupid, doin' somebody else when we had to make this thing look like an accident. We couldn't make it look like that with *two* stiffs -- no way in hell. And didn't we decide when we first started doin' this that the only freebies we do are for fun? When there ain't any witnesses around?"

"Still shoulda popped him," Rich grumbled, sitting back in his seat.

"Maybe so."

"*Not* maybe."

"All right, dammit." Ron knew his brother was right. But what was done was done, and what they had to do now was to start planning again.

The old man had broken contact, but Ron knew he'd be getting back in touch. When the next call came, Ron promised himself he'd handle the old fart differently.

The old man was nasty and didn't care how he treated them. Their father had treated them this way—coming in drunk at all hours, slapping them around whenever they got in his way and using the belt whenever he got a wild hair. This was why they popped him the first chance they got.

They'd popped him seven years ago. It taught them how easy it was. And though they'd done in more than two dozen folks since that special night, their desire for success and the sheer love of killing hadn't dimmed.

It continued shining brightly, as a matter of fact.

Like when Cobb started shooting off his mouth.

Ron suddenly had a terrific fantasy—he and Rich driving back to Cobb's store, taking the old man down to the basement and having a ball before finishing him off with some of the antique tools they'd seen hanging on the concrete wall down there.

Then the burner buzzed, disrupting his cool dream.

Ron checked the tiny gray dial. "It's him."

Rich scowled. "What're you gonna tell him this time?"

"One thing's for damn sure. I ain't gonna let him talk to us like gutter trash again."

***

Nathaniel Cobb frantically paced the apartment.

Those stupid twins had certainly messed things up.

Thirty years of his life, ten thousand dollars of his own money, and now it looked like he was going to have to shell out even more to keep this all quiet.

156

His thoughts went back to the irritating stranger, and he shuddered.

There was something frightening about that man...

Cobb reached up and smoothed out the few yellowish-white strands clinging tenaciously to his marble-like dome.

Something in the man's eyes warned Cobb of imminent danger. The stranger wasn't large, nor did he look physically powerful...but Nathaniel Cobb was certain this man could be trouble and needed to be taken out of the picture.

Cobb went to his console and switched it on.

He'd installed several different programs on his PC. One program included the complete inventory manifest of his store. Another was devoted to customers and contacts. There was one for local and overseas distributors. One for business transactions. And one listing of libraries telling him everything he needed to know about collectibles, gems, and rare antiques.

There was also a program consisting of a contact he didn't want anyone else to know about. It was password-protected, accessible only on his special high security program. The program was labeled *FileF*. Its contents consisted of just one name and one e-mail address in an encrypted file.

The address was for a man known only as "*Rbow*."

Cobb wasn't certain but was reasonably sure the contact resided in the Tristate area. He went into his own server, typed the message, "*require services immediately*," sent it to the appropriate address, and waited.

He didn't want to deal with the Murphy's in this matter. They were young and crude, stupid and greedy. And insolent—a quality Cobb detested. Cobb needed maturity here and knew he could get it from Rbow. He hadn't used him before, but one of Cobb's most reliable business contacts had rated the service very high.

Rbow (so the story went) was a former F.B.I. agent who had been in Drug Enforcement nearly twenty years, retiring early due to an injury sustained while attached to a Miami undercover operation. He was thorough, discreet, and one hundred percent professional. He was more expensive than the Murphy's, but one hundred percent reliable and top-quality.

And God knows I need total reliability and top-quality services...

Five minutes later, Cobb heard the *beep*.

His heart fluttering, he entered a *receive* and waited until it popped up on his screen.

Then he read the message.

His heart sank heavily.

> *"Out of town.*
> *Thursday OK?"*

After some furious thinking, the idea came to him like a spark of electricity. Feverishly he typed the message:

and sent it off immediately.

Then, grinning in delight, Cobb picked up the phone, dialed the appropriate number, and left the numeric message.

No reason why he couldn't kill *two* birds with one stone.

Maybe even *three*?

***

His senses alert, John leaned against the streetlamp at the corner.

He'd circled the block twice but hadn't seen anything out of the ordinary. Fortunately, there wasn't much street activity. Cobb's store windows faced the front on both floors. One second-floor window was dark, the other lit. There were two other upper-floor windows behind the building. One was lit.

Hoping to be seen, John decided to stay near the streetlamp for twenty minutes, then switch to the front of the building.

Being seen was the only way that would give him the advantage of shaking up his foe. He had already surprised Cobb by going into the store and asking questions. He considered this his greatest edge. Anything that would disorient the enemy or scare him changed the game and gave John the necessary edge.

Disoriented means defeated.

It would cause Cobb to screw up, make mistakes.

John *wanted* Cobb to make mistakes.

Your enemy is only as strong as his weakest link.

Find that link, and the enemy is in your hands.

It was the only way to discover what had happened to Buster.

John waited five more minutes. Satisfied with his plan, he moved away from the streetlamp and ambled to the front of the discount store on the other side of the street, facing Cobb's Collectibles.

***

Ron Murphy waited patiently for Cobb to pick up the phone.

"Yes?" came the shrilly voice after the fifth ring.

"We need to talk."

Silence.

Ron waited.

"I have another very important job for you," the old man said after a long pause.

"This about the dude we talked about earlier?"

"Yes."

Ron grinned. This was turning out just the way he wanted. He strongly suspected the old man had been shoved into a tight spot. And this meant even more of a price than what they had earned from doing the gimp.

"All right," Ron said. "But the price is higher."

A pause. "How much higher?"

"Double."

Another pause.

160

Ron could hear the old coot sucking in air. He expected Cobb to lose his nut again. Moments later, the old man asked, "Why?"

"I don't like the way you talked to me earlier."

Cobb didn't reply.

Ron suspected the old man was going to try negotiating. He knew right off that it wouldn't fly. Neither he nor his brother would stand for it. "If you don't meet our price, we won't do it."

Silence. The old man was probably thinking it over.

Ron was tempted to hang up but decided to wait. He told himself to give Cobb another minute before pulling the plug.

"All right," the old man finally said. "I guess I don't have much choice, do I?"

Ron felt flushed. A soothing warmth had gathered between his legs. He cursed himself for getting rid of the hooker so soon. "Nope. You don't."

"How can I be certain this will go as planned? Can you guarantee someone else won't get in the way?"

"Yep."

"How?"

"If there's someone else hangin' around, we'll act differently."

"How?"

"We'll take care of it."

"All right."

More silence.

"Deal?"

"Deal." Cobb hung up quickly.

Ron pocketed the cell. He felt greatly relieved. It would be a kick, telling his brother they'd soon be earning twenty thousand dollars for another day's work.

But just then, he began wondering why the old fart had given in so easily.

There had been no negotiating, no bargaining, no argument. Just a simple "why?" It made him suspicious.

However, he caught a quick vision of the cash they would soon be earning, and his suspicions and doubts simply vanished.

The old man knew he had to give in. It was that simple.

Ron wanted to laugh and do a cartwheel at the same time.

There would be plenty of time for that later.

***

Nathaniel Cobb replaced the receiver and grinned with satisfaction.

Those stupid, insolent twits. Do they honestly think they are a match for someone like Nathaniel Cobb? A man who has amassed a fortune swindling people and getting away with it for the last forty years? Selling these fools overpriced junk and convincing them their purchase was actually a valuable antique? Taking an antique from a grieving widow for pennies and telling her it was only a cheap copy? Or a clumsy attempt at restoration?

Who do these imbeciles think they are dealing with?

Cobb sat back in his armchair and laughed. He thought fondly of his treasures lying hidden within their cardboard backings.

Who else but a genius could have acquired such a prize? Who else but a man of insight could lay claim to such wealth?

He got up and moved silently into the next room, which served as his living room.

This room was quite large. Facing Main Street, it served as his favorite place for ultimate relaxation during the evenings, where he listened to Beethoven and Tchaikovsky, his two favorite composers, while enjoying a drink. Brahms was normally much too dark and brooding to suit his particular moods. Tchaikovsky brooded, but also managed to lift his spirits. Especially the ballet suites.

Beethoven's symphonies were Cobb's favorites. Numbers 5, 7, & 9 were the masterpieces he loved for different reasons.

Number 5 made him feel very special about himself and life in general. Cobb listened to it on a specific occasion—customarily when an obstacle was removed from his path. Cobb had played it very recently: when the Murphy boy told him Norton was dead.

Number 7 had been a gift from his mother more than sixty years ago, when he was just a child, aspiring to be a concert violinist. Its First Movement, the "*poco sostenuto*," never failed to uplift him -- especially when the passage

163

transformed into the "*Vivace*," an extremely invigorating piece of melodious elation.

Cobb preferred playing this work when things looked grim, and he needed something to lift his spirits.

Number 9, his all-time favorite, was played when his life reflected a significant personal victory. He had played it last night, with his latest acquisition. And since he considered his contact with Rbow another victory, Cobb would play it again tonight,.

Rbow would rid him of his enemies.

Rbow would make everything right again.

Cobb pulled the record from its special place on the shelf. He very gently removed it from its dust jacket, slipped it carefully onto the turntable, closed the cover, and went to the bar to pour a very potent cognac.

As the strings began their haunting *Allegro*, he closed his eyes and breathed in the beautiful sounds. After a few minutes, he opened them again and went to the window to gaze out at the thick blanket of the approaching night. And stiffened.

The Beast was standing out there. Across the street, beneath a streetlamp.

Waving!

"*Oh no*!" he gasped, dropping his drink on the wine-red carpet.

***

"What's the first thing we do?" Rich Murphy asked.

Ron relaxed behind the wheel of the truck, celebrating their good fortune with some high-grade coke. He sniffed a few times, then glanced at his brother. "Simple. We go back to Bern and wait."

Rich was silent. He'd just done a line but was more interested in this other business. "I think I know what happens next."

"Tell me."

"First of all, we go back, like you said. Then we pick out a good observation post and watch for a while. You don't think that asshole lives near the gimp, do ya?"

"Don'tcha remember? Pennsylvania tags. But I don't think this dude's too far away. Especially since his buddy's dead. You can bet your ass he'll be at the funeral."

"When's that?"

"Friday or Saturday. Should be in the mornin' papers. Then we'll know for sure."

"Might make it easier."

"That's what I'm hopin'."

"How much time we got?"

"Ol' man didn't say. But we'd better do this dude quick. Before the funeral."

Rich smiled. "Twenty thousand big ones. That's a shitload of change."

"Right. And we're gonna do it -- "

His cellphone buzzed.

Ron sat up sharply and grabbed the cell from the console. He checked the display. "The ol' man again."

Rich blinked. "So soon? This don't feel right."

Ron nodded. "Better find out."

***

Erika got up from the living room sofa and fixed herself another drink.

She knew she was overdoing it, but somehow it didn't matter. Her world was crumbling around her ankles. Two drinks after a small serving of pot roast wouldn't hurt anything.

She remembered her conversation with Al Peterson and felt the heat of anger bubbling up again.

How *dare* Paul try screwing her out of what was rightfully hers!

Especially when he was having an affair!

Would there be an end to this outrage?

She poured what was left in the bottle and drank…a little too quickly. The room began spinning, telling her she should stop.

She really didn't want to. The more she drank, the more relaxed she became. It didn't exactly mellow her or make things any easier, but it did quell the heat considerably. She didn't want to be angry, and she didn't want to hate Paul. She'd never been comfortable with such strong negative emotions. It made her queasy.

However, it occurred to her that it wasn't the anger that had been making her dizzy, it was the hurt. The feeling of betrayal. The knowing that her husband had not only shifted his affections toward another woman but had also turned his back on their relationship.

In her mind, he had killed the very memory of their years together.

The drinking seemed to help, making her determined to do more of it. It dimmed the anger and numbed the pain. It also numbed the senses, but who was counting? She was going to drink, and if anyone didn't like it, they could just take a running leap.

She got up rather clumsily and plodded over to the counter. The cognac had done serious damage to her balance. Her feet felt funny when she tried moving them. She had the strange feeling that her toes had jumped ship.

She vaguely remembered someone (was it Paul? someone else?) saying you shouldn't drink cognac the same way you drink whiskey. You had to *sip* cognac. Coax a drop or two onto your tongue and let it soak in before you swallowed. If you actually drank it like any other liquid, you'd be sorry.

She guessed that this procedure would work for someone who was thinking clearly. However, she knew that she hadn't exactly been too concerned with such protocol at the time, and the cognac bottle had been the one she'd picked up.

But now that the bottle was empty, such details no longer mattered.

She staggered back to the couch and fell into it.

The room began spinning again. She took a deep breath, but the room continued to spin.

Maybe some fresh air would help…

It was an effort, getting up. The couch seemed reluctant to let her go. It took three tries to get it to release its grip. Using the padded arm as leverage, she managed, finally, to push away the moment her butt cleared the cushion.

Once again, her toes felt like they'd gone into town for a leisurely stroll.

She ignored the sensation by walking on the outer edges of her slippers.

In no time, she'd reached the foyer.

Then the door began giving her trouble.

You like me, too, Mr. Door?

Wanna tango?

She eventually got the deadbolt working, then the chain, and finally the little metal catch over the knob, before bumping her forehead on the screen.

Groaning, she staggered out onto the front porch.

The cool night breeze enveloped her, but instead of making her feel better, it made her nauseous. She reached out for the thick wooden post. Wrapping an arm around it, she slid down until her butt landed on the top step. Her feet began doing funny things again, and for an instant she thought she saw her toes (all ten of 'em!) scurrying across the step like fat roaches, then jumping off the edge.

She said, or *thought* she said, "God, I am *so* seriously messed up!" and felt her lower lip buzzing like an angry bumble bee.

Then she laughed, and both lips began buzzing.

She gasped in surprise when she let go of the post. She hadn't done it intentionally — her right arm just collapsed.

Is my arm gonna jump in the shrubs, too?

I'll look pretty stupid, crawling around in there, looking for my toes...

A moment later, she realized she was rolling down the steps. She was shocked to discover that it didn't hurt. Or maybe she just wasn't feeling anything anymore, she didn't know. She thought she laughed again, but the blackness had drifted over and was soon right there, reaching out to devour her, and she didn't want to think about anything else.

When she stopped rolling, she saw the headlights of a car splashing her full in the face.

To her amazement, she found that she no longer cared.

If she was killed, that was that. And if it really happened, Paul could move in with his blond bimbo and they could live happily ever after.

Erika closed her eyes as the headlights drew closer.

***

One ring.

Ron waited.

Two rings.

Ron glanced at his brother. "Make the old fuck sweat for a change."

Rich grinned.

Three rings.

Ron pressed *talk*. "Yeah?"

169

"He was *here*! *Outside*!" Cobb sounded like he had come unglued. His loud, raspy voice sounded like someone was choking him. "Standing across the *street*! Looking up at my *living room window*!"

Ron wanted to smile. "Who?"

"Who else, you idiot? *Him*! The man who was *in my store earlier*! He *knows*, dammit! I *know* he does! He knows what *happened*! What we've *done*! Why *else* would he be out there — "

"Why'd you call?" Ron asked calmly, enjoying Cobb's predicament.

"Why *else*, damn you? I want him *done*! *Now*! *Finished*! *Dead*! Right this *minute*! I want you and your brother — "

"Wait a minute. You already contracted us to — — "

"I know what I contracted you for. I just told you, I want him *gone*. *Now*! I don't want to be a prisoner in my own home, and I think I've earned the right to demand — right here and now — that you take care of this, and in the way we agreed. Is that clear?"

"Sure is."

The old jerk was scared shitless and still trying to call the shots.

Ron knew they had him now, and it was time to start roasting him over the spit. "There's one big problem," he said after a pause.

A gasp. "What? What? What's the problem?"

"Problem is, we *can't* do him *right now, right this minute*." Ronald enjoyed mimicking the old fart. It was refreshing, like a rush from high-grade

170

coke or crank. His crotch had grown warm again. He wondered how long it would take them to hunt down the hooker.

"Why not? You're being paid — "

"Yeah. We're bein' paid. Just like the other guy. But it was different with the other guy."

"Listen to me, now—"

"*You're* the one should be listenin'. You're payin' us, but this is *our* show, and it's *our* asses out there. The shit starts, it's *us* out there, not *you*. We're takin' our time with this, just like we did with Norton. We'll take a coupla days, stake out the house. We'll watch him, see what he does, where he goes. When we pick up his routine, we'll take more time, then —"

"I'll d-*double* the offer," Cobb said quickly.

Ron paused—this time, for effect.

Damn... This asshole wants to double the original offer, fork out forty grand, just to have a guy snuffed two days quicker than planned?

This was turning out better and better!

"Whaddya mean?" he asked.

"I mean, I mean...f-forty thousand dollars. That is, *if* you do it in one day. *One day*! This means before midnight, tomorrow night. Is *that* clear enough for you?"

Forty thousand skins. If we do the guy in the next twenty-four hours.

That didn't seem out of the question, did it?

No. Especially with that kind of money at stake.

"You got a deal."

171

"Call me the instant you're finished—and I mean the *very* instant!"

Click!

As Ron pocketed the cell, he thought once again about doing that cartwheel.

***

John lowered Erika gently to the couch and propped up her head with a pillow. Then he hurried to the kitchen.

The girl was obviously drunk. She was rolling down the porch steps as he drove up to the house just ten minutes earlier. Good thing he'd pulled over when he did. He could tell by her momentum that she would have rolled into the street.

He found a washcloth in the kitchen and soaked it with cold water from the tap. He wrung it out, hurried back to the living room, and applied it softly to her forehead.

She stirred a little, moaning softly.

He wondered if he should check the house and see if someone else was around. A kid, maybe? A husband?

Then he remembered that she was getting a divorce.

He knew right then why she'd been drinking.

He remembered his own divorce not very long ago. Pam marching out the front door, taking things that were rightfully his. The insults. The screaming. The threats. The nastiness, the hatred.

All the terrible things slithering to the surface that had been developed from a relationship that had once been based on love.

172

As he gazed at the troubled woman lying restlessly on the couch before him, he wondered what had happened in this house, this tastefully decorated, comfortable place that had once been a home. As he studied her beautiful face, her long lashes, the thick blanket of dark hair covering part of her cheek, he thought of the first time he had seen her, outside the Holiday Inn. Their conversation later on, in the restaurant.

Although she seemed like a genuinely nice, warm person, he knew it was impossible to sum up anyone in just a few minutes. A human being was a complex organism, filled with love and hate, gifted with potential, marred by weaknesses and failures. A human being was a maze of complications and frustrations, neuroses and fears.

This woman could quite possibly be the same sort of loathsome bitch that Pam had been, the love of his life who had pulled every string possible to take everything from him, even though it had been Pam who had been the one to walk out of the marriage.

However, even though John barely knew this lady, he could tell that she was hurting, and very deeply.

John sighed tiredly. Knowing Erika could be out of commission for quite a while, he went over to the recliner, sat heavily, then pushed the chair back. He decided to stay here a while to make sure she got through this. Then he'd go back to Buster's and do more planning.

For the next two hours, John relaxed in the recliner and thought about Buster. And Cobb. And Pam.

And, of course, the troubled woman sacked out on the couch, just ten feet away.

***

Consumed by the darkness, Nathaniel Cobb desperately gripped the arms of his chair. "Is he…s-still out there?" he whispered nervously to his friend.

"*You need to look*," was the reply.

"I c-can't."

"*You really need to*."

"No."

"*Yes*."

"No!"

The silence overwhelmed him. Beethoven's *7th* had just ended. He had switched it off just minutes ago, in the middle of the Second Movement. It had been necessary. This present mood was not meant for the majestic beauty of Beethoven.

Nor Tchaikovsky.

Nor even Brahms.

This horribly dark mood was suited for silence only, as Nathaniel Cobb struggled for some way to survive the next few hours.

He was reminded of his childhood, when he was locked in the closet for wetting the bed. Locked in that tiny, foul-smelling room, forced to wear the very nightclothes he had soiled.

To remain in total blackness.

Locked out of his room, his world.

174

Being at the mercy of the two monsters dictating his confinement, his punishment. His stays were made longer and longer since his bed-wetting infuriated both of them more and more.

He could never forget the sheer terror coming from the dark, the coldness in his spine as he sobbed, pleading for them to unlock the door, to let him out.

The confinements had forced him inward, causing him to retreat into himself, since he couldn't break out under his own power. They caused him to turn to his only friend, who approached him in the darkness as he wept, comforting him until the light finally returned.

He did the same thing growing up: retreating inwardly during failure, turning to his dear friend in times of stress.

"I *can't* look," he repeated, his gaze carefully avoiding the dreaded window.

"*Yes. You can.*"

"But — "

"*I know you can. You know you can. Know it. Feel it. See it.*"

He wanted to sneak over to the window and see if he was still being watched. He wanted to but knew he couldn't. He didn't dare. Norton's friend might still be out there. If he were, he would make another horrid gesture.

The darkness had become his ally again, his companion. The darkness hid the terror, the fear. He knew he must caress it as never before. Even though his friend had urged him to do the impossible.

"Look outside, Nathaniel."

"No."

"Look out."

"No!"

The Murphy's would take care of the Beast and that would be that. Then Cobb could go back out into the light and do what he'd been planning all these years. To return to the basement, open the safe, and take them all out. Unwrap them. Hold them lovingly in his hands, then stand them up against the wall and talk to them, tell them his plans, then show them to his friend.

He smiled in the darkness. It would only be a matter of a few hours, and the other one would be dead. Then Cobb could finally go out into the light and enjoy what was rightfully his.

"Just a few hours more," he told his friend. "Then I won't have to worry about who or what is out there."

"Yes."

Cobb sat quietly. His mind went back to the auction. As always, his body stiffened at the dark, forbidden thoughts.

"What is wrong, Nathaniel? The auction again?"

"It upsets me, just thinking of it. Remembering. Always remembering. Knowing all this could have been avoided."

"Why didn't you buy the painting?"

176

Cobb frowned in the darkness. "You know why. You were there."

"Yes. I was there."

"And what did you see?"

"I saw you and that man Norton bidding against one another. For the painting. You bid ten, Norton eleven. You bid twelve, Norton thirteen."

The scene returned, making his scalp itch. He closed his eyes tightly and took a deep breath. "And then…and then…what happened?" he asked through clenched teeth.

"You bid twenty. Norton, twenty-five."

The scene had turned bright and harsh beneath his eyelids. He stiffened again in his seat.

"I looked into his eyes. They were mocking me, telling me that no matter what I bid, he would take the painting. It didn't matter because he wanted it and was going to steal it from me. I saw victory in those eyes. Victory and triumph. The sort of thing you see when your enemy knows he has won."

"And you panicked."

Cobb sighed. He reached up and wiped his moist brow. "I panicked. Those eyes..."

"Yes. They resembled…his…"

"Yes. His! The monster! *His* eyes!" Cobb felt his brow turn cold. "They looked…they looked like —"

"Like years ago, when the monster came upstairs and saw you."

"Yes." Cobb shuddered. He gasped when a sudden cold wetness gathered between his legs.

"He handled you. Just before she *came up to—*
"

"Enough!" Cobb squeezed his wet eyes shut. He suddenly felt weak. Spent.

"I'm sorry. I didn't mean to upset you."

"I…forgive you."

"Thank you."

"It was all so…so *horrible*. The auction. Seeing those *eyes* again. Knowing the beast was dead and yet, years later, going to an auction and seeing his *eyes* again. Feeling the same things…all over again."

"I understand."

"Then it got even *worse*…"

"*Worse*?"

"Yes. *Yes*! Turning around…and seeing all those…those *other* eyes…on *me*. The audience. They were sneering, too. They knew my pain, my torment. Yet they — "

"It was your imagination, Nathaniel."

"It was so *real*…"

"It must have been."

"I had to leave. To escape."

"*Yes*."

"Another second in that place and…and I would've…I would've come apart!"

"*Yes*."

Cobb tried to relax. Things were dimming, moving away. Moving slowly, but moving away, nonetheless. The icy feeling in his spine had vanished.

"I'm…better, now."

178

"I'm glad."
"Good things will happen."
"Yes."
"Very soon."
"Of course."
"Soon there will be no one to stand against us."
"No one."
"We'll wait for this moment."
"We'll wait together."
"Thank you."
"You're welcome."
"You'll always be my friend."
"And you will always be mine."

Nathaniel Cobb pulled his damp palms away from the arms of the chair and wrapped them around himself.

This way, he could hug both himself and his friend at the same time.

***

Erika opened her eyes and saw someone sitting in the recliner.

John?

Oh my God...

What happened? What have I done?

Moments later, he was standing over her, a worried look on his face. Reaching out, gently repositioning something cool on her forehead.

She sighed deeply and felt a warm sourness in her throat. She reached up and touched the cool, soft cloth he had placed on her forehead.

179

Deep concern showed prominently in his beautiful brown eyes. She tried speaking, but he waved her down.

"Don't try to talk. Just relax. You passed out on the steps."

She took another breath and felt the sourness growing. "How long…have I…been out?"

"About two hours."

"My God…" It all came back. Sluggishly at first, then bright flashes.

The cognac. My toes jumping ship. Holding onto the post on the porch.

Sliding, sliding…

Rolling…

Bright lights.

"I remember."

Paul…

Damn you for making this all happen!

She discovered that her eyes were wet. "Was that you? The headlights in my face?" She pointed toward the front door.

He nodded. "Good thing I happened by. You might've rolled out into the street."

She closed her eyes. The warm tears drifted slowly down her cheeks. "You could have…run me over."

It would have made things so *much easier…*

"It was okay. You stayed on the walk. At least, long enough for me to bring you inside."

She shook her head.

He doesn't understand.

"What I meant was, you could've run me over and saved me a ton of aggravation."

He didn't reply.

She tried sitting up but lay back down when the hot throbbing bolted through her skull. Moaning, she grabbed her temples. The washcloth fell. John picked it up and helped her lie back.

"Relax." His voice was soft, reassuring. "You need to tough through this one."

She forced a smile. With one hand, she reached up to wipe way the tears. John handed her the cloth.

"Thanks." She used it to blot her eyes. "You keep helping me."

He looked a little embarrassed. "Seems like it."

I have my very own White Knight. I'm so lucky...

"Want me to make coffee?" he asked.

"Does that really work?"

"No, but I thought I should offer."

She laughed, grimacing when the throbbing rushed back. "Please don't make me laugh. I'm too depressed and irritable. And it makes my head hurt."

"The divorce going bad?"

She thought of their talk earlier and tried to remember the details, but her mind remained much too cloudy. "Did we discuss that?"

"You mentioned it."

She groaned. "He's taking all he can from me."

"I know this won't help much right now, but a lot of people have gone through the same thing."

"You, too?"

He nodded.

She clearly saw the hurt in his eyes. "Painful?"

"Excruciating."

"How'd you get through it?"

"Time. And Jack Daniel's."

She smiled despite the throbbing.

Cognac. Jack Daniel's. It all amounted to the same thing, didn't it? The same timeworn remedy for failure and hurt.

He got up and looked down at her. "I guess I should be going."

"Do you have to?" The prospect of being alone made her shiver.

"I just don't think you want company now."

"Actually, that's *exactly* what I think I need."

"I'll stay if you like. If you don't think the neighbors will mind."

"I don't really care about the neighbors. Please stay with me. I guess I could use some coffee, after all."

***

The Murphy twins waited in their truck in the Burger King parking lot on East Main in Bern.

It was almost midnight; traffic was very light.

They'd checked out Cobb's place first, staking out different sections of the block at half-hour intervals. They'd come up empty, and after waiting nearly two hours for any sign of the Town Car, they left Wheeling and headed straight for Bern.

Ron's discovery of the Lincoln had brought a smile to his lips. He knew right then that this would be the easiest money they ever made.

However, something wasn't quite right. The Town Car wasn't in Norton's drive. Instead, it was parked in front of the house at the other end of the block.

"Whaddya think the Town Car's doin' *there*?" Rich whispered after a long pause.

"No idea. But we'd better find out."

"How?"

Ron ran a hand through his short blond hair. "Well, since we only got twenty-four hours to wrap this one up, it's gonna be tight. We can do this, but we'll have to wait a few more hours. We can sneak in Norton's house okay, but we don't know why the dude's at the other place. But we really need to find out what's goin' on, and if we wait a few hours, he'll prob'ly make some kinda move. Then it might be easier to take 'im out. But we still gotta be extra careful. Too much damn jack ridin' on this one."

"Whaddya wanna do first?"

"I want you to mosey on down the street and have a look at that other place. Make sure nobody sees you. Use the bushes. We need to know what he's doin' there. We can't see any lights from here, so we gotta do all this from a different angle. Go on over, then get close—but not *too* close. Like I just said, we can't be seen—by anyone. When you're finished, c'mon back. Got it?"

"Gotcha." Rich slipped quietly out of the truck and hurried down the street.

***

Erika sat on the couch, sipping the strong black coffee John had made.

"Feeling any better?"

She shrugged. "A little. At least the tom-toms have quit. That cognac sure is powerful."

"That's the stuff heavy drinkers use. An amateur like you? You should stick to highballs."

"How do you know I'm an amateur?"

John smiled. "I can tell. Why? Am I wrong?"

"It just bothers me that you can read me so easily. What else can you see? Other than the fact that I'm not a drinker, and obviously can't hold what I put in there."

"You're also hurting."

No reply.

"Care to tell me about it?"

She was looking down at her lap. "It's not a pretty story."

"Divorce seldom is."

"My husband…well, he wants the house, and as much of everything else as he can get. He's also messing around, and has been for quite a while, it seems. But he's got money, and he thinks he can use it to buy a bigger settlement than I can get."

"Is he right?"

"I don't know. Maybe. My attorney hired a private investigator to snoop around, maybe get some pictures."

"Then you could be worrying about nothing."

"What's bothering me is what's happened to the relationship. We were so much in love…once. The marriage started off just fine. We couldn't get enough of each other. We could talk to one another. We shared things."

Her face clouded over. "Then, almost overnight, Paul turned into a total stranger. That last argument we had, he…he looked at me with such *contempt*…"

"You've got to forget that."

"I can't."

"You will."

She frowned.

"Believe me. You'll forget, in time. Maybe not today, or tomorrow. Maybe not even next year, or in five years. But one day, you'll notice that the hurt is no longer there, and when you look back, you'll remember how your life changed and how much of a better person you are because of it."

"Is that how it was with you?"

"I still remember how Pam practically ran out the door. It was almost like she was escaping prison—or some terrible personal hell. It made me wonder if she considered me some sort of monster." He sighed. "But it doesn't hurt anymore. The more I think of it, the more I remember early signs. Signs I couldn't see at the time."

"How long were you married?"

"Three years."

"Not very long."

"Nope."

"Were you married just once?"

He nodded.

"How come?"

John shrugged. "Gun-shy, I guess."

"How long ago did that happen?"

"Ten years."

She gave him a wide-eyed look. "You've been *alone*? For the last *ten years*?"

He sighed. "More or less…"

Erika shook her head. "Now *that's* a long time."

"In more ways than one."

Erika smiled shyly. "I guess you really *are* gun-shy…"

John shifted uneasily. "More coffee?" he asked, getting up.

She nodded, pushing her legs out from underneath her. "Let me get it, okay? Don't forget—you're the visitor."

"I don't want you waiting on me if you don't feel right."

"I'm fine. And I'm not waiting on you. Just getting coffee."

Chapter 4 - Wednesday

"Dude's with a chick!"

Out of breath, Rich Murphy jumped into the passenger seat of the pickup and pulled the door shut.

"Really? Strange." Ron looked puzzled.

"They were both in the kitchen, drinkin' coffee."

Using the dirt path behind the houses, Rich had crept over to the house at the end of the block. A snoring dog in the back yard of the second house had prompted Rich to stay particularly quiet as he'd passed, reminding him to walk on the grass to cushion the sound of his footfalls.

He managed to sneak up the backyard of the corner house, using the fruit trees as cover. A buckeye about fifty feet directly behind the house provided sufficient concealment. Rich used the thick trunk to hide himself while inching closer to the building.

The kitchen light was on. He could see movement from within, but the laced drapes prevented him from distinguishing any useful images.

Since the backyard wasn't lit, he found it easy to reach the rear wall. There were no signs of a dog, and he heard no growling or yelping near the house or the neighboring property. It was just a matter of staying close to the trees and keeping an eye on the kitchen window.

A flowerbed sat directly beneath the windowsill. He was careful to stay in the dirt, mindful of where he stepped. The smooth bottoms of his tennis shoes would make depressed prints in the dirt but wouldn't be obvious unless someone was searching for signs of disturbance.

Satisfied that he hadn't been seen, he gazed in the window.

A man and a woman sat at the kitchen table, talking and drinking from mugs. The man was the dude he'd seen at the Norton place. Rich recognized the curly brown hair.

Once again, he felt confident this job would not pose much of a risk. This dude was pushing forty and didn't look very formidable. He was definitely no match for the two of them.

The chick was a fox. Lots of black hair, a pretty face, and nice-sized titties visible in the baggy sweatshirt. Definitely had a body that could make a guy slobber over. She was no kid, but that didn't mean she wasn't hot.

"What else were they doin'?" Ron wanted to know.

Rich shrugged. "Just talkin', drinkin' coffee. Like I said."

"Not holdin' hands? Playin' around?"

"Didn't see 'em touch one another. Not once."

"How were they lookin' at each other?"

"Nothin' special." Rich noticed his brother's pensive silence. "Whatcha thinkin'?"

"Maybe this guy lives in that house and maybe he doesn't. I keep thinkin' of those Pennsylvania tags. Who's this chick? And what's he doin' there, this time of night?"

"A visit. maybe?" suggested Rich.

"Yeah. But why?"

"What's it matter?"

"Matters."

"How?"

"If we can't pick him off alone, then we'll need bait to get him."

"You mean the chick?"

"Exactly."

"Smart."

"Here's the plan. We watch the house. All night, if we have to. He comes out, fine. We watch what he does, then take it from there. He doesn't come out, then we go in and get 'im ourselves. Hell, who knows? They might just be hidin' the banana when we go in later—which'll make it easy. Don't have much time – "

"What about the chick? I mean, say we go in and find her, instead?"

"Like I said, we might need her as bait. Then we'll have to do her anyway, so why worry? Forty grand, bro. Nothin's gonna fuck us outa *this* one."

***

"About your friend," Erika said, watching John closely. "Is there something you're not telling me?"

She wanted to ask John about everything that was happening but didn't want to pry. Although John had told her about his friend's death, what he *hadn't* told her was the source of the darkness she clearly saw whenever he mentioned it. It wasn't

189

your average darkness, and she couldn't help noticing the anger in his eyes whenever the subject came up. She realized that even though this was not something he might want to discuss, there were many questions she had to ask. She only hoped her questions wouldn't make his darkness even worse.

His silence told her he was holding back. Especially since his mood had changed so drastically during the last few minutes, when he lowered his face and began staring at his hands.

"What makes you think that?" he finally asked.

"For one thing, you're not looking at me."

More silence.

"*Please* tell me what's wrong…"

After a pause, he said, "Are you sure you want to know?"

"I really do."

"It's not…it's not very pleasant."

She blinked. "I kind of figured that one out on my own."

He went silent again and went right back to looking down at his hands. Then he raised his head and gave her a most unsettling stare. "I have a strong suspicion Buster was murdered."

Erika's jaw dropped. "My God. Are you sure?"

"Reasonably."

"But *why*? I mean, why would someone kill a nice man like Buster? What makes you think he was murdered?"

"Something strange happened when I left the hospital and went back to the house." There was a

190

painful expression on his face. She could clearly sense that he had gone to a very bad place.

"Trust me, John." She watched him, noting the cracks around his eyes that hadn't been there moments earlier. "I'll believe whatever you tell me."

He smiled. "At first, I didn't even believe what I guessed had happened. It was only after my trip to Wheeling that I knew for sure. After I'd seen…after I'd actually *talked* to the man. Then I knew."

"What man?"

He sipped his coffee. The angry expression remained.

Erika felt for him, knowing that she was now facing a man who was hurting just as much as she was.

She suddenly discovered that she no longer felt sorry for herself or for the breakup of her marriage. She knew she'd mend and would eventually go on while this man continued mourning for his friend— that sweet guy who'd always managed to lift her spirits whenever she walked into the Post Office.

John began talking, and when he was finished, Erika sat there, her mouth open, her eyes filling the sockets.

"I remember that painting," she said, the memories drifting back sluggishly, as if they had come back from some distant place in her mind she seldom visited. "And I remember the man bidding against him."

John stiffened in his seat. "You do?"

"I was there. At the auction."

"Are you *sure*? I mean, this was almost a year ago."

"It was our seventh anniversary. Paul's and mine. In December. Just before Christmas. I remember, because it was the first and only time I'd ever seen your friend somewhere other than in the Post Office."

"And you actually *remember* what happened?"

"Yes."

"And who was bidding against him?"

"A weird old man. He owns that antique place in Wheeling, next to the pharmacy just off Main. Guy gives me the creeps. He's tall and skinny, with buggy eyes. Reminds me of a spider or something out of a horror flick."

"His name is Nathaniel Cobb." John's expression remained tense. "And you remember all this because of your anniversary?"

"Paul decided we'd go to an auction, maybe find something nice. And we did. We bid on an Early American – "

"What else do you remember?"

"I don't think I'll ever forget the look on that old man's face when your friend was bidding against him. I'd never seen anyone look so *angry*. I mean, he was enraged, and barely containing himself. He was shaking so badly, and his face was so red, he looked like he would explode."

"Anything else?"

"The funniest thing happened. Right in the middle of the bidding, the old man groaned loudly enough for all of us to hear, then stomped out of the room without a word."

***

At one o'clock, Rich Murphy was getting restless.

He'd been watching the house down the block, the one with *Larson* painted neatly in white on the black mailbox. The Town Car parked in the drive did not move -- nor was there any other sign of life.

"This sucks, Ronnie."

With Norton, the job had been much easier. They knew he lived alone, where he worked, shopped, spent his leisure time.

They knew nothing about this guy. They hadn't even seen him before yesterday. It was like he'd popped into the picture like magic.

But things had suddenly gone down the shitter. It looked like this dude wouldn't go away. He'd somehow figured out what had happened to Norton and was hanging around, asking questions. He'd even gone to Wheeling, found the old man, and got him all fired up.

"Nothin' else to do right now." Ron had pulled his seat back. He was relaxing on his left side, his chiseled arms folded across his muscular chest.

Rich had always envied the way his brother could relax—even when things got tense, or all messed up. Rich had always been the worrier of the two. He didn't like it, but it was the way things were. Even as kids, Rich always worried about trouble they could get into, while Ron stayed relatively calm and kept things manageable.

Still, Rich didn't like all this waiting around. Not even with all that money hanging in the balance.

"How 'bout I sneak on over there again and — "

"We stay here."

"How long?"

"Till somethin' happens."

Rich studied the dashboard clock. "Not much time left."

"I'd rather wait 'em out than have you go over and fuck it all up. Forty thousand skins, remember?"

Frowning, Rich squirmed into a comfortable position in the seat.

Waiting around was a bitch sometimes. Even with so much money out there, waiting for them to snatch it up.

***

"Did you go to the police?" Erika asked John after finishing her coffee.

She couldn't believe Buster Norton was murdered and hoped John was just imagining all this. But even though she didn't know much about John, she could tell that he really and truly believed what he'd told her.

"I talked to Sergeant Grubb. My big mistake was telling Buster's sister what I suspected. Julie's nice, but not the calmest, most tactful person I've ever met. She apparently made quite a stink at the station. Grubb was waiting for me when I got back from Wheeling. He didn't appreciate getting reamed by Julie. I think he accepts my murder theory, but

194

when I told him the evidence I had to work with, he told me I was on my own."

"Does this mean you're gonna go with this by yourself?"

"Have to. I already went to Wheeling, like I said, and talked to Cobb."

She frowned. "I don't believe you actually *talked* to that man."

John shrugged.

"But why? I mean, if he did as you think and had your friend killed, isn't he kind of dangerous to be messing with?"

"That's why I went to see him. To stir him up. He's definitely the excitable type. I know I set him off. You upset someone badly enough, they start making stupid mistakes. Then you can nail them."

"But if you're right, and Cobb did have someone kill your friend...aren't you afraid he'll have them come after you?"

"That's what I'm hoping," he said, getting up.

"Why?"

"Then I'll know where they are. And that I was right about this all along."

***

At two o'clock, Rich nudged his brother.

"Ronnie! Look!"

Ron opened his eyes and sat up sharply.

The headlights of the Town Car blazed to life in the Larson drive. The car backed out onto the street, stopped, and began moving in their direction.

"Push your seat back and *duck down*!" he whispered anxiously. "Those lights hit us, he'll see us just as clear as daylight!"

Rich reached down, found the lever, and forced the back of the seat all the way down. He used his own weight to depress it, gasping as the high beams of the Town Car splashed dangerously close to his face.

Ron lay back, waiting tensely until the blinding swash inched away. Then he slowly raised forward and watched as the Lincoln stopped in front of Norton's driveway before pulling up the drive.

"Think he's callin' it a night?" Rich asked.

"Hope so."

"How come he didn't stay with the babe?"

"That don't matter. Not to us, anyway. All we gotta worry about is gettin' him without anyone suspectin' anything."

As they watched, the man got out, closed the car door, and went up the porch steps. Before approaching the door, he turned around.

"Duck, dammit!" Ron shrunk down, nearly catching his chin on the steering wheel.

"Shit!" Rich slammed the side of his head onto the console. "What the fuck was *that* all about?"

"Dunno. Just wait."

"Think he saw us, Ronnie?"

"Not sure." Ron slowly raised his head. "You can get back up. He's inside now."

Rich pushed himself up, gawked at the empty front porch, and smiled. "Looks like we're about to make ourselves a big chunk of easy cash."

196

"We'll give him an hour or so," Ron said. "We gotta wait, see which lights go off. When it feels right, we'll sneak inside and do the deed."

**

John went up the front steps and turned.

As he regarded Erika Larson's place at the other end of the block, he wondered if she was getting ready for bed. He imagined her in front of a mirror, brushing her hair and removing her makeup. He also envisioned her brushing her teeth, wriggling into a nightgown, then getting into bed. Sleeping alone, while her jerk of a husband was fooling around with another woman.

John got out Buster's keys and slipped inside.

The house was dark except for the kitchen light, living room lamp, and hall light, which lit up the staircase. Before going upstairs, John turned off the lights in the kitchen and living room, leaving the one in the upstairs hall burning.

Moments later, he began thinking of Cobb once again.

If the old man were planning to send another assassin, John would need to set some sort of trap. This wouldn't be difficult, since John had been a light sleeper, thanks to his days in Iraq. It wouldn't take much time or effort to rig up something that would trip up someone trying to sneak in.

John went into the kitchen, turned the light back on, and began looking for things that might prove useful for handling an intruder.

**

At four o'clock, Ron Murphy decided the time was right.

The downstairs lights had gone off more than an hour ago. The house had been totally dark ever since.

"Feels like it's time to rock," he told his brother.

"I feel it, too," Rich whispered, checking his pockets.

Their plan was simple. Sneak in the house, take the dude by surprise, and feed him the chloroform. They had a packet ready: it would be simple to hold him down and give him a big dose. Then they'd bundle him up, carry him outside, and stick him in the truck. Their next stop would be Wheeling. They'd take him to one of the seedier places in town, near the docks, and clean out his pockets. Then they'd run him over, dump him in the river, and the job would be finished.

Piece of cake.

And they'd be forty thousand richer for it.

"Let's go over this one last time." Ron wore his solemn business face. "We need to get it up there, fresh, so it's second nature. This way, no slipups."

"All right."

"You go in first. Here's the knockout juice." He handed his brother the packet, which was sealed carefully in plastic. "Use your key, sneak inside, then check the first floor. Have your penlight on and make damn sure he's not downstairs. Worse comes to worse, we might have to use those steps again. Give me the signal when it's clear."

"No problem."

"I'll go in and double-check the first floor while you're upstairs. But wait till I join you before you do anything. Gimme a flash of the beam to lemme know where you are. I'll join you, then we'll do it. But have the juice ready in case he wakes up. Feed it to him if you gotta. If not, wait till I get there. Got it?"

"Got it."

The brothers eased the doors of the truck carefully shut and hurried across the street, toward the house at the corner.

**

John waited tensely in the upstairs hall closet.

He sat in the heavy wooden chair he'd taken from the spare room. The closet door was open about ten inches, enabling him to see the hall and the railing at the top of the staircase.

John had found a hard rubber mallet in the kitchen pantry. The handle, about a foot long, was thick and solid enough to serve as a formidable weapon. It lay comfortably in his lap.

His trusted pocketknife, which he had been carrying with him everywhere for the last fifteen years, rested in his trouser pocket. As he had learned as a sniper, the only knife worth carrying was one that could be sharpened to the consistency of a razor blade.

Someone was coming. He could sense it, feel it.

He suspected that this "sense" had been that same instinct he developed as a sniper in Iraq. He also couldn't shake the overwhelming feeling that Cobb would make some sort of lethal decision before John had the chance to tell anyone his suspicions about Buster's death.

Or maybe what had been nagging at him most of all was that tingling sensation that had started up so suddenly the moment he'd turned into Buster's drive only hours ago.

The image of the battered pickup sitting in the Burger King parking lot flashed brightly in his head. He remembered seeing the same truck before, and in the very same spot. As before, it was pointed directly at Buster's house.

He strongly sensed someone inside the cab, watching the house.

John sat tensely in the dark, his senses at the ready.

It was frightening that everything had come back so easily. He felt as if he'd been on permanent standby, secretly yearning to be recalled after all these years.

As if he hadn't left the desert at all.

He would never forget how he'd gathered twigs and rubble from destroyed buildings he used to cover himself so he could spend the night undisturbed within enemy lines. Placing dry, brittle sticks and long, jagged strips of scorched wood, covered in sand, at three-foot intervals, starting at fifteen feet from his makeshift bunker, which would alert him of approaching footsteps.

Other than the shotgun mounted on the living room wall, John had been unable to find ammunition or any other firearm anywhere in the house. Even if he had, he considered the shotgun too bulky, too impractical. He hadn't had the opportunity to find out exactly what Buster had owned, nor had he been afforded the time to perform a thorough search of the house.

But it hadn't been necessary. If someone had to be taken down, John was confident he could do it without a gun.

Once again, he thought of Buster.

The fact that there had been no sign of a struggle suggested that Buster had been overpowered. In John's view, his friend hadn't had time to resist. Or cause trouble. He was convinced Buster had been taken by surprise and was shoved down the staircase.

Buster hadn't been a small man. Six feet and over two hundred pounds. He'd lifted weights in college and worked in a lumber mill for two summers between semesters.

Buster was no weakling. Even with just one healthy leg, he would have been more than capable of causing a world of hurt to anyone bent on sending him down a flight of steps.

This told John that there had been more than one assassin.

Suddenly tired, he pulled the blanket up to his chin, squirmed into a comfortable position, and closed his eyes.

Just fifteen minutes later, he heard someone moving about, downstairs.

***

Rich had no trouble opening the front door.

The same key that had opened the door the first time opened it again. It was a special key he and Ron had bought from a Columbus locksmith several years ago, which could open more than seventy-five percent of the old Yale locks on houses built half a century ago.

Rich pushed open the door about three inches and remained totally still, listening.

Silence.

He knew he didn't have to guess where his brother was. Ronnie was close — that much was certain.

Rich opened the door a few more inches.

More silence.

The dude was probably sound asleep.

Didn't matter, even if he was awake. They knew what they were doing. Together, they were unbeatable.

More than two dozen kills to your credit gives you helluva edge...

Squinting, he tried penetrating the darkness but could make out just a slight haze coming from the kitchen. It wasn't the kitchen light, but some nightlight shining low in the room, lighting the carpeting.

When his senses told him it was clear, he opened the door wider, listened, then slipped quickly through the opening.

***

Ron crept out of the bushes.

He saw no sign of life outside the house. He knew Norton's friend hadn't snuck outside through another doorway. Why would the dude suspect anyone was after him in the first place?

Well, he *had* suspected *some*thing, hadn't he? He'd even gone to Wheeling to question Cobb. But that was probably just a fluke. Ron considered himself good at figuring things out. He knew it wouldn't be long before the explanation came to him. But by that time, Norton's friend would be dead, and nothing else would matter.

Ron and his brother were professionals, and professionals considered every conceivable avenue. Even though there was no earthly reason for Norton's friend to suspect anyone was after him, Ron was careful to consider every possible chance of a fuckup.

He waited on the front porch, listening, his senses alert. At one point, he even rested his ear against the wall to pick up vibrations.

His brother was inside, exploring the first floor. Ron decided to wait exactly five minutes before slipping through the opening Rich had provided at the front door. He would then close the door silently behind him and stand quite still, the long-barreled .357 in his right hand.

The gun would be used to frighten if the need arose. It was loaded, but Ron knew better than use it. Especially at this time of night. It would be totally insane to alert the whole town.

As silently as a cat, Ron slipped through the opening. Seconds later, he eased the door shut. Just before it had the chance to brush the rubber liner, he eased it to a stop. Then he turned and watched as his brother slowly climbed the staircase, one cautious step at a time.

***

Rich meticulously checked the first floor before approaching the staircase.

The place was as quiet as the grave.

His penlight stuck between his teeth, lighting the way with a long sliver of bright yellow, he crept on tiptoe across the living room floor. Out of the corner of his eye, he saw Ron sneaking in, taking his position near the door. A brief glint of light revealed the stainless finish of his brother's revolver. Ronnie was holding it in his right hand.

Rich smiled as he approached the foot of the staircase. He knew his brother would provide the perfect blockade; no one would get past him. Especially with that cannon in his hand.

Rich began climbing the stairs.

The main section of each stair was covered with a layer of worn carpeting. This was good; it provided an excellent cushion for his footfalls. He and Ronnie both wore tennis shoes, favoring this style of footwear for extreme comfort, as well as for quiet and agility. And since they had already tested the staircase, they both knew they had nothing to fear. A couple of steps creaked, but only if you placed your weight on the inner edges. A simple test told them that if they put pressure on the outer portion of each step, they wouldn't make a sound.

204

This precaution hadn't been necessary with Norton. That situation had been different—surprising him coming out of the john, breaking his neck, then carrying him up the stairs and positioning him for the fall.

This would be much simpler.

It would also be fun.

Rich couldn't wait.

Just five more steps....

Forty thousand skins...

As Rich lowered his right foot on the fourth step from the top, something thumped noisily to the wooden table directly below.

***

John tried peering through the door opening, but it was much too dark to distinguish any activity. He thought he might have glimpsed a pinpoint of light, but he couldn't be certain if it was that or his imagination.

He decided to wait until his trap put his foe into a state of shock before making his next move. He'd learned that you could gain precious seconds-- even if the enemy knew about you—by causing confusion. By upsetting the enemy's concentration, you could gain the advantage you needed to do what was necessary.

The trap was simple and effective.

He had found mint-flavored dental floss in the downstairs bathroom medicine cabinet. He also found some tiny eyehooks in Buster's metal toolbox in the kitchen cupboard.

John screwed an eyehook into the wooden border on the inner wall of the staircase, about two inches higher than the step. He then screwed another hook to the opposite side, on the outer edge of the corresponding rail, at the same height. Finally, he positioned a third hook into the corner of the rail, at the top of the staircase. The floss was then tied to the first hook and passed across the step, then slipped through the second hook, before running up the stairs, parallel with the wooden border. The floss then ran through the corner hook. John fastened the loose end to the vertical wooden railing of the balcony.

He then balanced a thick black Paper Mate permanent marker in a standing position on the edge of the balcony floor. It was positioned next to the wooden railing, its back resting against the floss, which was tied snugly.

Any sudden downward movement, such as pressing the floss into the stair carpet, would pull the line taut, thus causing the marker to be pushed forward, propelling it to the cocktail table below. Since the floss was the same color as the green carpeting, it was virtually undetectable—especially in the dark.

Just moments after John had heard the faint footsteps on the stairs, he heard the marker clattering on the wooden surface of the table.

The game was on…

The mallet gripped tightly in his right hand, John slipped silently through the closet opening.

***

Richard Murphy stood frozen on the step.

The penlight clenched tightly between his teeth, he desperately searched for the source of the sound.

Several things came to him at once.

His first reaction was that someone—the dude, most likely—was standing at the top of the stairs, watching. Ron had startled him, making him drop something.

He pulled the penlight out of his mouth and pointed it at the top of the stairs.

Nothing.

No movement in the shadows.

He turned, lowered the penlight, and inspected the living room floor.

The table below had stuff on it, but it was too dark for the penlight to pick up everything. He couldn't tell if something was there that wasn't there before.

But *some*thing had fallen, causing enough racket to alert anyone within earshot.

An accident?

Or some sort of trap?

He moved the penlight back toward the top of the staircase, scanning as much area as possible, but the sliver of light couldn't take in much. As he did so, his ears combed the silence, alert for anything coming from the upper rooms.

Perhaps the fallen object had been a fluke. If it had been something else, he should have heard some sort of noise coming from one of the bedrooms.

Confident their plan was still a go, Rich turned on the step and gave his brother a thumbs-up sign. He knew Ronnie would be watching him and would see the movement, even in the dark.

Rich eased off the step. Then, reaching the top landing, he made his way down the hall.

***

Standing totally still, John blended in with the darkness.

Whoever was moving around down the hall had reached the top step and was most likely trying to guess what had gone wrong. John figured this person had been spooked by the sudden noise and would stay there for a while, listening closely to the silence. When he finally decided that whatever he had heard was no doubt an accident, he'd betray his position by continuing down the hall.

Staying close to the wall, John took a careful step toward the staircase. Then he saw the pinpoint of light bouncing in his direction.

His head filled with bright, choppy colors. The rage inside him had grown quickly, becoming hot splashes moving steadily up his spine. He clenched his jaw tightly and took a deep breath. His temples began to throb, but he ignored the discomfort.

Buster. Dead. My friend killed. For a fucking painting!

John pulled his arm back. Strong images of Buster lying at the bottom of the staircase flashed loudly in his head.

The pinpoint of light suddenly stopped. John heard a soft gasp just before the light moved in his direction, toward his face.

Just as the bright beam was about to meet his eyes, John brought the square hard rubber head of the mallet brutally down.

Onto the assassin's head.

Bonk!

A loud gasp echoed down the hall.

In the very next second, the house blazed with bright lights.

***

Ron cringed in terror.

Hands trembling, he twisted around, reaching for the living room light.

The place screamed loudly in brilliant light.

Then he saw his brother flying down the wooden staircase.

It happened in slow motion, Rich twisting and rolling down the steps. Moving like a rag doll, arms flailing, head bouncing as his skull slammed into each step. An eternity later, he landed on the living room floor with a sickening thud.

Ron's jaw dropped. A soft squeal escaped his throat. His feet numb, he scurried awkwardly across the room.

A dream. This feels like a dream.

He was imagining this!

It…just…didn't…happen!

He dropped to his knees. His broken brother lay on his back at the foot of the staircase, head twisted, blood oozing from his nose and opened mouth.

"Richie…God, what the fuck happened?"

Ron dropped the gun onto the floor and reached out. His thoughts were racing. Telling him one thing, then another.

His eyes were deceiving him.

This was only a dream.

A dream. Yes. Had to be a dream, *had* to be!

He'd somehow drifted off while watching the door and was having a terrifying nightmare. Rich wasn't lying here at all. Not really. He was upstairs, getting ready to apply the chloroform to Norton's sleeping friend.

A dream.

Gotta be a dream.

Gotta be!

He gently picked up his brother's head and held it close.

No dream.

This is the real thing…

Richie's dead… My brother…

Dead!

He knew his brother was dead but didn't want to move the lifeless head for fear of twisting it the wrong way. Just in case… He cradled it tenderly, resting it on his left thigh as he feverishly felt for a pulse.

Please…

Dream…

Has to be, has to be!

Please *let there be a pulse please let there be a fucking pulse!*

Suddenly they were in their own little world again. Ron and Rich. Together. As they had been all their lives. Especially when they were kids, their old man beating them and locking them up before going out and bringing in his drunken friends.

Just Ron and Rich. The two of them, locked in their room, listening to the loud, drunken hysterics in the living room and trying to block it all out. Dreaming. Telling one another their own special aspirations.

When they grew older.

How they would get rid of their old man.

How they would sneak out through the window, then sneak into the bastard's bedroom when he was sleeping it off.

Putting him out of their misery.

Killing him. And whoever else wanted to push them around.

Maybe even get paid for it -- like in the movies.

Ron was preoccupied with his brother, and not aware of what was going on at the top of the staircase. He had heard something up there, near the very top, but everything else had switched off when he'd picked up his brother's bloody, lifeless head.

He just didn't care anymore. Rich was dead, and he realized only then that they had never talked about what would happen if something went wrong. If one of them died during a job.

Then he looked up and saw a madman at the top of the stairs, looking down at him with such fury, his eyes seemed to be on fire.

The madman's arms were extended above his head.

The wooden leg of an armchair was gripped tightly in each white-knuckled fist.

***

John let the chair fly.

It sailed down, smashing into the duo at the foot of the stairs and driving a strangled shriek from the man kneeling.

The sounds were loud and revolting. A splintered *crack*! as the arm of the chair smacked the kneeling man full in the face. A dull *thump*! as the bulk of the chair crushed into the man's body. A loud *thud*! as the back of the man's head slammed the carpeted floor.

John waited more than a minute before leaving his sanctuary. He pulled his penknife from his pocket and descended the stairs slowly, his eyes fixed on both men.

Rather, *boys*.

The one lying at the bottom of the staircase didn't move. John bent, felt for a pulse. There was none. He put his palm near the boy's nose but felt not even the slightest trickle of warmth.

Frowning, he thought of Buster again and the rage came right back.

No need for rage here. This psycho was gone.

The other one watched him silently. He lay on his back, one eye slashed so severely, the clotted blood had forced it shut. The other eye, light-blue and cloudy, remained wide-open as John knelt before him. The boy's swollen mouth was moving, the blood-covered lips quivering awkwardly.

A hot sourness filled John's gut. A heavy dizziness made the room flip sideways. His eyes had become wet; he reached up and wiped them with his fingers.

Snap out of it, Callen...

This isn't Iraq!

He turned. The stainless, long-barreled revolver lay on the floor just a few feet away.

Did they threaten Buster with it? Stick the slab barrel in his ear while they forced him up the staircase? Poke him in the gut while they pushed him down the stairs? Shove it in his mouth while they laughed and told him what they were going to do? While they nudged him up the stairs? While they made him stand at the top, gazing down at his doom?

Did they tell him what they were going to do?

Did they make him aware of what was going to happen?

Buster knew; John was sure of it.

His friend knew he was going to die.

Buster had suffered the ultimate fate at the hands of these disgusting psychos.

The hot sourness moved upwards, settling in his chest. Making his entire body hot.

His eyes were wet again, this time, from blind rage.

Growling softly, John kicked the big revolver out of harm's way. His eyes were fierce red slits as he knelt before the second youth and looked directly

213

into the bloody, wide-open blue eye. He lay down the knife and placed his hands on both sides of the young man's head. "This one's for my friend," he whispered close to the boy's ear.

Without hesitation, he jerked his hands in opposite directions, snapping the boy's neck and driving one last squeal from the gaping lips.

The snap of the boy's neck echoed loudly through the house.

**

Grubb's men carefully chalked the scene, examined the bodies, and cordoned off the front of the house.

"We're sendin' their prints to Washington," Grubb said to John on the street. "You got somewhere to stay?"

"I'll find a place." John watched as the medical unit slid the stretcher with the first body bag into the back of the van. "There's a motel a couple of miles down the road."

Grubb was watching him closely. "You actually think those two were wet boys?"

John nodded.

"Couldn'ta been a simple home invasion?"

"Not when one of them was carrying chloroform, tape, and twine. You saw the three-fifty-seven. And unless I miss my guess, that beat-up Ford pickup parked at the Burger King might give you some evidence about them as well."

Grubb pursed his lips and pulled the toothpick out of his mouth. "What else ya thinkin'?"

"I'm thinking they were the two who murdered Buster."

Grubb replaced the toothpick. "Still can't figure it. No evidence to indicate foul play. Run it by me a second time, why ya think they were paid to do in your friend."

"I think it's all about a painting Buster bought in Wheeling last year."

"You actually think someone wanted a *painting* bad enough to have Norton killed for it?"

"Or the frame. Since Buster didn't really go for expensive originals, I'm betting on the frame. Unless it was a setting that really moved him, according to his sister, he didn't like spending more than twenty or thirty dollars on any of his paintings."

"You got somebody in mind?"

"A dealer in Wheeling. Cobb's his name. Heard of him?"

"Can't say I have. But I'll take your word on it. One thing puzzles me, though." He was looking at the open doorway, where one of his deputies was dusting the doorknob.

"What's that?"

"Those two in there. *Kids*, for Chrissakes. No more than twenty, and damn muscular. Six-one, six-two, two hundred, all solid. One's got a Smith three-fifty-seven mag, the other a switchblade and a knockout pack." He shrugged a bony shoulder. "No offense, but you're prob'ly older than both of 'em put together, and don't go much more than one-seventy-five."

"One-sixty-nine, actually, but what's your point?"

"How the fuck didja manage to get the drop on 'em?"

"Lucky, I guess."

Grubb shook his head and scowled. "Nope. Don't like it. If these really were wet boys, they woulda done your ass in, real quick. They're young, strong, and armed. What I don't like is, the one got his neck wrung like a turkey."

John shrugged. "Self-defense."

The big man sighed. "Tell me somethin', Callen. I got somethin' to worry about here?"

"What do you mean?"

"What I mean is, I gotta worry about *you*?"

"Only if someone else tries to kill me."

Grubb frowned. "How come that don't exactly give me a big, warm fuzzy?"

"I didn't realize that's what you were looking for."

"One thing I *ain't* lookin' for is more paperwork to fill out. It ain't exactly my thing, ya know what I mean..."

"All I care about is finding out what happened to my friend. Once I'm satisfied, I'm outa here, and you can take that to the bank."

Grubb pulled off his cap and scratched his gray-black brush cut. "Ya don't mind my sayin' so, I hope to hell you find out. *Real* quick."

John nodded.

"Just tell me one thing."

"If I can."

"The way these two bought it. Got anything to do with your sniper trainin'?"

"Survival training was pretty extensive. And it stays with a guy."

"Thought so."

"Came in handy, didn't it?"

"Good thing you didn't forget what they taught ya."

"As I just said..."

Grubb moved away. "Well, go git yourself a room. We're ready to seal off the house. But don't go far. I'll need to ask ya more questions. For the record."

John got in his car. As he pulled away, he was thinking of what he could do next to show Cobb his hand.

***

Nathaniel Cobb sat tensely in his armchair, hoping the quiet strands of Tchaikovsky's "*Pathetique*" would quell the cold dread that had enveloped him the past few hours.

He turned to his friend, who faced him in the darkness. "I'm really worried."

"*About what?*"

"Norton's friend."

"*What worries you most?*"

"The look in his eyes. The day he came to my store. The way he faced me, studied me, tried to read my thoughts." Cobb shivered and gripped the chair even tighter. Gripping it seemed to give him a sense of security. He felt as if he might vanish forever if he let go.

"*Did he manage to read your thoughts?*" asked his friend.

"He looked like…like he might have..."

"*But you're not sure.*"

"Of course not."

"*Why worry, then?*"

"It was this feeling I had. And still have."

"*What feeling?*"

"The feeling that this man is evil. I fear he will be the source of my downfall."

"*What is the basis for this feeling?*"

"I've already said. I saw evil in his eyes."

"*A foolish notion, Nathaniel.*"

"I know. But very real."

"*Kill it.*"

"How?"

"*Put it in the back of your mind, where the darkness is so deep, you'll never be able to find it again. Snuff it out. Like a candle.*"

"I…don't think I can."

"*You can.*"

"How can you be so sure?"

"*You are special. You have managed to accomplish your dreams despite the monsters. Despite what they did to kill your dreams. You own this store, run a very profitable business, and deal in valuable art and treasures. You have a reputation in this city. People respect you and come to you when they're seeking something rare and precious.*"

"And I've acquired the paintings," he whispered, his eyes suddenly wide-open in the darkness. "It's taken me thirty years, but I've done it."

"Yes. You have."

"And now that I've done it, it will make me -- make *us* -- very rich."

"*Yes*."

"Rich enough to flee this filthy, disgusting city."

"Yes."

Nathaniel Cobb leaned back in his chair, closed his eyes, and sighed deeply.

Just one more day, and the monster would be gone.

Then he could finally put together the puzzle that would make him—and his friend—very rich.

***

After spotting the familiar light-blue Town Car parked in front of the East Main Coffeehouse, Erika pulled over and parked.

Getting to the bank early that morning had suddenly become unimportant. She arrived early every morning and knew they could function this morning without her help. Anyway, she wanted to ask John about the police cars she'd seen in Buster's drive earlier that morning.

The place was packed and, as usual, smelled strongly of coffee, burnt toast, and fried bacon.

John was sitting at a corner table near the front, sipping coffee and gazing out the window. Erika walked over and stopped just a few feet away, watching him.

A moment later, he noticed her standing there, smiled, and put down his coffee mug. He stood. "I'm sorry, I didn't know you were standing there. Please. Sit." His cheeks flushed. "When did you get here?"

"Just a few moments ago." She sat. "I didn't want to interrupt you. You seemed deep in thought."

"Do you have a few minutes? Would you like some coffee?"

"I have time. And yes, I'd *love* some."

He signaled for the waitress, who came right over with a fresh pot and clean mug.

After she left, John said, "It was an exciting night. After I left your house, things got pretty hot."

"I can imagine. I was getting in my car to leave for work and saw some of our neighbors and just about every policeman in town standing in front of Buster's place. I wanted to see if you were okay, but I didn't know if they'd let me through. Besides, your car was gone."

The creases around his eyes deepened. He lowered his voice. "Two men came to Buster's house last night and tried to kill me."

Erika gasped.

"They were both young, big, and strong. Twins. Grubb's running their prints as we speak. He expects to hear from Washington shortly. It happened just a couple of hours after I left you. By the time you were ready to leave for work, the cops had already come, picked up the bodies, and sealed off the house."

"They actually tried to...*kill* you?"

220

"They were both armed. One had a three-fifty-seven, the other a switchblade. The one carrying the switchblade also had chloroform."

"My *God*..."

"I'm pretty confident they were pros, but Grubb isn't so sure."

Erika quickly discovered that she was trying very hard not to appear as frightened as she felt. This was terrifying, and she wasn't sure how she should react. "What happened? I mean, you're here, and in one piece. How did you manage to – "

"They're dead, Erika."

She felt her jaw drop.

Dead. He just said dead. This meant...it most likely meant that he killed them. Both of them. The man sitting across from her, looking so calm and handsome, had just killed two young men.

She just gazed at him and found herself wondering, once again, how she should react.

Just then, he reached across the table to cover her hand. His touch, both warm and comforting, somehow made her feel less frightened.

"It was self-defense."

She snapped herself out of it. "I'm sure it was. It's just that, well, call me a wimp if you like. But three deaths in just two days? All of them murders? And just six houses down? On my street?"

"You're not a wimp."

To cover her uneasiness, she picked up the sugar bowl and tried putting some in her spoon without spilling it. She knew how clumsy and awkward she must look. John was a soft-spoken, personable man. There was no way she wanted to upset him by saying something stupid. He'd already been through enough—why make things worse by letting something ridiculous slip out of her mouth?

But the fact remained: she was having coffee with a man who had just murdered two people. And, despite what she knew about the situation, this was something she just didn't think she could accept.

He was watching her. It felt—at least, to her—like he knew what was going on in her head.

"It was war, Erika."

She gazed at him stupidly.

"They were the enemy. They'd killed my friend."

Just then, she found her voice. It felt funny—kind of pinched and far away—and didn't even sound like her normal voice. "But you still can't be sure Buster was murdered. Or can you?"

"Why else would that painting disappear?"

She sighed. "It's just hard to accept the fact that someone would want to kill that nice man."

"We all have enemies."

Paul's image immediately filled her head.

Their argument quickly returned, bringing back the feelings of hatred, betrayal, and revenge with it. She'd been married to the man for seven years. She'd lived with him, loved him, shared her life with him, carried and miscarried two children for him.

And now here she was, battling this same man for the house they had once shared. Hiring an attorney to fight him and an investigator to take dirty pictures of her husband with another woman.

Forcing the tears back, she realized John was right. *We all have enemies. Most of the time, they're right in front of us. And we don't even know it.*

"I know," she told him in a voice so soft, she could barely hear it above the chattering customers and the clinking of silverware. "The sad part is, we really don't have to do much to make them, do we?"

He sat back and suddenly looked very sad. "It has always been my firm belief that making enemies can actually be the easiest thing in the world."

Erika drank some coffee and struggled to say something that would dispute what he had just said. Unfortunately, she had to acknowledge the fact that he was probably right.

"I need to find out," John said suddenly.

"Find out?"

"The whole story."

"About your friend?"

"There's got to be some way I can find out about that auction. Where Buster bought that painting. The painting itself. Do you have any idea how I could find out a few things?"

The idea came to her in a flash. "I have a friend in St. Clairsville who works at the courthouse. Lizzie's got connections all over. And her husband's an attorney. My attorney, in fact. Let me talk to her and see what she can come up with."

John smiled. Erika was pleased to see some of the lines disappearing around his eyes.

"Thanks. This means a lot."

Erika felt very warm inside. For the first time in years, she felt genuinely comfortable in the company of another man.

***

At eleven o'clock, Sergeant Grubb knocked on John's motel room door.

"Slumming?" John opened the door and stepped back.

Looking somewhat grim, Grubb came right in, went over to the round table, pulled out a chair, and sat. "Got a fax from Washington on those two you did in." His scowl didn't exactly give John a warm fuzzy. "Looks like those boys mighta been helluva lot smarter than we've been thinkin'."

"No sheet?" John closed the door and sat down facing the cop.

"Not a damn thing the Feds could find."

John said nothing.

"But what we found out locally gives us a rough idea you mighta been on the right track." Grubb pulled a folded piece of paper from his shirt pocket and opened it. "Ronald Philip Murphy and Richard Arthur Murphy. Born nineteen years ago in Moundsville, grew up there. Mom skipped when the twins were around five. Neighbors say she got tired of the old man battin' her around. When she left, the old man started beatin' on the twins. He was a boozer, worked construction. Carpenter, apparently. He also liked hookers. Brought 'em home, locked the twins in their bedroom, then had himself some wing-ding parties."

224

"The father still alive?"

"Bastard croaked seven years back. In his sleep."

"Natural?"

"Asphyxiation. Smothered to death."

"He had help, didn't he?"

"Seems like it. Moundsville found imprints of the old man's teeth discolorin' the inside of his mouth. A sure sign somethin' was shoved against his face."

"Any suspects?"

"I talked to one of Moundsville's finest. He was there when they brought the old man in. Pisser is, Murphy was one of those mean assholes everyone hated. Like they said, how many pages of suspects did I want?"

"Who'd they think did it?"

"They suspect the twins stuck a pillow over the old man's face and kept it there. Like Moundsville told me, the fucker had it comin'. The kids were twelve then, and already so wild, nobody wanted to lock 'em up and have the taxpayers foot the bill. 'Sides, there was no evidence, and Moundsville wanted the case closed. You know. One less badass to worry about."

"What happened to the twins?"

"A relative took 'em in, somewhere near Columbus. Westerville, they think. An aunt, maybe the wife of an uncle—we ain't sure. Moundsville was eager to be rid of 'em. Damn kids always causin' trouble in school, startin' fights." Grubb scowled. "Moundsville wanted to know why we were interested."

"What'd you tell them?"

"They coulda been wet boys."

"And they said…?"

"They weren't surprised. When we got the fax, we were sure somethin' had turned up. But Behavioral Sciences pulled up a blank. The Murphy's never had been printed."

"That doesn't prove anything, does it?"

"Just that they never got caught."

"Got anything at all?"

"At least a dozen unsolved murders in the Ohio Valley can be blamed on a professional team. In other words, somebody had to know the people and the area. Take the other day, for example. Hooker disappears here, in downtown Bern. Local broad, hung out at the Waterin' Hole. Somebody saw the Murphy's there. A hooker friend of the one missin' said she saw those two leavin' the bar with her."

"Why would they kill her?"

"Maybe they just liked killin'. Or maybe the hooker asked too many questions, and they had to shut her up." Grubb shrugged. "Who knows?"

"Well, at least now you might suspect they'd been paid."

"Yeah. But by who?"

"I'm working on it."

Grubb shook his head. "Like I said before, watch yourself. I don't wanna have to come after your ass."

"I didn't think you liked me that much, Sheriff."

Grubb pocketed the paper and stood. "It still bugs my ass how you managed to do in two strong, professional boys like that."

John shrugged. "I had the advantage, like I said. I was expecting them."

"Shame you couldn't catch 'em alive for us."

"Wasn't thinking of that at the time."

"Does a cop's heart a world of good when a pro's brought in alive. Sorta restores a sense of order, ya know? Two of 'em woulda put our butts in the papers. Maybe even on the tube."

"Sorry."

Grubb reached for the doorknob. "Like I said, watch it. Whatever you're doin', make sure you get it done right. All I gotta say." He opened the door and slipped outside.

***

"Lizzie, I need a very large favor."

"Sounds serious, Erika."

"It is. Believe me."

"Tell me what you'd like me to do."

"You know anyone working over there who keeps up with the auctions in the Ohio Valley?"

"I can find out. What kind of auction are we talking about?"

"Hmmm…I didn't think of that. Are there categories or something?"

"Yep. And there are a *lot* of them."

"Give me some examples."

"Let's see... First, we have the Police Department, for unclaimed and surplus property, lost, stolen, or seized. Then there are Sheriff auctions that sell foreclosed real estate. You've also got state and municipal, which offer surplus property to the general public. We have mini storage, which dumps storage contents seized for non-payment of rent. Utility company and corporate auto sell vehicles previously used. Of course, we've also got Department of Defense, for government property, U.S. Bankruptcy Court, for real estate and personal property, and General Service Administration, which also handles personal property. U.S. Marshal's Service deals with confiscations. I.R.S. auctions handle seizures, U.S. Customs Service, seized, forfeited, and unclaimed personal property. Small Business, also for personal property. Estate auctions are the most popular. They -- "

"This, I'm pretty sure, would be an estate auction."

"OK. At least we've got that narrowed down."

"It took place last year. A couple of weeks before Christmas, as I remember."

"You're sure?"

"Yes."

"Can I ask you a personal question?"

"Fire away."

"What's all this about?"

"It's complicated. I'd rather tell you in person."

"OK. I've got a friend in Wheeling who works in the library. It used to store shelves upon shelves of boxes stuffed with microfilm, but now everything's digital. He worked on the paper for years but got fired not too long ago. I also know Jeanie Nagel fairly well. She works here in Records and just might be able to do us some good. That is, if this is really important — "

"It is."

"Tell me what you know about this auction. And mind you, this'll cost you lunch—at least."

***

At twelve o'clock, John's cell buzzed.

It was Erika. "Busy right now?"

John used the remote to kill the volume on the TV, which was doing a special on the life of Hollywood legend, Spencer Tracy. "Got something?"

"Meet me at the St. Clairsville Holiday Inn, okay? I'm there right now."

He didn't reply.

"Something wrong?"

"I was just thinking."

"About what?"

"The first time I saw you there, you had a drunk stuck to your shoe."

"No problem. I'm wearing different shoes."

John laughed. "Good one."

"Every once in a while, I come up with one."

"I'll bet it's more often that that…"

A pause. "Don't be too long."

"I'm already headed out the door."

***

229

Erika was sitting in a corner booth with a pretty redhead when John walked in.

The redhead was about the same age as Erika and at least twenty pounds heavier. She was dressed smartly, but couldn't hold a candle to Erika, who looked fabulous in her light-blue suit.

"John Callen? Lizzie Peterson, a very good friend of mine."

John shook Lizzie's hand and sat down. The bartender came. Erika ordered another round for herself and Lizzie, while John ordered a Jack's on ice.

"Lizzie's doing the legwork on this auction thing," Erika said after the drinks came. "She works at the courthouse in town."

He sampled his drink. "Find out anything?"

"I've got a contact in Wheeling handling the poop on local artwork. Estates, dispersals, that kind of thing. Carl used to be a reporter and is still a decent investigator. I'm sure he'll come up with something shortly."

"What did you tell her?" John asked Erika.

She shrugged. "Everything. Is that all right?"

"If it tracks down whoever paid to have Buster killed."

"I also have a friend in Records," Lizzie added. "Working on registrations. Valued works of art are insured and recorded. A lot of this stuff is accessible to the public."

"I appreciate all this."

"No problem." Lizzie shook her head. "If some psycho had someone killed for a stupid painting, we

230

really need to expose him." A look of disgust covered her face.

John was trying to imagine the events of the auction. Buster and Cobb going at it—first Buster, then Cobb, with Buster winning in the end. Cobb stomping off, making phone calls to find someone who would bring him the painting, one way or the other.

"Erika told me two men...tried to kill you last night," Lizzie whispered uneasily.

John nodded.

"And they're dead now?"

"Yes."

"This is sounding more and more like something out of one of those true crime shows."

"The Sheriff paid me a visit earlier this afternoon and read me the fax from Washington. The boys were twin brothers. There's no record of them with Behavioral Sciences, but several unexplained deaths in the Ohio Valley can possibly be traced to them. The Moundsville cops think the twins killed their father a few years back, but they've got no proof. The boys were nineteen, which means they might have been murdering people at a ridiculously young age. Especially if they started with their father."

"My God!" Erika sounded genuinely shocked.

"Well, we're both glad you got them," Lizzie said. "This kind of stuff scares the crap out of me. Two boys sneaking around, killing people for money?"

231

"And for fun," he added. "Judging by what the Sheriff told me, the police think they did in a hooker when they came to town. Eyewitnesses saw her leave the local bar with them. Cops are looking for her now."

"What the hell's this world coming to?" Lizzie said. "Kids murdering their own *father*, as well as *other* people? Then they made a *living* doing it?"

"I guess you've got others on your side now," Erika told John.

He watched her as she played with her swizzle stick. He wasn't thinking of Buster, the old man, or the twins he'd killed only hours before. He was thinking of the beautiful woman sitting near him, smiling at him. He was watching how her thick black mane swept over her shoulders, giving off a gloss in the dim bar lighting. How her light-blue suit made her large almond eyes sparkle. And how the tiny dimples on either side of her mouth appeared magically when she spoke.

"I guess so," he replied, feeling a satisfying warmth for the first time in years.

***

At twelve-fifteen, Nathaniel Cobb was ready to leave his sanctuary.

Dressed smartly and showing no outward signs of stress, he was prepared to conduct business as usual. Even with very little sleep, he knew he would be more than able to maintain his natural high level of professionalism.

It was his close friend who had convinced him to be strong and face the world.

232

"You must leave now," his friend had said. *"Get up and turn on the lights."*

"No." Cobb found that he was content in the darkness, where it was safe and warm. Sitting in his favorite chair, listening to what was left of the *Pathetique*. "I want to stay here and think."

"You must get up. Turn on the lights. Stand tall and proud. Go downstairs. Act like nothing happened."

"Why?"

"People will come to your shop. When they see it closed, they'll think something has happened. They'll ask questions, maybe even go to the police. If the police get involved, they will ruin everything."

"I understand." Cobb knew his friend was right, that the authorities would indeed wonder why the shop wasn't open.

He didn't need the authorities thinking about him.

This must be kept quiet.

Downstairs, he unlocked the front gate and pushed it back into its heavy metal base. He flipped the *CLOSED* sign to expose *OPEN* to the street, unlocked the door, then went back to the rear of the store, to his tiny office.

He had just finished mixing his own special blend of amaretto coffee when he flicked on the portable TV on the table beside his desk.

The news came on.

The well-dressed, sober-looking gray-haired man was talking about two young men killed in an attempted home invasion in Bern, Ohio.

233

"…and the two men, Ronald Philip Murphy and his twin brother, Richard Arthur Murphy, both nineteen years of age, were armed when they broke into the home of the deceased Larry Norton, whose funeral will be held this Saturday…"

Nathaniel Cobb froze.

His hand, holding the brown coffee mug with *NATHANIEL* inscribed in bold black lettering, twitched violently. The mug slipped from his grasp and dropped to the linoleum floor. It smacked against the base of the chipped steam radiator and shattered into hundreds of shards, strewing hot coffee all over the floor.

***

At three o'clock, Erika called John's motel room.

"John, can you come over to my place?"

"Sure. When?"

"I'll be finished here at the bank in about half an hour. It takes me five minutes to get home. How about if you get here shortly afterward?"

"If you're sure it's okay."

"Why wouldn't it be?"

"Your divorce."

"What about it?"

"My showing up in your driveway. Your being seen with a strange man. Not that I'm actually what you'd call *strange*, but you know what I mean…"

Erika smiled. John's consideration had taken her completely by surprise. It made her wonder how long it had been since she had been treated this way.

"You needn't worry."

234

"You're sure?"

"Yes."

"We could meet at the Coffeehouse," he suggested.

"And sixty people would see us together, rather than one or two elderly neighbors who wouldn't think twice about noticing your car in my drive. Especially since they've already seen it at Buster's."

"I guess you've got a point."

"Three-thirtyish?"

"It's a date…well, you know what I mean."

Erika laughed and hung up.

***

"Lizzie's got something for us."

"She works fast," John said, surprised.

Erika poured coffee and brought the mugs over to the kitchen table. "Not really, but her contacts do." She sat facing him. "So far, we have the name of the artist who did the painting your friend bought, and Lizzie's friend Carl is working on that, as we speak."

"Carl?"

"Wheeling Library."

"How'd they find the name?"

"Auction records. At auctions, all transactions are painstakingly detailed for tax purposes. Everything is recorded: buyer's name, date and time of sale, the artist's name, the auction type, the auctioneer—the whole nine yards. Everything was on the fiche Carl found in the vault."

"What's the name of the artist?"

"Alexander Summerville."

235

"Never heard of him."

"Neither have I."

"He's probably a local."

"No doubt."

"But it's really no surprise Summerville's not a big name. Buster wasn't interested in names, just the scenes themselves. The others he's got are either cheap prints or originals by other locals. Nobody big, nobody famous, and certainly nothing rare. The only one I'd ever seen before is the one in the living room. It's a print by Susan Hunt. I think her name's hyphenated, but I can't remember the rest of it. I remember seeing something similar by her years ago, in some dog-eared magazine. She was fairly well known, but since Buster got hold of a print, I don't think he paid much for it. He probably paid more for the frame."

Erika nodded. "But the fact is, Buster was undoubtedly killed for the Summerville. And even though Summerville was quite possibly local, it's worth something. At least, to Cobb."

John sat back in his chair. "And if it's worth so much to a dealer, what's that tell you?"

"The dealer knows something about the painting that no one else knows?"

"Or something he doesn't *want* anyone else to know."

***

At four o'clock, Nathaniel Cobb tried once again to contact Rbow.

His message was short and quite clear:

236

"Need services asap.
Can we talk?"

His hands shook as he typed. Despite his excellent typing skills, it took him forever to get out the e-mail without error. At first, his index finger kept moving between keys. Then his thumb had fits with the space bar. He had to lean back in his chair and take deep breaths.

His friend emerged from the darkness and tried consoling him, but it was useless. The bottom had fallen out of everything, and it didn't seem like there would be any way to escape.

"Rbow will help," his friend said.

"He seems to be too busy to communicate with me!"

"Maybe something will come about to change his plans."

"Maybe. And maybe a miracle will suddenly cause lightning to strike the animal who killed the Murphy twins."

His friend grew silent. It made Cobb feel triumphant, since his friend always seemed to have the right answers.

However, Cobb's feeling of triumph was short-lived. He thought of his enemy out there, walking around freely. Coming into his store. Looking at his things. *Touching* them. Contaminating everything. Then leaving, walking outside, crossing the street, and leaning against the streetlamp. Looking up at the second-floor windows.

Smiling.

Waving.

The same monster that had killed two strong, young boys.

That last thought made him cringe. It felt like something heavy had dropped in his stomach, like a croquet ball onto a tiled floor.

"He'll come back," Cobb whispered, his throat hot and constricted. "He'll come back and stand there like before. Looking at me. His eyes...slithering into my soul. Squirming inside my head...sifting through my private thoughts."

"We'll be fine, Nathaniel."

"No. We won't."

"But we will."

"He'll find out what happened. What we did. He'll go to the police."

"He can only find out if we tell him."

"He needs to be dead!"

"He will be. Soon."

"Rbow must help. He must free himself of his other commitments. I'll pay whatever he wishes."

"He'll be in touch."

"How can you be so sure?"

"Have I ever let you down?"

Cobb sighed. "No. You haven't."

"Well, then..."

Cobb rose stiffly from his rolltop desk and moved to the cabinet. He picked up a bottle of very old Benedictine brandy and carefully poured two inches into an elaborately engraved brandy snifter.

The monks will soothe my worries for tonight...

238

He poured two inches for his friend and left the second snifter on the counter of the cabinet. His friend never drank, but Cobb poured a glass anyway. Just in case.

He went over to his armchair and put his drink on the table beside the chair. He got out Brahms and put it on the stereo.

The *Symphony No. 1* in C Minor would suffice for this occasion.

The exquisite brooding of Brahms would be so excruciatingly perfect.

Cobb sat back, sipped the aged liqueur, and patiently waited for the dark, disturbing music to soothe his shattered nerves.

***

At six o'clock, Lizzie Peterson, acting very excited, showed up at Erika's.

"You didn't just win the lottery, did you?" Erika said.

"Almost as good, my dear," the redhead replied, smiling. "Where's your guest?"

Erika pointed down the hall.

"The *bedroom*?" Lizzie asked in a whisper, blinking.

"*Bath*room, you scum puppy." Erika frowned. "Did you forget? Your husband's my divorce lawyer. It wouldn't be very bright, my jumping someone's bones while Al just hired someone to get dirt on Paul, would it?"

"Actually, you're absolutely right."

"Good. So put a lid on it, okay?"

Lizzie tilted her head and glanced at the ceiling.

Erika could tell her friend had something on her mind. "Go ahead, spit it out. You know you want to…"

Lizzie shrugged a shoulder. "Not to cause trouble or anything, but if I had that guy in my house, I'd be looking for all kinds of dark corners."

Erika knew better than admit her friend was right. She really liked Lizzie, but the girl frequently had trouble keeping her mouth shut. "I hear you, believe me."

Lizzie plopped on the couch. "Good. For a minute I was afraid seven years of marriage might have done a major job on your hormones. *And* your desire for some good, hot sex."

"No chance of *that*."

Lizzie opened her mouth to say something but closed it when she saw John coming down the hall.

Lizzie brought us good news," Erika said, shifting their attention to the main issue.

"I could use it." John sat in an armchair.

"To begin with," Lizzie said, "Carl came up with some really juicy stuff. For starters, Alexander Summerville wasn't even a full-time artist."

"What's that got to do with anything?" Erika asked.

"It gets better. Summerville, believe it or not, was a pawnbroker." Lizzie took a piece of paper from her handbag. She put the bag on the cushion beside her and unfolded the paper. "Let me start from the beginning. Carl came up with this. Alexander Summerville was born August tenth, nineteen -oh-eight, in Bridgeport, Ohio. His parents were well off. His father had something to do with the railroad, and his mother came from money. Asphalt, we think, going by her maiden name.

"Summerville was an only child. His parents began having problems with him when the boy started school and showed an early interest in girls. He was chastised severely, but it didn't seem to have any effect. In fact, soon afterwards, he began exhibiting a marked interest in both sexes."

"That's not really much of a thing anymore." John looked bored.

"Like I said, it gets better." Lizzie went back to her notes. "Summerville became a pawnbroker after graduating from high school. Since his father helped finance his business, Summerville never had any major problems. He'd always had an interest in art, which helped in his acquisition of rare pieces. He displayed artistic talent, although most critics agreed that the man was more unbalanced than he was gifted. When Summerville was in his thirties, both parents died in a fire, leaving him quite wealthy. However, the man didn't trust banks, and hated paying taxes. It was rumored that he had much of his assets converted into cash, then buried as much of it as he could in several different places on his properties."

"Properties?" Erika asked.

"Summerville had invested in several parcels of land. He lived in Bridgeport but owned estates and raw land all over the Ohio Valley. Bethesda. Belmont. Cambridge. He owned a small ten-acre farm in Flushing he rented out from time to time.

He even owned a square block in the St. Clairsville business district that was recently bought by the County to revamp into apartment buildings."

"What's this have to do with Buster's painting?" John asked.

"When Summerville died thirty-two years ago, there was no trace or record of where he'd buried his money."

"Was there a widow?" Erika asked.

"Summerville had been married three times. The first two ended in divorce, and his third wife just disappeared. No one really knows what happened. But everyone who knew Summerville suspected that she eventually grew tired of his eccentricities, and just ran away."

"Leaving all that money?" John looked skeptical.

Lizzie nodded. "Summerville's third wife had a child from a previous marriage. A boy. When Summerville married this woman, his boyhood obsession returned. Several people said he was hopelessly infatuated. They think he molested the boy, but there isn't any recorded proof. Since his wife feared her husband, she always sided with him to avoid becoming the target of his wrath herself. As a result, any reports of molestation are unsubstantiated. But the boy grew up to be unbalanced himself. He was always close to his mother but went through such traumatic events when she married Summerville, he was never the same."

"Is the boy still alive?" Erika asked.

"Yes."

"Any data on him?"

"His name is Nathaniel Cobb."

***

At six-fifteen, Cobb received an email from Rbow.

The message came through as Cobb angrily paced his living room, obsessing over the monster that had killed the Murphy twins and was now harassing him.

The tiny *beep!* jolted him from his rage, forcing his head around so severely, the tiny *pop!* in his neck made him gasp. A moment later, he unclasped his hands from behind his back, straightened, and hurried back to his laptop.

He sat tensely, his pulse hammering. After long, agonizing moments, he managed to click on *receive* with the few muscles in his right hand still able to do their job.

Then he saw the short message and gasped.

"Will call tomorrow a.m."

Cobb read it over and over. Tears came to his eyes. He sat back and let the warmth caress his tense body. The message was like a heavenly elixir instantly forcing the cold darkness from his tortured soul.

Moments later, his friend's voice, standing very close, drifted over.

"I was right, wasn't I, Nathaniel?"

"You were right."

243

"Rbow will deliver."

"Yes."

"And you will be free."

"*We* will be free."

"Yes. Of course."

"Norton's friend will be dead, and there will be no one else looking for us."

"Yes. No one."

"The treasure will finally be ours. With no worries."

No reply.

"We'll know where to look."

A pause. "*Yes.*"

Cobb frowned. "You don't sound excited."

A sigh. *"I am, Nathaniel. I am excited."*

Cobb smiled. His friend sounded strange, but that was okay. Sometimes his friend's moods came on quickly, without warning. That was okay, too, since they were so close. They were soulmates, and soulmates always remained very close.

"I'm glad." Cobb got up and went to the stereo cabinet. He suddenly felt triumphant. Beethoven, this time. Yes. He decided to put on the magnificent *Fifth*, in C minor, and settle in with a glass of sherry.

Cobb found the record, slipped it gingerly from its paper dust cover, turned it on, and went to pour a drink for him and his very good friend.

"Better days are ahead, my friend."

"Yes," his friend replied.

"For *both* of us."

***

244

"You're telling me Cobb is the stepson of Alexander Summerville?" John asked in disbelief.

Lizzie went back to her notes. "Cobb was born in the South Hills section of Pittsburgh. He was always a quiet boy, withdrawn and antisocial. His father ran off when Nathaniel was around four, so the boy and his mother were on their own for three years when she met Summerville. They were soon married, and Nathaniel found himself in another city, attending school with different kids. Apparently he was very small and, coupled with his shyness, of course, this would present a red flag for being bullied. But what his stepfather did later on was much worse than what his peers could ever do."

"That's right," Erika said. "Summerville was a sex maniac. And he didn't care who he did it with."

John frowned. "I don't care how bad Cobb had it. Or what his stepfather did to him. He killed my friend."

"That's going to be hard to prove," Lizzie said.

"Most definitely. But I'm still going to do it. Somehow."

"What does Summerville's artwork have to do with all this?" Erika asked.

"That's the real key to the puzzle," Lizzie said. "It's rumored that Summerville drew maps of where he buried his treasure. These he put on the backs of the paintings, which were then covered with a thin piece of Masonite to hide them when viewed from the back. Since he was so paranoid, the common consensus was that only one map actually led to the treasure. Summerville, of course, was the only one who knew which map actually held the treasure, and kept this important detail locked up in his demented little mind."

"What blew this all up?" John asked.

"Summerville was audited by the IRS. He panicked, of course, and realized that his maps might be discovered—especially if the IRS seized his property. A close friend of his wife—Cobb's mother—said that Summerville was so terrified the Government would get his wealth, he took frantic steps to conceal its hiding place. So, not knowing what else to do, he placed all six paintings in his pawnshop."

"Wasn't he afraid of someone buying them?" Erika asked.

"Summerville had an extremely limited talent—which was why he was never able to create his own works. None of the six were actually very good. From what I learned, they weren't even considered good accent material."

"In other words," John said, "no one even noticed them."

"That's right. And when he died, the paintings were auctioned off."

"Why didn't Cobb get them?" John asked. "Wasn't there a will?"

Lizzie shook her head. "I checked that out with Probate. Summerville left Cobb just one silver dollar."

"Nice guy."

"Exactly."

"I thought the asshole loved Cobb."

246

"Apparently he wanted the boy only for sex—or whatever he called it. As far as the paintings went, they were all sent to the auction block. The grand total came to slightly more than two hundred and fifty dollars." Lizzie shook her head. "Not much money for all that trouble, huh?"

"Who bought them?" Erika asked.

"Locals. Carl contacted three of the buyers. All three said they were approached by Cobb, who offered them twice the amount they'd paid for the paintings."

"Weren't they suspicious?" John asked.

"They thought Cobb was buying them up for sentimental purposes. At least, that's what they got from their brief conversation with him."

"I'm wondering what happened to Cobb's mother," John said.

"No one has seen her for many years."

"Summerville must've been a real sweetheart to make her run away from all that wealth," he said.

"He probably scared her away," Erika said.

"I don't suppose anyone has suspected Summerville of killing her?" he asked.

"There was never any trace of her body. At least, not in the Ohio Valley. There were many unclaimed bodies found after her disappearance, but none of the dental records matched."

"Anyone check her relatives in the Pittsburgh area?" he asked.

"Yes. But by that time, her parents were dead, and most of her relatives and friends had either died or moved away."

John sat back. "The old man drew maps of where he hid his gold, covered them, then died before he could get to it. Then the asshole's unbalanced stepson bought them all up so he could have the gold for himself."

"That's about it."

"How come Cobb never asked Buster if he could buy back that last painting? Why the hell did he pay two wet boys to kill him, instead?"

"Maybe he did ask," Erika said, "but Buster turned him down."

"Or maybe he lost it so bad at the auction," Lizzie said, "that he decided to make your friend suffer for it."

"I'm going with that," John said. "From what Erika said about his behavior, I'd guess that's exactly what happened. Which makes me even more determined to nail his ass."

***

After Lizzie left, John had supper with Erika in her home and spent the next two hours talking about John's plan to bring Nathaniel Cobb to justice.

"Cobb already sent two men after you," Erika said, sipping wine. "What do you think he's up to now?"

"If he's already sent two men, he considers me a strong threat. After all, I was Buster's friend. I went to Cobb's store after Buster was killed. Cobb probably thinks I know enough to have him put away."

"And what if he found out about the Murphy twins? He won't stop just because they didn't

248

succeed, would he? Don't you think he'll do something even more desperate?"

"I'm sure he already knows about the twins. It's been on the news. A Wheeling news wagon even showed up at Buster's while the cops were finishing up. In a small town like this? A double homicide would not only make the Wheeling stations, but it might also have even reached Pittsburgh."

"What do you think his options are now?"

"He's even more desperate, so I'd bet he most likely will pay someone else to come after me."

"Do you think anyone can link him to the Murphy's?"

"Wet boys don't take checks or credit cards. Many don't even accept payment until the job is finished. However, Cobb isn't thinking rationally. His paranoia's probably kicking into overdrive by now."

"But you're not the only one who knows about this now. I know about it, so does Lizzie, her friends, the Bern police—"

"Like I said, I don't think he's rational anymore. I'm sure he thinks I'm the only one who can nail him."

"But if there's someone else he's getting in touch with, don't you think you should be telling Sergeant Grubb about it?"

"I don't think Grubb likes to take chances. He's already told me how close to retirement he is. If I were in his shoes, I wouldn't risk my butt for a total stranger. Anyway, he's still pissed at me for killing the twins."

Erka's dark brows bumped together. "But they tried to *kill* you!"

"He thinks I should've brought them in alive."

"I didn't think our police department was that stupid."

"I don't know if it's stupidity, or just naivete. Grubb didn't like looking at two dead teenagers."

Erika turned pale.

"Sorry..."

"You had to do it. I understand."

"Do you?"

"I think so..."

John noticed that her expression had changed somewhat, softening a little. However, there was still something in her eyes that told him she was more than just a little nervous in his presence.

"Something wrong?" she asked after a pause.

"Wrong?"

"You're staring."

"I know."

"But nothing's wrong?"

He didn't reply.

This time, her expression was even clearer. It said, simply: *Liar*.

"You can tell me," she said softly.

He could tell that she really wanted to know what he was thinking. It was then that he decided he could get two things off his chest. The first thing had been bugging him the last few minutes. However, the second was something that had been bugging him since he'd first met her.

"I was thinking of two things. First, you're looking at me like I'm something from another planet. I killed two men, and I killed them violently. But as I told you before, killing is what I did in Iraq, and I did it as well as I could, then forgot about it. It was extremely difficult to forget, and I didn't actually get there. Drinking helped somewhat. I spent a great deal of time getting drunk to forget, and it worked to some degree.

"But I was sober when they brought me back to the States, and this was when things got bad. Everything came back like a cyclone, and it messed me up for the longest time. But that's water over the bridge. And it's something someone like you could never understand."

She didn't reply.

"But if you consider what the Murphy's had in store for me, I'm sure you'd agree that the way I killed them was both quick and merciful."

"I do agree." Once again, the hard expression came back. It wasn't very flattering on a beautiful woman like Erika. It made her look older and world-weary. "It's just so difficult for me to accept the fact that I'm with someone who has actually killed people. I'm strictly small-town, John. To make matters worse, I was raised a Catholic. I learned about Iraq in the news. I was almost out of high school before I found out the facts of life. Sex was something I knew nothing about and only heard about through movies, or when a bunch of us girls got together for one of those parties our parents never knew about."

251

"Really?"

"I didn't find out very much about life from my parents. Like I said, I found out through my friends, and with the help of a couple of immature young men in business school."

John didn't reply. The thought of someone as fine as this woman being brought up just as dysfunctional as everyone else was something that hadn't occurred to him.

"What was that second thing you were thinking?" she asked suddenly.

"I was just wondering," he said after a long pause, "how a seemingly intelligent man like your husband could let someone as fine as you walk out of his life."

Erika went silent.

"I'm sorry," he said, angry at himself. "Sometimes my big mouth gets me in trouble."

Erika reddened. "Not *this* time."

***

Feeling genuinely elated over Rbow's email, Nathaniel Cobb sat in the darkness with his friend. "It's finally going to happen," he said, smiling.

A slight pause. "*Yes*..."

"You don't sound happy." Cobb sensed doubt in his friend's soft voice. "In fact, you sound quite sad. As you did before."

"It's only that...that I suspect our relationship might end...or change...when you find your treasure."

"*Our* treasure."

"*Yes*."

252

Cobb frowned. He didn't like what his friend was implying. "You are my very good friend. Good friends don't abandon one another when one of them becomes rich."

"Of course. But strange things happen when a treasure is uncovered."

"Like what?"

"It is not my place to say."

"You're speaking in riddles." Cobb's right eye began to twitch. "You've never spoken this way before."

"It is because of things…that I know."

"What do you know?"

"There are things about this treasure. Things that must not be known. That must forever remain buried."

"This treasure was accumulated by an evil man." Cobb's face contorted as the dark memories swept past. "A vile man. A man I loathed. A man I prayed many times would die — "

"And he did, Nathaniel. He did indeed die."

"But only after he'd corrupted and ruined the lives of myself and my mother."

"Yes. But death is death. And he troubles you—us—no more."

"And I will soon claim his treasure."

Once again, his friend made no reply.

"I hated him with my heart and soul," Cobb whispered, mostly to himself. "He…did things to me. He…soiled me. I'd wake up screaming. My pants… would be wet." He sighed deeply. "Then they'd come in. They'd come in and…and *laugh*.

253

They'd *laugh...both* of them! Her laugh was forced, because I know she felt sorry for what was happening but had no control over that bastard. She was afraid of what he might do if she—"

"*She was just like him*," his friend said suddenly, in a dark, unusually cruel, voice.

Cobb paused in his rant. This was so unlike his friend, this sudden flash of temper. His friend was always calm, always collected. Why this outburst?

"Mother was afraid of him. Summerville was a monster, but she didn't know this until after they were married. He did awful things—things that should have gotten him arrested and committed. She was always afraid to argue, to side with me. He was a monster and turned wild when people argued with him. He would curse and yell...and throw things, break things. Mother was very slender, very fragile. She fell ill very easily. He took advantage of her. I understand why she tried to appease him—"

"*I don't*," replied his friend.

"I think I knew her better than you did," Cobb said.

"*Do you?*"

"Yes."

"*We won't argue amongst ourselves, will we?*"

"Friends do not argue. Especially very close ones."

"*The important thing is, they are both gone.*"

"Yes." Grateful the argument had been quelled so easily, Cobb sighed in relief. "They are gone."

"*Your mother left.*"

"She'd had enough and was afraid to stay with a monster."

"And she'll never come back."

"No. I guess she never will."

"No," his friend echoed in a soft voice. *"She never will."*

Cobb sat in silence, his attention shifted now to Rbow.

"You are quiet once again."

"He will be contacting me very soon."

"Yes. Sometime in the morning."

"I am very excited."

His friend grew silent and, after some thought, said, *"I believe you are."*

"Are you not excited, as well?"

After a pause, his friend said, *"Yes. I believe I am."*

Cobb relaxed in his chair. He wanted to put on Beethoven's 7th but quickly decided against it. Silence seemed more fitting right now.

Chapter 5 - Thursday

At eight o'clock the next morning, John sat in the Town Car across the street from Cobb's Collectibles.

He hadn't slept much the previous night and had spent most of it pacing in his motel room, trying to come up with some sort of plan. Erika had called, but he hadn't replied. He didn't want her involved in this nasty business, and he certainly didn't want to have to worry about her when he was going after Cobb or someone Cobb might have paid to do what the Murphy twins had failed doing.

In John's view, the only thing that made sense was staying close. The old man would undoubtedly make another move—especially if he'd heard about the Murphy's. Cobb would most likely consider him a threat—especially if he suspected John had been responsible for killing the twins.

Now, as he sat behind the wheel, watching the morning traffic, he struggled to devise a foolproof scheme. He knew that if Cobb were sufficiently shaken up, he'd start making stupid mistakes. What mistakes he made would vary, according to his mental state, and John knew that whatever happened, he couldn't let himself be distracted—not even for an instant.

This meant keeping as close to the old man as possible. If Cobb was contacting another killer, John wanted to be around when the big event took place.

At eight-fifteen, Nathaniel Cobb received a message from Rbow in his email box. It said:

"Go to 7-Eleven
across from Hardee's
near I-70 exit ramp
wait for call."

His nerves jumping like short circuits, Cobb dressed hurriedly, picking up anything within reach. He scrambled for the door, his fingers fumbling with the door locks, deadbolt, and chain. He managed to get the door open but tripped over his shoelaces, which, in his haste, he had neglected to tie. The shoes were expensive imports. During his incredible display of total clumsiness, he'd managed to scuff the glistening side of one with the sharp heel of the other.

"*Patience*," his friend whispered behind his ear.

Cobb felt his gut tighten. "It's hard to be patient when you're so clumsy!"

"There is no need to be clumsy. Take a breath, then fix your shoes."

Moaning in frustration, he did as his friend suggested. Feeling some of the pressure leaving him, he bent and carefully tied his shoes, then hurried down the stairs, holding on tightly to the rail so he didn't trip.

He got in the BMW, then spent the next two agonizing minutes clumsily fitting the wrong keys in the ignition slot. He finally found the right key and, after finally managing to concentrate on what he was doing, succeeded working the gearshift properly.

To his relief, he was cruising down the block precious seconds later.

"Soon," he muttered nervously as he drove. "Very, very soon."

***

John followed the BMW out of town.

Making sure several cars separated him from Cobb, John was careful to remain relatively invisible while keeping the glistening ride firmly in sight. Since it was morning rush hour, staying hidden was not difficult.

He knew he had to be close enough to see what Cobb was doing but also had to be certain the old man wasn't aware of anything. John was reasonably sure Cobb had no idea what vehicle he was driving. This in itself would give him an edge.

About two miles later, the BMW pulled off the Interstate and into a 7-Eleven at the first light.

John drove on by, stopping at the Hardee's and parking on the other side of a delivery van a few yards from the rest rooms. He stayed behind the wheel, watching as Cobb got out of the BMW and hurried to the payphones. The old man moved abruptly, indicating agitation. He was dressed sloppily: shirttails dangling, half the buttons unbuttoned.

The old fart must have dressed in a hurry.

When Cobb reached the phones, he stopped and examined each one of them closely. This done, he put his arms behind his back and began to pace.

John sat back and relaxed. He could tell Cobb was anxiously waiting to hear from someone he had no doubt contacted.

Someone who was forced to remain anonymous.

This was getting better and better.

***

Cobb paced the cracked pavement for nearly ten minutes before the payphone at the end began to ring.

He snatched it up quickly, grimacing at its sticky surface. "Y-Yes?"

"Who's this?" spoke a soft, low-pitched voice.

"Nathaniel Cobb."

Silence.

Cobb stood rigidly, his heart pumping like a jackhammer. Was this Rbow? Yes. It had to be. Who else would have arranged this?

But what if someone else were calling? What if—

"*Find out, Nathaniel,*" whispered his friend.

Yes. He needed to find out. At once. "Are you—"

"I understand you require my services."

Yes. It was definitely Rbow. Who else would have asked that question?

"Greatly."

"Give me details. Be vague. And brief."

259

The words came out automatically. Cobb had no trouble organizing them. "A man is causing me much aggravation. I don't wish to see him any longer."

"How will I know this man?"

"He'll probably come to my store again."

"I'll need to see this man. Give me a signal when he leaves."

"What sort of signal?"

"When he leaves your store, flip your *OPEN/CLOSED* sign."

"And then?"

"Flip it back after one minute."

"Very good idea."

"My fee is twenty-five thousand dollars American."

"That seems reasonable."

"Deposit the amount into my bank account by wire."

"Your bank account?"

"Check your e-mail."

"Good enough. I -- "

The line went dead.

Cobb swallowed deeply, replaced the receiver, and returned to his car.

Soon, he thought, a big grin on his face.

Very, very soon...

***

Back in his apartment above the store, Cobb hurried into his office and logged onto his computer to check his messages.

Sure enough, Rbow's bank and address had been included with the e-mail address in his secured program. The bank was located in Costa Rica, with an account number, phone number, and Post Office box.

Cobb picked up his phone. His heart was thumping erratically as he began dialing.

***

John watched Cobb's Collectibles from the Town Car across the street.

Erika had tried calling him a second time. Once again, he let the call go into his voicemail.

It was ten o'clock, and he was getting restless.

Cobb hadn't yet opened his shop. This made John think the old man might be preoccupied with some other more important matter. He figured it most likely had something to do with that mysterious phone call he'd received at the 7-Eleven.

He wondered if Cobb had slithered into his piggy bank to gather up a second load of serious cash for another wet boy.

Whatever was going in, John had to somehow shake up the old man again. The best way of doing that, of course, was making another appearance in the store. This would let Cobb know John was sticking around and not going anywhere. This way, the old man's nerves would shatter, and he'd make a foolish mistake. If John worked this right, whatever he did just might chafe Cobb's ass enough where the bottom would fall out and cause his world to crumble all around him.

John sat back and waited patiently for the store to open.

***

At eleven o'clock, Nathaniel Cobb opened his store.

Neat as a pin, he smelled strongly of Aqua Velva and body talc and was freshly shaven. He wore his favorite gray three-piece sharkskin suit and a black-and-white cotton tie. A fresh carnation tastefully adorned the lapel of his jacket. His antique gold pocket watch rested in his vest pocket, its glittering chain dangling between the shiny black buttons of the vest. A bright smile lit up his seamless face. He felt better than he had in days.

He stood at the storefront, looking out.

Cars and buses filled the street. Shoppers and well-dressed men and women rushed past. A bus had stopped at the corner, dropping off elderly women carrying large vinyl bags and folded umbrellas. The parking lot on the other side of the street was packed. The bored attendants paced slowly, hands in pockets, one of them spitting frequently and looking up at the cloudy afternoon sky.

Rbow was out there, somewhere; Cobb was certain of it. The transaction has been made, the money transferred, and now it was time for Norton's meddlesome friend to join Norton in the Hereafter.

Ode to Joy.

Cobb looked out at the crowd and wondered if Rbow was visible. If he was among the shoppers scuttling by, or the freshly dressed corporate types rushing past.

"*You really don't expect to see him, do you?*" his friend asked.

"I sincerely hope not." Cobb straightened to his full, six-foot, one-inch height and turned to gaze at his friend. "I would like this business to be as anonymous as possible."

"*I can clearly understand that.*"

"It shall be much better if I never see him or know what he has planned. Watching it on the news will be acceptable. It will be like, well, like I am just learning about it."

"*Your reasoning is as sensible as ever, Nathaniel.*"

"Thank you. Now please go back upstairs. We shall talk later. Right now, I prefer to be alone in case something unexpected -- "

"*I understand.*"

"You do?"

"*Yes. We shall talk later.*"

Cobb once again faced the front. The sun had emerged from the clouds and begun climbing, filtering in bright rays that lit up the curio cabinet in the storefront display. The antique frames in the other display glittered. The large brass Remington copy revealed sinewy muscles in the horse's legs. The cracks and creases in the saddle upon which the tired, range-weary rider sat, head bowed, scarred hands grasping the reins, showed boldly.

With a sigh, Cobb ambled to the rear of the store, to make a fresh pot of coffee.

***

Confused, John watched the old man disappear inside.

He couldn't stop wondering if Cobb had been talking to himself.

Was he actually standing there in the doorway, carrying on a conversation with someone who wasn't there?

Or was someone standing hidden in the background?

From their one brief conversation, John could tell the old man was weird. That, plus the known fact that Cobb had gone psychopathic for the sake of a stupid painting and had done the same sort of thing when John began asking questions.

Not to mention what John had learned from Lizzie the day before.

He glanced at his watch. 11:15. He'd wanted to go inside for a repeat visit, but when he'd seen Cobb in such a demented state, he reconsidered.

What's making me gun-shy?

Maybe it was the fact that Cobb had unexpectedly shed a new light on the situation. In just a few minutes, he convinced John that he was just a cherry or two shy of a fruitcake and should be treated very carefully.

But I already knew that...

Maybe John's reluctance stemmed from something else.

Maybe Cobb *hadn't* been talking to himself.

The old man could have been talking to someone hiding in the darkness of the store. This

264

suggested that the old fart might have set a trap and was waiting for John to come right in and face his fate.

The new killer could have already been in the store.

All John had to do was wander inside. He suspected that he would then be knocked out, dragged to the back, taken out back into the alley, murdered, then disposed of.

John began thinking of alternatives.

However, just a few minutes later, he saw his chance.

***

Cobb heard the commotion and cringed.

He put down his coffee cup, jumped up from his chair, and rushed out of the office.

A rowdy young family had invaded the store. The father and mother were furiously trying to control their two children, who were carrying on loudly. The little boy was screaming while the little girl stumbled around, giggling and touching everything within reach.

"Natalie!" The plump mother was hunched over, scrambling after her daughter. "You mustn't touch the pretty things!"

"Mine!" shouted the little girl, swatting an ashtray stand and making it reel until it bumped against the polished pedestal next to it. "Mine-Mine-Mine-Mine-Mine!"

The father, a tall, slender man wearing tight jeans and a Western shirt opened halfway down, cursed softly as he tried to quiet the screaming boy.

"May I help you?" Cobb nervously watched the mother grab her daughter before the child could swat a brass spittoon resting on the marble top of a hand-carved table.

"Mine!"

The woman picked up the little brat and smiled sheepishly at Cobb, giving him the familiar, *sorry-I-can-take-care-of-this*, look. She pointed a short, chubby index finger at her daughter, who wasn't paying the least bit of attention.

"No, thanks, we're just look — "

"*W-A-A-A-A-A-H-H-H-H*!!!" screamed the little boy, making the walls vibrate.

"Please!" His face squeezed tightly into a tangle of wrinkles, Cobb covered his ears. "If there's something I can get for you..."

The little girl squirmed in her mother's arms, reaching out for something to touch. The child's short, fat legs pumped furiously. "Mine! Mine!"

The mother shrugged, then lowered her daughter to the wooden floor.

"Please!" Cobb shook with rage. "There are many priceless antiques in my store!"

"Yeah." The father displayed two gold front teeth with his bearded grin. "Looks like you got some real neat shit, all right."

The little boy took a deep breath and wailed.

Cringing, Cobb turned away from the father to see what mischief the little girl was getting into.

Then he saw the man in the doorway.

Norton's friend!

My dear God!

His arms crossed, the man leaned against the doorway.

He was *smiling* again!

He's back!

The evil bastard's back!

A harsh finger tapped Cobb on the shoulder, making him jump.

He spun around.

The father had picked up a large glass ashtray and was examining it closely. "How much for this?"

Cobb said nothing. He turned to the storefront. Norton's friend had pulled away from the doorway and moved five feet closer. He now stood in the center of the room, still smiling.

Another tap, and Cobb jumped again.

"How much?" The father was holding the ashtray just a few inches from Cobb's nose.

Cobb struggled to concentrate on the item in question. It took him two tries to pull his gaze away from the other man. "Uh…I think that item is…is going for — "

"W-A-A-A-A-H-H-H!!!"

"Natalie, come *here*!"

"Mine!"

"I'll give you five bucks for it."

"Nata-l-e-e-e-e-e!"

"Mine! *Mine*!"

"For goodness sake!" The throbbing in his head had made his whole body tremble. Cobb fought hard to maintain his professionalism. "That's a rare piece. It was taken from an estate sale, and has been traced back to the Roosevelt era — "

"W-A-A-H! W-A-A-H!"

"Shuddup, Edward Stuart." The father turned back to Cobb. "Five bucks?"

Norton's friend had moved closer.

Cobb had the horrible feeling the walls of the store were closing in on him.

The throbbing in his head grew worse...

*Rbow...I need you...*how *I need you!*

"Control, Nathaniel." Cobb's friend had suddenly appeared and was whispering softly in his ear. *"Rbow is out there, and your troubles will soon be gone."* The throbbing grew softer as his friend's voice grew clearer. *"Chill, and maybe you can direct this family of imbeciles out of here. Then you might be able to deal with Norton's friend by simply closing up and making him go back outside, where Rbow will be waiting for him."*

The father pointed to the ashtray.

"No. Heavens, no. This piece is twenty-eight dollars — "

A toothy laugh. "You gotta be *shittin'* me!"

"No — I — "

"Natalie-e-e-e!"

"It's even got a *chip* on one side." The father wrinkled his nose.

"Eddie, we better leave." The mother was cradling the little girl, shaking her gently. "These two need a nap."

"No-o-o-o!"

"W-A-A-A-H!!!"

268

"Shuddup. I think we better go. We been shoppin' all mornin' and these two are gettin' tired."

"*Please...*" Cobb took the ashtray from the jerk's hand and carefully replaced it onto the surface of the battered dressing table. The thundering footsteps on the wooden floor hurt only as long as it took the irritating family to leave the store.

The loud *jingle!* of the sleighbell above the door had become the most beautiful sound Cobb had heard in a very long time. Even better than the stringed passages of the Tchaikovsky "*Pathetique*" he'd listened to earlier.

The silence that followed was both heavy and invigorating. It was even more beautiful than the jingling of the sleigh bell, though both sounds had the distinction of a freedom Cobb hadn't thought of—or appreciated—before this moment.

Cobb sighed deeply, then turned to the empty doorway.

It took him several long moments to realize Norton's friend had also gone.

***

John sat in a window booth in the crowded restaurant halfway down the block from Cobb's Collectibles, sipping coffee and thinking about what had just happened in the store.

When he saw the family go inside, he knew something interesting might happen. He wanted to be right in the middle of it, to make things even more confusing with his sudden appearance.

His plan was to make sure Cobb saw him, then leave with the family. This way, if there was someone else in the store, John wouldn't have to worry about being trapped.

Although he'd only been in the store a minute or so, John hadn't seen anyone else. He hadn't been able to check out the office, but that couldn't be helped. He'd been watching the rear doorway during the commotion but hadn't seen any activity. While this didn't mean much, it suggested that, if someone *had* been in the office, this person was determined not to be seen nor heard.

If Cobb had indeed engaged someone else in this, this person wasn't in the store. The important thing was that John had clearly shown Cobb that he was still a force to be reckoned with, and there was nothing Cobb could do to change this.

John finished his coffee and signaled the waitress for a refill.

***

Keeping his distance behind the entrance door, Nathaniel Cobb stared at the *OPEN/CLOSED* sign and wondered if his world was about to shatter.

Norton's friend had tricked him, and he shook each time he thought of it.

He was absolutely sure the bastard had made those morons come in the store. He paid them to come in and make trouble, causing Cobb to avert his eyes from the door. He followed them in a little later and stood there, grinning that village idiot's smile, making a mockery of everything.

270

"A mockery," he mumbled between clenched teeth. "A disgusting, pathetic mockery."

"*I helped you when you needed me,*" his friend said, moving closer.

"Yes," Cobb replied, sighing. "You did."

"*I had no idea something like that was going to happen. Otherwise, I would have warned you.*"

"I know. I appreciate it, I really do. And I know you would help me more if you could. Believe me, I'm very, very sorry for not asking for your help. I promise I'll never offend you again."

"*You promise?*"

"Yes."

"*Cross your heart?*"

"Cross my heart."

"*Good. And now that I'm here, we must decide what has to be done.*"

"Yes."

"*Rbow must be warned.*"

"But I can't give him a signal. Norton's friend has seen to that."

"*There is something you* can *do...*"

Cobb pushed his brows together. "And what is that?"

"*Norton's friend is still out there.*"

"Obviously."

"*And so is Rbow.*"

"Yes."

"*You must bring the two together -- am I not correct?*"

Cobb blinked. Funny, how he hadn't thought of that. It was so obvious, yet he hadn't thought of it.

He once again considered himself lucky to have such a terrific friend who always looked out for him. "Yes. You are most definitely correct."

"And how can you do this?"

Cobb grew silent.

"Go for a walk," his friend said after a long pause.

"A walk?"

"Close up, walk down the block, then grab a paper at the newsstand. Norton's friend is bound to follow. He will think you're up to something and won't want you out of his sight. When you spot him, it will be easy giving the appropriate signal to Rbow."

Cobb smiled.

"Is this not a good idea?"

"It is a wonderful idea, and I thank you so very, very much."

***

Cobb left the store with the *CLOSED* sign displayed prominently on the entrance door.

John jumped up from his window seat and dropped some bills on the table. He rushed outside. Cobb was marching down the street in a brisk manner. He moved with long, fluid strides.

Keeping a comfortable distance behind staggered clots of people, John maintained a moderate clip, occasionally risking a quick glance behind him to make sure no one was slipping out through the front or dashing from the alley next to the store.

Cobb stopped briefly at the intersection, then turned right.

John crossed the street with the crowd and stayed with the flow, his eyes straight ahead, alert for sudden movement.

Cobb continued moving at the same fast clip.

John crossed at the intersection. He kept his pace, staying close to the buildings for cover. He knew he could easily slip into a doorway or storefront if Cobb suddenly turned around.

Then, before he realized it, the old man had disappeared.

John slowed, stopping in front of a store window. He turned around.

No one suspicious.

He moved farther down, glancing at the hand-painted sign dangling by two rusty chains over the doorway of the store facing the corner.

WALSH'S CORNER NEWSSTAND
magazines, paperbacks, newspapers, DVD rentals
"C'mon in, see what we got!"

John glanced inside.

His back to the window, the old man was standing in front of the newspaper rack, a paper opened in front of him.

John scowled.

A newspaper?
What the hell?
He knows I'm watching him. And here he is, reading a damned newspaper?

273

John's mind went berserk.

Moments later, the reality

(bait)

hit him with the force of a sledgehammer.

That bastard just suckered me!

There's someone out here among the crowds –

Without hesitation, John forced himself to walk calmly past the newsstand window. A group of three fleshy middle-aged women waddled by. John kept close, maintaining his position about five feet behind them. One of them glanced back at him. He smiled. She smiled back.

The women stopped at the end of the block, waiting for the light. They crossed the street, making their way for the buffet restaurant at the end of the block.

John held the door open for them before following them inside.

***

The short, round-faced man sat in the rented van, looking through a pair of binoculars.

The lunch crowd would make things difficult. Cobb's mark would be harder to spot, making the hit complicated.

Rbow didn't like complications.

He kept a watchful eye on the street. So far, no one seemed suspicious, but the crowds could be concealing the mark. Small, scattered groups of women shoppers, smaller groups of the white-collar crowd, and an occasional street bum panhandling suggested nothing out of the ordinary.

Cobb turned at the corner.

Rbow kept an eye on the newsstand at the far end of the block. Cobb seemed to be headed there. Since Rbow had parked the rented white van in the lot near the intersection, he had an excellent point of surveillance. If anyone were following Cobb, it would be easy to spot him.

This job wouldn't be difficult once he'd spotted the mark.

Rbow's specialty was his success at approaching people. He was able to approach anyone, at any time. He was friendly, kind-faced: the last guy you'd expect to arouse suspicion. He'd been doing this sort of thing for fifteen years and hadn't even come close to being caught.

Of course, it helped, looking the way he did. He'd been told all his life that he resembled Uncle Billy in the movie, *It's A Wonderful Life*. And no one would ever suspect Uncle Billy of doing anything evil, would they?

Forgetful? Yes.

Silly? Childish? Most definitely.

Other than that?

No. Especially when Uncle Billy wore his huge, disarming smile.

And also the priest's garb he'd picked up for occasions like this.

No one would ever suspect a priest of doing a hit.

Especially a priest looking like Uncle Billy.

Chloroform would be used to get the mark out of commission. He had a packet specially made with an aerosol spray that responded to the slightest

275

pressure, exploding through a vent in the plastic the instant the packet was squeezed. He would then drag the mark into the nearest alley, retrieve the van, return to the alley, put the mark in back, and perform the euthanasia.

Otherwise, he'd have to use a gun with a suppressor, and he didn't want to do that. Guns were cumbersome, dangerous, and extremely noisy. He'd only used a gun a few times, and only as a last resort. The best-known untraceable bullets were hard to come by, and sometimes shattered before reaching their target. Mercury-dipped slugs were acceptable, provided they were prepared by someone you could trust. Black talons were getting more and more difficult to obtain, and anything involving guns -- especially lately -- made people nervous.

And asking questions.

Chloroform would suffice for this one.

When Cobb was halfway down the block, Rbow spotted a man in casual clothes crossing the street in Cobb's direction. The man was walking at a moderate pace, glancing behind him at frequent intervals. He looked to be in his late thirties, medium height, and thin. Other than being good-looking, nothing about the man suggested anything special.

Cobb suddenly disappeared inside the newsstand.

The man in casual clothes stopped about halfway down the block. He turned to the storefront window and began looking at the display but kept

276

glancing around him. Moments later, he started walking again, this time at a slower pace, until he reached the newsstand window. He looked inside, glanced behind him again, then went right back to the window. At one point, he tilted his head, reached up, and scratched the back of his neck. He glanced behind him and tilted his head again.

Seconds later, he seemed to stiffen as if someone had snuck up behind him and poked a rod up his ass. Moments later, he resumed walking just as three matronly women plodded past.

The foursome went down the block and crossed the street. The women disappeared in the restaurant.

So did the man.

Rbow got out of his van.

That was the mark, all right.

The idiot should be wearing a sign that said: *I'M COBB'S MARK*.

Rbow's round, red cheeks spread into a delightful grin.

This wouldn't be difficult at all.

***

Erika parked in the lot across the street from Cobb's Collectibles.

Just as she got out of her car, she spotted John's Lincoln Town Car. The Pennsylvania tag told her it was probably his rental. It was parked along the curb, just a few spaces from the lot she'd just pulled into.

Worried when she hadn't heard from him all day, Erika had left work early. Despite half a dozen attempts at phoning him—not to mention a personal query at the motel desk—there was no word.

Al Peterson had called that day, telling her of the progress his investigator friend was making. Apparently Al's guy had been able to get some crackerjack shots of Paul and Stacy together, and had arranged a time and place to surrender the valuable evidence to Al.

However, Erika discovered that she didn't care nearly as much as she had in the beginning. She still wanted the house and still wanted to expose Paul for his infidelity...but she was surprised that her entire focus had suddenly changed.

Not changed, as much as it had *shifted*.

Yes. Shifted. This made her realize how different things had become since John Callen entered her life.

And how did she feel about all this?

The only thing that seemed to make sense was that John needed her help, and she realized that she felt much better about herself and life in general when she was with him. His mere presence somehow dimmed the guilt feelings—and the hurt—that had developed from her failed marriage, even though the reason for the failure had largely been her husband's fault.

She wondered if this new development would help her through the divorce. It certainly seemed possible. Since she had met John, she found herself thinking of other things and agonizing less and less about the breakup of her marriage.

278

It had been a long time since she had experienced the intense pleasure of being needed, being wanted. Being appreciated. And after so many long years of not experiencing such delights, Erika realized that, since she met John, she had been enjoying all that she had been missing.

But with all this realization came something else. It was happening in spite of Buster's murder and what John had done to the psychotic Murphy twins. This new phenomenon was wonderful and pure. It had burst joyfully out into the open, convincing Erika of the obvious. She was falling in love with another man. And unless she was mistaken, this man could quite possibly be falling in love with her.

But despite all this, she had to take a breath and focus on other facts that seemed to be even more important than a brand-new love. These facts were both terrifying and very simple: John had gone after an old man responsible for killing his friend, and this same old man might be getting in touch with a killer to deal with John.

And it was at that moment that Erika found that she was determined to make sure nothing happened to this new man in her life.

How? she wondered.

She had no idea. All she knew was that she was going to do whatever it took to make sure nothing bad happened to John Callen.

***

From a corner table of the buffet restaurant, John drank coffee and carefully eyed the lunch crowd.

The room was filled with well-dressed, white-collar types, with hordes of chattering female shoppers mixed in.

So far, he hadn't seen anyone suspicious. No one seemed even slightly interested in him.

He wondered if he'd given himself away earlier, while he was looking in the newsstand window. Fortunately, there were more than enough pedestrians and street traffic to hide him from professional eyes, as well as the women he'd followed into the restaurant, which might have contributed to his anonymity.

Even so, he knew he'd better be careful...

He had to get back to Cobb, and he had to do it without incident. It was obvious the old man had left the store to lure him away.

He supposed he should hide within another crowd, head back to the store, and shake up Cobb again. As before, he could wait until another group of potential customers went in, then follow. Nothing could happen in front of witnesses.

John examined the crowd again. Some had left, others had come in. A short, blocky man about fifty-five sat at a table near the doorway, smiling at the waitress serving him. The man was wearing a dark jacket, slacks, and black shoes, and had on a clerical collar. He had a large, round face, a thick shock of curly gray hair, and the expression of a cherub. He resembled someone John had seen in an old movie.

Which one was it?

Okay, movie buff. Care to step up?

A moment later, it came to him. Thomas Mitchell. Vivien Leigh's father in *Gone with The Wind*.

John glanced at his watch. 2:15. He decided to return to Cobb's store and give the old fart another healthy round of genuine annoyance. After pissing him off, John could leave, then wait until Cobb did something stupid again.

He got up, left money for the coffee, and went down the hall, to the rest rooms.

***

Rbow followed the mark down the hall that led to the rest rooms.

The crowd had become heavy in the last half-hour. He had to elbow his way down the hall. Two people chattered loudly on the pay phones and two others argued about world events. Rbow squeezed through, giving both a beaming smile.

He knew the john might be crowded, but he had his packet ready, just in case an opportunity suddenly came up.

The mark stood at the urinal, his back to the door. No one else was in sight, but a pair of scuffed Oxfords showed clearly behind the door of the end booth.

No problem: he'd need only ten seconds to get this done.

The best way of doing this was to chloroform him at the urinal, when the mark was distracted and his hands were busy, drag him into a stall, break his neck, and leave him there.

His left hand grasping the packet in his coat pocket, Rbow cautiously approached the man at the urinal.

***

John turned toward the shadow slowly approaching him.

The short, dark figure turned out to be the cleric he'd seen sitting near the front door.

John zipped up, then flushed. He had the feeling the cleric was standing directly behind him. The man hadn't passed on his way to the sinks or toilets, nor had he stepped to John's right to use the other urinal.

Strange.

Just as John was about to move away, the door opened sharply. Two well-dressed guys in their late thirties appeared, having a good-natured argument about software.

"It's getting to be a relic," one of them said as he approached the sink to comb his thinning hair. He put down his tan leather briefcase on the tiled floor, then got busy with his comb. "Once the Chinese perfect the chip, everything else is obsolete." He laughed as he pocketed the comb, then washed his hands. "Name anything more convenient than having your personal computer installed in your brain."

His friend shook his head. "Convenience really doesn't matter. Something about that scares the hell out of me."

282

His companion said, "Afraid you won't have room enough up there for a chip?"

His friend laughed. "That's probably it."

The other grinned as he made his way for the urinal.

John saw the cleric once again as he moved toward the sink. The little guy stood close to the urinal, smiling at him. John smiled politely back, then finished washing his hands.

A gay priest.

What else was new?

***

For the sake of appearance, Rbow finished at the urinal, washed his hands, and left the bathroom.

Close, but no cigar.

Since he hadn't really counted on doing the hit so soon, the encounter hadn't bothered him much. One thing he'd learned in this business was patience.

The mark had seen him, but this didn't bother him, either. The mark probably had him summed up as just another friendly old coot, or a fag, and wouldn't consider him a threat.

Rbow went back out into the restaurant and looked around.

The mark had disappeared.

***

John squeezed through the small crowds on his way back to Cobb's Collectibles.

It was now 2:25. He decided to return to his car, keep watch, and wait an hour or so before returning to the shop — just in case Cobb was expecting him.

He was about halfway down the block when he heard someone shouting behind him. The crowd had dispersed; some had crossed the street while others had gone into the pharmacy. John turned. The cleric hurried in his direction, a big smile on the man's face.

"Excuse me! Excuse me!"

John stopped walking and waited for the other man to catch up. The cleric was gripping something in his hand. At first glance, it looked like a white handkerchief. As the man grew closer, John could see that the cleric was holding the handkerchief very carefully.

Moments later, the man caught up to him.

"Yes?"

"Excuse me," the cleric said breathlessly, "but I believe you dropped your handkerchief. I was in the restaurant with you, and I'm sure I saw this fall from your pocket as you were— "

"Not mine. Thanks, anyway." John turned away, but the cleric nudged him by the crook of the elbow.

"Are you sure?" The cleric looked concerned. "It's monogrammed, and if you'll just — "

"I said, it's not mine." John frowned. He hoped his expression conveyed the distinctive message that the hankie wasn't his. But anything similar would do just as long as the preacher man made tracks.

It was at that very moment that John felt the familiar twitching sensation at the back of his neck. It was the same feeling he'd experienced years ago, when he was stationed in Iraq.

The cleric was still smiling. "Maybe if you saw the initials — "

The pudgy hand suddenly came up.

John moved out of the way.

He wondered if his memory of the cleric in the restaurant bathroom had just sent over a red flag. It could have been the realization that the man had been standing behind him a little too close and too long, and had moved away only when the two computer nerds came in.

Or maybe it was the smile the cleric had given him at the wrong moment.

The twitching sensation had been the final straw.

John jerked away. The handkerchief shot up in a lightning-quick arc, engaging John in a strong whiff of something reeking of medicine—a disturbing stench that made the hair stand up on the back of his neck.

Knockout juice?

Compliments of Nathaniel Cobb?

His reflexes kicking in, John reached out to grab the wrist of the hand holding the handkerchief.

He quickly discovered that his instincts had been right on the mark. He knew right then that his senses, dormant for more than a decade, had not failed him and were working just as efficiently as they'd been when the two killers had snuck into Buster's house.

The cleric's arm, he quickly discovered, belonged to someone deceptively strong. It took most of John's strength to push it away from his face. As he struggled, a sharp burst of explosive pain near his solar plexus turned his vision double. He realized right then that the cleric had used his free hand to deliver a martial arts blow. It was well-aimed and expertly executed. This man knew what he was doing.

Waves of dizziness enveloped him as the oxygen was sucked from him in one powerful jolt.

Then it dawned on him.

Not a cleric at all.

Another wet boy, this one far more dangerous than the Murphy twins.

This one you wouldn't suspect in a million years.

This was someone you'd entrust your kid to. Or your wife. Or even your bank account if it was requested.

You couldn't possibly know that what lurked behind that innocent, concerned face was a monster vicious enough to slit your throat while the friendly mask covering it was stretched in a beaming smile.

John held on to the killer's arm with both hands. As he did so, he felt himself being dragged into the alley next to Cobb's Collectibles. The alley was small and narrow. The metal corner of a green dumpster protruded dangerously in their path.

John had the sinking feeling his face was about to be slammed directly into it.

He continued to resist, but the other man was much stronger. The more John tried pulling away, the easier the killer dragged him. The killer was using John's weight and resistance as leverage. His technique was extremely effective.

The dumpster grew closer; John could smell the spoiled food, mildew, and grease emanating within it. He tried twisting the man's arm behind him, but suddenly there was another hand to worry about, this one closing around his neck.

John raised his knee to get the other man in the groin. Anticipating this, his adversary twisted his torso, taking the full impact in his solid left buttock. All the while, his hand continued closing tightly around John's throat.

John felt his breath weakening. He twisted his head and tried to get into position to bite the man's wrist.

Then, just as he began feeling another sudden burst of dizziness, he heard someone shouting his name.

***

Erika saw John walking around the corner

Her first instinct was to get out of the car and rush over to him.

However, some inner voice told her to wait. If he had a plan, she surely didn't want to mess it up. She'd come to help, not complicate things.

If he went into Cobb's store, she could wait a few minutes, then slip inside and see what was going on. The fact that Cobb might have someone else in his store had occurred to her. And she was determined not to let John walk blindly into an ambush.

But what could she do?

Turn into Wonder Woman?

Get real, girl. You're in the Big Leagues now. The man you want to protect was a killer in Iraq. Just the other day he killed two young, strong, armed men. Now he's going after an old man, and you're worried about him?

Just then, a short, stocky man in a dark suit entered the picture. The man was following John, waving some sort of white material at him. John stopped and turned. They began talking. John shook his head. The other man held up something. And then --

They were *fighting*!

Oh my God!

In just seconds, the man in the dark suit was dragging John into the alley.

Erika practically leaped out of her car. Dodging rush-hour traffic and ignoring whistles and catcalls from men in passing trucks, she ran across the street.

When she slipped into the alley entrance, she froze.

The man in the dark suit wore a collar

(priest?)

around his neck and was in the process of strangling John. John struggled, but the priest bore

288

down on him, pushing John toward the side of the dumpster.

Do something, girl! Even if it's wrong!

"John! *John*!"

Her cries rang out, shattering the tense silence.

The priest jerked his head toward her.

In that same instant, John grabbed the man's wrist, twisted it, extended his leg in front of the priest's ankle, and forced him roughly to the ground.

After landing on his back with a sharp grunt, the priest punched John in the face.

Erika cringed.

John suddenly went berserk, jumping on the other man and wrapping his hands around the priest's neck. Twisting and jerking, the priest punched John in the sides and kicked him in the legs. John, seemingly oblivious of the blows, kept up the pressure. The look on his face made Erika think of an old horror flick she'd seen in high school, when she'd gone to the movies with a few of her girlfriends. It was a werewolf movie, and it scared her for weeks afterward.

The priest's face abruptly turned red, then blue. A gurgling sound escaped his throat. Phlegm spewed out, catching John on the chin. John kept up the pressure, rocking on top of the man and digging his fingers and thumbs into the soft flesh of the man's throat.

The priest went limp.

"John!"

No response.

John kept rocking and digging. A soft growling sound trickled out of his throat.

"*John*!" Trembling a little, Erika reached down and gently touched his arm, flinching at the heat in it.

He cringed at her touch, twisting around and gaping at her as if he had no idea who or what he was looking at. Recognition gradually returned, and he shook himself out of his trance.

"E-Erika?"

"It's me, John." She forced a smile. Gathering courage, she took a breath and carefully touched his arm again. "You...okay?"

He slowly removed his hands from the dead man's throat and sat back on the cleric's thighs. He gazed at his hands. Erika was shocked at their redness, how they resembled claws. He tried massaging them, wincing when he suddenly realized how stiff they had become. Moments later, he sighed deeply. "I think so..."

Erika watched him closely, hoping that whatever had happened had passed. She wondered if the Iraq nightmare had come back to John during the scuffle. Then she wondered if John would still be alive if it hadn't come back. She considered it very strange that the man John had just killed, obviously very strong, very powerful, had been dressed as a priest. But since so many other strange things had been happening lately, she decided not to let this paradox bug her.

She had heard or read somewhere that the smell of death, according to soldiers who had killed in combat, never goes away, and does something to you when you smell it again. It is similar to the taste of human flesh. A wild animal never forgets it.

Erika thought of the werewolf again.

"Thanks to you." John suddenly smiled.

Erika wanted to return his smile but had other things on her mind. "John…who *is* he? He's not a priest, is he?"

" Just another killer Cobb sent after me."

Erika was staring. "But he doesn't *look* like a hired killer."

"He also doesn't look very strong, but he would've turned my ass into worm-food if you hadn't happened along."

She watched as John picked up the handkerchief the other man had dropped. There was a small plastic packet inside. He sniffed, then quickly turned away. "Chloroform."

Erika watched as he searched the man's pockets. She gasped when he found a switchblade and a small, pocket-sized automatic.

"Standard issue for priests nowadays, I guess."

"What do we do now?" she asked. "We can't just leave him here."

"He's going in the dumpster. I'll call Sheriff Grubb a little later and give him a heads up. I'm sure he's gonna hate this, but it was unavoidable. He'll call someone in Wheeling, and they'll have to hash it out among themselves. After I dump this wet boy, I'm going to pay Mr. Nathaniel Cobb one last visit, and we're going to have it out, once and for all."

"But…are you sure? I mean, what if he tries to kill you?"

"Cobb isn't the type. Doesn't want to dirty his hands. You've seen him; there's not a mark on him. Not a blemish, nor wrinkle. And his hands look like they see weekly visits to manicurists. Cobb obviously pays big money to have his laundry done. On his own, he's pitiful. A pathetic old man messed up by his mother and father."

"I…want to help you." She didn't want John to kill Cobb. She hoped that he might not do it if she was with him.

The fact was, she didn't like what had just happened. That deadly animal thing. She didn't want whatever she had seen happen to John happen ever again.

"You've done more than enough." He put his hand on her shoulder and smiled. "And I'm truly grateful. But there's no way I can let you into this last part. I could never forgive myself if I did something that got you hurt."

"What about you?"

"I'll be all right."

"Please tell me what happened. I mean, after I distracted him. You…didn't hear me…"

"I'll tell you later." He straightened, stepped over the priest, and turned to the dumpster.

Feeling helpless, Erika watched silently.

John dragged the body closer to the dumpster. He bent and, grabbing the other man around the torso, pulled him upright and leaned him against the side of the dumpster. It took a mighty effort to

292

heave him up and shove him inside the bin. He then rested against the side of the dumpster for a few moments to catch his breath. Once he'd recovered, he pulled the lid shut. Then he stepped away from the dumpster and wiped himself off. "I guess I'll see you later."

Erika shook her head. There was no way this man was going to write her off so easily. "No, you won't."

He blinked.

"I want to know what you're going to do."

"It's best that you don't."

She thought of the incident at the Holiday Inn, when he'd got that drunk away from her. Then at her own place, when he'd scooped her up from the street. Her White Knight was about to fall off his horse and she would *not* let that happen.

"What's the problem?" he asked.

"I'm worried about you."

"I'll be all right."

"I was expecting you to say something like that."

He didn't reply.

"You're going into a strange man's store. This man has already paid three people to have you and your friend killed. Doesn't that tell you Cobb is crazy?"

He nodded.

"And you're going into his store when he's probably expecting to see either you or that killer he just hired to do what those other two couldn't do."

Another nod.

293

"I just don't think you know exactly what you're going to do. Nor do you know how you're going to do it. For instance, how do you intend to sneak in there?"

"The front door, I guess."

"What about the bell?"

"What bell?"

"The one attached to the door. The one that jingles every time the door opens more than two inches."

He blinked. "Now I remember. You're right, there *is* a bell. The two times I'd gone in, I was preoccupied. How did you know?"

She shrugged. "I've been in that store before. I remember it."

John didn't reply.

"He'll be ready for you. And what if he's armed? What if he decides to do his own laundry for the very first time in his life?"

He thought that one over before replying. "Any suggestions?"

"I think I might have something in mind."

***

In his office, Nathaniel Cobb drank cinnamon coffee while listening to the silence.

"*He'll be in touch*," his friend said.

"I hope so," Cobb replied. "It's been hours since I returned from the newsstand. I hope he found Norton's friend."

"*I think he did.*"

"You do?"

294

"Rbow is a professional. I'm sure he knows exactly what he is doing."

"You're right, of course."

"Yes."

"And we'll soon be getting an e-mail, informing us of his progress."

"I'm sure we will."

Cobb frowned. "I still can't help feeling nervous. This man has spooked me. It's like he can — "

"See inside your soul. You've said this before."

"But it's true."

"Yes. But impossible."

"I know it seems impossible, but it was exactly how he made me feel. Like when I was little, and the monster came in and…and *grinned* at me — "

"I remember."

"Yes. You were there, too. Not at first, but when they started locking me in the closet for doing — for doing what…what I couldn't help -- "

"Someone had to help you."

Tears crept down Cobb's cheeks as the nightmare returned.

Summerville snuck silently up the stairs while little seven-year-old Nathaniel, shaken awake by a nightmare, was squirming out of bed. Summerville had been so quiet that Nathaniel couldn't hear him. The big, bulky man peered into the room, his veiny blue eyes growing as he took in the sight of little Nathaniel huddled in the middle of the room, quietly sobbing, his soiled undershorts pushed down to his knees.

Summerville came in as silently as a stalking cat, bloodshot eyes wild, thin lips parted and drooling, one huge hand moving toward little Nathaniel's damp penis, his other hand encircling the slender body, clamping firmly over the boy's startled, wide-open mouth —

"*He died much too easily,*" Cobb's friend said.

"Yes!" Cobb, blinking furiously, shook himself out of the horrible memory. "Yes…" He sat for long moments, trembling while waiting for his breathing to normalize.

When he realized it was safe…that he was no longer back there again…that the horrible, drooling monster was truly dead…he sighed deeply.

"*Heart attack. He was nearly eighty. They were thinking of monsters like him when they made that statement about the good dying young.*"

"Yes. But-- "

Just then, he stopped.

The bell above the shop door jingled.

***

Erika walked into the large, dreary store and instantly felt the nausea returning.

The spacious room was packed with merchandise. Mixed smells of air freshener, mildew, and rotten wood soured the warm, uncirculated air in the room. Dusty items were piled on top of dressers, on tables and shelves, and stacked on the wooden floor. Paintings hung from every square inch of available wall space. Antique mirrors with ornate frames covered other sections of the walls. Erika could see her reflection everywhere.

296

She suddenly felt helpless and vulnerable. She had entered forbidden territory—the domain of a monster who paid people to murder others to suit his needs.

She moved to the western section of the room. Scratched, ancient-looking armoires, with short, chiseled legs, stood next to one another in uneven rows. Erika opened a door and was attacked by a heavy waft of mildew. Her eyes watered; she wiped them with an index finger. A faint pine smell lingered in the air.

She suddenly had the feeling she wasn't alone.

She turned.

Nathaniel Cobb stood just a few feet behind her, watching her intently.

***

Cobb found the attractive brunette at the armoires.

He glanced at the ancient cuckoo clock on the wall above the mirrors. 3:00. The clock was a couple of minutes slow. He'd been talking with his friend, had started once again on Summerville, and lost all track of time.

Now there's a customer, and I must return to my professional, courteous manner...

She was standing in front of an open door of an armoire. She looked about thirty or so, with raven-black hair and the face of a model. She was tall, maybe five-nine with the two-inch heels -- which made her only four inches shorter than Cobb.

He felt uncomfortable—as he usually did in the presence of a woman. Summerville had corrupted

297

this desire, among others, when Nathaniel was just a boy. And even though he had tried many times to prove himself with the opposite sex, he'd never been successful. He'd always felt extreme terror when his attentions focused on his penis, and a painful burning sensation consumed him whenever the subject of sex entered his mind.

His friend tried to help, but both knew this affliction ran deep, and could not be cured with kind words or positive thinking. Because of Summerville, Cobb associated sex with pain—as well as discomfort and inadequacy—and realized nothing short of shock therapy could change this condition.

However, while watching this woman, he felt a strange warmth, and found himself approaching a state of contented pleasure despite the burning sensation in his crotch.

"Oh! You startled me!" She whirled around, her right hand covering the front of her neck.

"May I help you?" he asked, smiling while focusing on her beautiful almond eyes.

She smiled in return, making Cobb feel even warmer. Her beautiful face became even more striking when she smiled. Those eyes. They made you feel so *special*...

"A very good friend of mine told me about your store, and I just had to come see for myself what treasures you have."

"Really?" He was delighted people talked about his place. "What is your friend's name? Maybe I can remember him. Or her..."

"Her name's Brenda. Brenda Canfield. She lives in St. Clairsville, and she was here last month, looking for German beer steins."

He scratched his scalp. He couldn't remember such a woman, but there had been so many customers. Perhaps her friend hadn't been striking enough for him to remember.

At least, not nearly as striking as this beauty.

And he didn't remember anyone buying any of the beer steins he had on display.

"Could you possibly describe your friend, Miss?"

"She's about my height, with reddish-brown hair and blue eyes."

That didn't quite narrow it down. Her description fit a thousand women in the Ohio Valley. But it wasn't important. The important issue was that this woman would most likely purchase something. She dressed well and carried herself wonderfully. Her leather bag probably went for a couple of hundred dollars. And the leather pumps looked like they reached two hundred, easy. The dress was obviously a designer and fit her very well.

"I can't honestly remember your friend, Miss, but may I help you in any way?"

She grew serious. "I was wondering if you had any armoires like this one, only with less shelves. I'm looking for something like this, but my clothes are mostly suits and dresses, and my closet space..." She smiled and shrugged.

"I understand, believe me." Grinning, Cobb gestured to his left, where another huge piece stood, its back to the one they were facing. "You live in a newer place, I'll bet."

She nodded. "One of those condos outside of town. They're about five years old, I guess, and they have no storage space whatsoever." She pouted. "Honestly, I don't understand what these builders are thinking when they design these places. They obviously don't have any conception of what to do with clothing, or things you don't normally use every day."

"Exactly." Cobb pulled open the double doors, stepped back, and gestured proudly.

The piece was nearly seven feet tall and five wide, with three long drawers on the bottom and a stack of deep shelves on each side.

"This is perfect for what you're looking for. As you can see, there are eight shelves for many pairs of shoes. Each shelf is deep enough for three pairs. The drawers can easily store unmentionables and folding items. The rest?" He held up his pink palms proudly. "You could easily hang twenty suits and a dozen other outfits here."

"It's really big. What's the price?"

"Fifteen-seventy-five. But I'm willing to drop ten percent if you decide to take it."

"Fifteen-seventy-five..." She thought it over, tilting her head, pushing her hair away when it fell in front of her face.

Cobb felt the strange burning sensation again. He forced his mind on the sale. This woman was a potential buyer—why ruin things by fantasizing over something unattainable?

"Do you deliver?"

"I have an arrangement with a small moving company down the street," he said, focusing again.

"How much extra is that?" She twisted to her left and bent to inspect a gouge on the carved wood.

He pulled back, forcing his gaze from her firm thighs and cursing himself for letting her catch his wandering eyes. "The delivery is included in the price."

She bent again, this time to her right. "That's very nice," she said, reaching out to touch the inner wall of the armoire.

"Yes." He caught a strong whiff of her lilac perfume and forced his eyes away again. It was extremely difficult keeping his eyes off her. "It's the way I do business, and I've been doing things this way for many years."

"Brenda told me you were nice." She smiled, flashing her big brown eyes at him.

"Thank her for me. And tell her that when she comes in again, I'll give her an automatic ten percent discount on anything she wishes to buy."

"That's extremely generous of you."

"Not where a valued customer is concerned," he said solemnly, holding up a skinny index finger. "As far as I'm concerned, good customers are what make business thrive. When someone gives my shop a referral, I make a sale. When I make a sale, I move merchandise. When I move merchandise, I take one more step toward my ultimate goal."

"And what *is* your goal?" she asked.

Cobb thought of the Summerville paintings. Searching for them, then buying them, one at a time. Finding out where they were being auctioned. Bidding. Counterbidding…until they were all in his possession. Going through the motions of operating an antique business all these years, while all he ever wanted was to find the fortune the monster Summerville had left buried beneath one of his many parcels of ground.

Then, finally, selling this wretched place and flying down to Rio, buying a condo near the beach, and living in total luxury for the rest of his life.

"To enjoy good fortune and good health," he replied, smiling his practiced smile. "And to maintain a fine, upstanding reputation among my peers." He spread out his hands. "After all, what else *is* there in life?"

***

The moment Erika had walked into the store, John, close behind, snuck over to the other side of the big room and blended in amongst the clutter.

While Cobb went over to assist Erika, John slipped silently down the muddled aisle that led to the office down the hall.

Just before he went into the hall, John lowered his face to the floor. He could see their feet in another section of the room. From what he remembered, they were standing amongst the dressers and armoires.

His plan was to sneak into Cobb's office and snoop around. He didn't think Erika was in any

302

danger. But he didn't want to be too far away, nonetheless.

Cobb's office was small—maybe ten by fifteen. A long table had been shoved against a wall and topped with a microwave, coffeemaker, and one of those small refrigerators. A filing cabinet shoved against the opposite wall faced the desk. Beside it, an ancient radiator served as a shelf for three tall stacks of old hardbacks.

Coffee brewed: the smell of cinnamon was strong.

John knew there was no way to search the filing cabinet without making racket. The metal unit was obviously very old. A huge dent disfigured the side. It would be literally impossible to pull open a drawer without alerting Cobb when it banged open or scraped against the runner. And if he wanted to check it after Cobb had gone upstairs later on, he'd be forced to play hide'n seek with the bastard all night...

John examined the two doors on the other wall. Both were locked and deadbolted but could be opened. Unfortunately, if John tried to open one of them, he wouldn't be able to re-bolt it from the other side, and Cobb would discover it when he returned.

Despite the obvious disadvantages of a thorough investigation, an inner voice was telling him to check the basement. There could be something down there that might incriminate Cobb, connecting him with Buster's death.

Buster's painting?

The frame?

Cobb might have his skeletons hidden in the basement, or other incriminating evidence that would prove that he wasn't such a good egg after all.

John cautiously approached the door on the left. He gingerly slid the deadbolt out of its niche.

***

"Do you live alone?"

Erika stiffened. "I beg your pardon?" She turned and gawked at the old man.

Cobb flushed. "My goodness! What I *meant* was, will you be sharing this magnificent piece with someone else? A roommate, perhaps?"

Erika wanted to smile. Inwardly she knew when someone was interested and prided herself in knowing when she should be on her guard.

This was why she was here. She hadn't told John her intentions but thought she might be able to use her feminine wiles to keep Cobb occupied. The man was a creep, but she was confident Cobb was thinking only about her for the moment. And unless some other customer came into the store, John wouldn't have to worry about Cobb for the next fifteen minutes or so.

"I'm divorced and live alone."

She wondered what John was doing at this moment. She'd seen him out of the corner of her eye while Cobb was busy with the armoire. It looked like he was headed for the office in back. She was worried about some sort of a trap but knew she had to play this out.

"I see." Cobb was beaming. Erika wasn't sure if it was because she'd told him she was divorced or because he thought she might actually purchase the smelly monstrosity. You just couldn't tell about old men. They were either perverts or just plain crazy.

This man, unfortunately, seemed to be both—and worse. Erika couldn't accept the cold fact that Cobb had actually paid money to have someone killed. This told her she needed to be constantly on her guard. Cobb would pay dearly to keep his good name, and if she or anyone else stood in his way, he'd merely open his wallet and have another potentially bad situation solved.

No fuss, no muss.

"Would you like to give me some earnest money for this piece?" Cobb asked, his eyes dropping to her bag. "We can discuss payment in my office, or if you prefer — "

"Actually, I'd like to look at it a little more, if you don't mind."

"Not at all." The old man's smile was still there, but Erika could tell it was forced. It seemed to say, *You're taking up my valuable time, sweet cheeks, and if you don't soon show me some green, I'm gonna show you the door...*

His jaw quivered; some color had left his cheeks. He obviously hadn't cared for her reluctance.

He wanted her money. Now.

"Take your time. I'll be closing soon, but if you need more time to think about it..." Cobb turned.

305

"If you need me, I'll be in my office." Then he began moving briskly toward the back.

Erika swallowed loudly.

John!

"Uh...Mr. Cobb?"

His footsteps stopped abruptly.

"Yes?" He turned and flashed a toothy smile.

"I have a question."

"Certainly." The lecherous grin returned as he walked back to where she was standing.

***

Piles of clutter choked most of the basement area.

Chairs, rockers, and furniture pieces had been shoved against the block walls and stacked as high as the seven-foot ceiling would permit. Odds and ends were scattered throughout the room and gave the appearance that they'd been dropped off and immediately forgotten.

A light bulb hung from a stained porcelain sconce drilled into a wooden beam. This single source of light enabled John to see almost half the room. But what caught his eye was the huge red Wells Fargo safe pushed against the far wall, directly beneath the wooden staircase.

He walked over and inspected it.

The light was interrupted by the staircase, slicing the metal unit into thick bars of blackness. The safe had a combination lock and wheel. Cobb was probably the only one with the combination. Short of using dynamite, John held no illusion of opening it.

There had to be some other way...

He knelt and began looking around. He didn't know what he was looking for, but it certainly beat wasting time wondering what he should be doing.

A large oak desk dominated the corner, just a few feet from the safe. If he could go through the drawers, he might be able to find something that could possibly —

John's heart skipped a beat.

Someone was walking around directly above his head.

***

"Are you serious about this piece, madam?"

Cobb's patience was wearing thin. This woman was becoming a nuisance, asking him question after question but showing no sign of reaching for her checkbook.

It was apparently true that beautiful women were selfish bitches.

Later, he and his friend would have a lengthy discussion about the shortcomings of beautiful women.

"I've been giving you my valuable time, and you're asking me these ridiculous questions — "

"They might seem ridiculous to *you*," she said sharply, "but they're important to *me*. And even though you seem to think I'm wasting your valuable time, I'm also wasting my own. If I'm going to spend sixteen hundred dollars — "

"As I've already explained, I intend to give you ten percent off — "

"All right. Fifteen hundred, then."

"It'll be considerably less, I assure you."

It was becoming an enormous effort to maintain his professionalism. Cobb wanted to go back to the office, sit, relax, enjoy another refreshing cup of coffee, and discuss this unpleasant matter with his good friend.

"The point is, I don't intend to spend this much money on something I don't know anything about."

Cobb placed his hands in front of him and interlaced his fingers. Sometimes this relieved the pressure; other times, it kept him from saying something distressing. "Madam, if I may be so bold, with the questions you've asked me, you no doubt know just as much about this piece as the craftsman who originally fashioned it nearly a century ago."

The woman's dark eyes grew larger. "If you're going to stand here and *insult* me — "

"I was merely being blunt. I am a very busy man. And, as much as I would like to give you a detailed history of each piece in my store — "

"I've had *more* than enough of this, thank you!" She spun around and stomped toward the store entrance.

Cobb was relieved. That armoire had been taking up valuable space for several years and he really wanted to sell it. Its mark-up was quite high, but he'd always hoped someone would come in and buy it, no questions asked. He'd expected this beautiful-but-irritating bitch to take out her checkbook and scribble the correct sum, but right now it didn't matter. All he wanted was for her to leave his store.

Now.

Just before she stormed outside, she spun around and gave him another glare. "Wait till I tell Brenda how rude and insulting you were to me. You'll never see *me*—nor *her*—in your stupid store again!"

Before he could give her his most dazzling smile and bid her a good day, she'd yanked open the entrance door and sent the sleigh bell ringing into oblivion as she bolted outside.

***

The door slammed shut the moment Erika reached the sidewalk.

She decided to wait a little while, then come back and see if she could open the door. Luckily, it was still rush hour. The sidewalks were just as flocked as they'd been an hour earlier. One person trying a shop door wasn't anything to call attention to. And there was always the chance that other customers might just go in first.

Erika hadn't wanted to call it quits with Cobb, but she hadn't liked the way the old man was looking at her. It gave her the creeps. The way he was eyeing her purse was just as disturbing as the way he was gawking at her legs.

She figured she'd given John enough time to do what he'd planned. He'd asked her to keep Cobb busy for fifteen minutes. That would give him plenty of time to snoop around and find another way outside when the time came for him to leave. A quick glance at her watch told her she'd occupied the old man for nearly half an hour. This made her feel John would be okay.

And anyway, she wanted—*needed*—fresh air.

She felt like she'd been rolling around in filth. The need to strip and jump in the shower had become overwhelming.

She reached the pharmacy next door, adjacent to the alley where John had finished off that guy in the priest's garb.

She eyed the dumpster and shivered.

A body lay inside that big, ugly metal thing. The body of a very bad man. A man who tried to kill John.

She suddenly felt the need to put some distance between herself and the dumpster. Before she realized it, she found herself heading back to Cobb's Collectibles.

A thorough study of the front window told her the lights had been switched off. Cobb wasn't in the store. He was either in the office in back or in another part of the building.

She moved over to the entrance door. The *CLOSED* sign faced out, but the burglar bars hadn't yet been pulled. Cobb could have just slammed the door shut, flicked off the lights, and gone back to his office.

Hopefully, John found something useful and left through the rear door.

But just in case...

Erika reached out and grasped the knob.

It didn't budge.

The door was locked.

***

Cobb slipped into his office and froze.

The strange cold feeling made the fine white hairs on the back of his neck bristle.

Someone's been in this room...

"I feel it, too, Nathaniel." His friend had followed him into the room and was standing close behind him.

"You do?"

"Someone was here while that woman"—he forced out the word, making it sound like a grunt—*"came into the store and started asking you those stupid questions."*

"You didn't like her, either?"

"She was a slut. I saw how she fluttered those store-bought lashes and gave you that disgusting smile. And that perfume... She smelled like a French whorehouse. I nearly gagged. And the way she bent over and showed you her panties..."

"I think you're right. She was a tease."

"A slut. A trollop."

"But she was so...so *beautiful*..."

"They generally are. Their beauty is their strongest weapon. Their beauty and their sex. It is how they make it so easy for themselves. And so difficult for us. Look at your own mother, how she — "

"Leave her out of this," Cobb said coldly.

"I was only using her as an example."

"I don't *care* what you were doing. She was my mother. She brought me into this world. She was a wonderful person who — "

311

"*She married Summerville…*" It was said flatly.

"Yes. But she only did it for me. I had no father of my own, and she was having a terrible time raising me, trying to make ends meet –– "

"*I understand.*"

"I'm sorry. I'm upset." Cobb took a deep breath and shuddered.

"*That slut upset you, brought back the darkness we both shared.*"

"You're right. But as I said, Mother needed help, and Summerville came into her life at a time when she was most vulnerable."

"*I hated him.*" His friend's voice had suddenly turned raspy.

"So did I."

"*She let him do…what he wanted.*"

"She was afraid. Summerville had a power. It was his presence. His size. And his eyes…they could slither inside my head, make me see all sorts of evil. All sorts of terror. He made me feel *dirty* when he looked at me. And his *touch*..." Cobb shivered, then wrapped his arms around himself. It was difficult, holding in the sob. "I felt *so* sorry for her!"

"*Her choice.*" It was said flatly.

"But as I said, she was vulnerable."

"*I blame her for everything.*"

"You always have. But you've got to see things from her perspective."

"*She married him, and when he came into the picture, nothing was ever the same, and I will always blame that bitch — *"

312

"Don't call her that." Cobb's face had turned bright red.

"You know how I feel."

"Yes. But — "

*"If it wasn't for Summerville, we wouldn't be —
"*

"If it wasn't for Summerville, you wouldn't have come to be!" Cobb realized he was on edge, but it was no wonder. Norton's friend. The Murphy's. That family of morons in his store. And, of course, the beautiful bitch who had come in and teased him unmercifully.

Now, to top it all off, his very best friend was badmouthing Mother!

"I don't wish to talk about that," said his friend. *"I came when you first started calling, and — "*

"I don't wish to talk about my mother. Or stand here and listen to you call her names."

"We shouldn't be arguing, Nathaniel."

"I know. But you know how I feel."

"Yes. I also know how we must come to terms with many bad things in our lives."

"Later," Cobb said.

"When?"

"When Rbow informs me that Norton's friend is dead, and we can finally focus on the treasure."

No reply.

Cobb waited, but his friend remained silent.

"You don't agree that everything will be fine when we uncover the treasure? When we move away and start our new life in a better place?"

Silence.

313

"Don't you?"

"No. I don't."

"But why?"

"Later. Later you will see. And understand."

"Why later?"

"It will be the right time. Right now, we must see why the cellar door is unlatched."

"You weren't in here when someone came in and -- "

"I was with you. Watching out for you. As always."

"My wonderful friend."

"Always. And now we must go downstairs and see that nothing is disturbed."

"Yes. But -- "

"But what, Nathaniel?"

"I'm frightened."

"Of what?"

"What if...what if someone *is* down there? An intruder. Someone who wants to rob me."

"There is a butcher knife behind the microwave. The one I told you to buy years ago, when you told me you needed protection, and couldn't bear to touch a gun."

"I remember."

"Pick it up and we shall go see if anyone is downstairs."

"And then?"

"And then we will take it from there."

Trembling, Cobb approached the knife. Its wooden handle was cold and harsh, and made him grit his teeth. He almost dropped it but recovered

314

when his friend approached and said, *"I'm right here with you."*

Cobb and his friend moved quietly toward the cellar door.

***

The cellar door squealed open.

Footsteps shuffled slowly toward the doorway.

John squeezed between an upright barrel and a stack of cardboard boxes.

The figure in the doorway did not move.

John peered cautiously around the side of the barrel.

No luck.

For one thing, the top three or four stairs extended several feet beyond his vantage point. For another, the single bulb just wasn't powerful enough to provide sufficient light.

Then he heard the voice.

Cobb's voice.

"Anyone…down here?" in a tense whisper.

John didn't move.

Ten seconds of silence.

"I know someone's…down here."

John waited.

"If you come out now, I'll…let you go."

John looked around for a weapon but couldn't distinguish anything in the darkness. As always, his penknife lay in his side pocket, but he couldn't dig for it without giving away his position.

"I think I should call the police and -- "

Just then, he stopped.

John heard whispering.

315

Cobb was talking to someone.

A moment later, heavy footsteps slowly descended the stairs.

***

Erika examined the window next to the metal door.

It looked just like any other window. A latch sat in the center. The frame probably moved in an up-and-down motion. But could she open it?

And—more importantly—could she get it open without causing a lot of racket?

She figured it was worth a try.

After all, John was inside with Cobb. And Cobb had locked the front door.

Erika opened her bag. She kept a small vinyl kit of short-handled screwdrivers and an adjustable wrench she'd bought at the hardware store in Bern. She'd always had a problem finding the right tools and never liked having to search for something when faced with a sudden emergency.

If the window was unlocked, she could use a screwdriver to pry it, then jam her fingers in the gap. This way, she might be able to raise it. She knew doing this would probably destroy her nails, thus triggering Peggy's wrath the next time she went in for a manicure. But it couldn't be helped.

She opened the kit and found the screwdriver. She laid her bag on the lid of the trashcan next to her, moved closer to the window, and stuck the flat metal tip of the screwdriver into the tiny gap. Then gently pushed the small yellow handle downwards.

The window began moving upward.

"*Why bring the police into this*?" His friend's frantic whisper scared him. "*You don't think —* "

"Of course not," Cobb whispered back. "It's a scare tactic. If there's a boy downstairs — "

"*Not a boy, Nathaniel.*"

"Who, then?"

"*A bum undoubtedly wandered in, probably through that back window that never locks. We need to go down there and get rid of him.*"

"I c-can't do that!" Cobb trembled at the mere thought of such a thing. "You know I abhor violence!"

"*Let me do it. I'll handle it. You know I can. I've done it before.*"

"Are you sure? I mean, can you honestly deal with something like this?"

"*You don't remember, do you*?"

Cobb stared blankly at his friend.

"*No. Of course you don't.*"

Cobb still didn't speak; he was wondering what his friend was talking about. He figured it was hiding in the darkness of his mind, just like the other terribly unpleasant memories he'd hidden there years ago.

"*Let me show you.*"

"All right." Despite his innermost fears, Cobb let his friend accompany him down the staircase.

***

Once the footsteps descended halfway down the stairs, John recognized the shiny imports, the creased dress slacks, and the flawless suit emerging from the darkness.

John kept his position as Cobb looked around. John could see something in the old man's right hand. Something long and tapered, extending from the bony hand like an enormous claw.

A butcher knife.

John wondered if Cobb would be able to use it. A man who paid others to do his killing didn't seem the type to have the stomach to soil his own hands.

Cobb was most likely scared and putting on an act.

More whispering drifted over from the stairs. John peered around the side of the barrel, trying to look beyond Cobb. Still at a disadvantage, he could see nothing but Cobb's lower body and the large, tapered object in his right hand. However, the closer Cobb got to the cellar floor, the more John could distinguish two different whispers.

There was someone else. The bastard had a friend.

Another paid killer?

John's heart skipped a beat as Cobb reached the bottom step.

***

Cobb lowered a shoe to the concrete floor.

"He's hiding behind that wine barrel."

"Are you sure?" Cobb's heart fluttered.

"Yes."

"Can you recognize him?"

"He is in the dark."

"What do we do?"

318

"From now on, we don't speak. I shall enter your mind and we will communicate this way. We don't want him to know what we are planning."

No. Of course not.

"All right, then. Turn left. Appear as if you are heading for the antique rockers stacked along the far wall."

Why?

"A distraction. I shall be watching the rear and will tell you what I see."

Of course.

Cobb moved stiffly in the appropriate direction. After he'd taken two shaky steps, his friend said, *"Put the knife in your other hand and straighten your right arm."*

Why?

"We don't want him to see it."

Oh...

"Don't want him to know we're armed. He can certainly see in the light, but I don't think he will be able to distinguish what you've got in your hand."

Cobb switched the knife, lowered his arms, and resumed moving toward the rockers.

After ten more steps, his friend said, *"Stop."*

Why?

"To throw him off. Just stand there. I shall watch him from the rear. Bring your left arm toward the front, so the knife is out of his range of vision. This will give him something else to think about. I will tell you what I will do if he starts moving toward us. And when I act, you will black

319

*out and let me take over. Then I will be able to do
what is necessary—as usual. All right?"*

Of course. Cobb once again wondered what his
friend was talking about. But he did as was
suggested. He stood stock-still, his left arm in front
of him, the knife held directly in front of his crotch.

His friend spoke again.

"He's moving."

Cobb's body went rigid. The knife twitched in
his grasp. *What now?*

*"When I tell you, spin around and let me take
control of the knife."*

What will you do?

"I told you, I will handle this."

But —

"He must be dealt with."

*We can't murder someone who's come inside to
stay warm and dry for the night!*

*"If he is here for that, why hasn't he come out
of his hiding place?"*

Maybe he's scared.

*"No, Nathaniel. If he were scared, he wouldn't
be moving toward us right now."*

Cobb shivered. *Is he...doing that?*

"As we speak."

Then what can we possibly —

"Let me handle this!"

Very well. What will you —

*"Black out, Nathaniel. Let me take over. Do as
you usually do. Hide in the darkness, where you feel
safe. Right now!"*

320

Before Cobb could comply, strange sounds coming from the top of the stairs made him gasp.

The cellar door suddenly slammed shut.

***

After five minutes of painstakingly slow work, Erika managed to create a gap more than an inch wide between the chipped window and the sill. Her heart racing, she reached up and shoved her fingers into the gap.

In no time at all, she managed to create a space large enough to permit her body to slip through. Taking a breath, she faced the opening, her pulse racing as she studied angles. She soon realized she would have to jump at least a foot to gain the height necessary to propel herself through the opening.

She needed something to stand on.

The trash can.

She grabbed it by the metal handles and began dragging it, stopping when it was directly beneath the window. She shoved her bag between the side of the can and the brick wall so it would remain hidden. Then, gathering courage, she raised a knee and rested it on the lid.

Moments later, she began inching her head and torso through the opening.

Using her elbows to pull herself forward, it wasn't long before her stomach rested on the sill. But just as she was about to grasp the radiator for balance, her left foot flew up, upsetting her equilibrium and propelling her into a nosedive.

Arms flapping, she shot forward. Her right arm came down, breaking her fall. She landed on her shoulder, whacking the side of her head on the linoleum.

Bright stars flashed across her vision. A hot core of redness screamed from somewhere deep in her shoulder. She gritted her teeth as the sizzling heat danced from her shoulder into the back of her neck.

As she landed, her left leg flew upwards, flipping her over. The side of her open-toed shoe slapped against the cellar door, slamming it viciously into its frame.

***

John was less than five feet away from Cobb when he heard the crash.

It sounded like someone had slammed the basement door shut.

When Cobb spun around, John saw the butcher knife. John raised his hand. Using the flat edge of his palm, he brought his arm down, slicing into Cobb's extended wrist. Cobb's blood-curdling shriek made the concrete walls vibrate. The butcher knife leaped from Cobb's hand, skipping across the uneven concrete floor. Cobb watched numbly, then looked down at his hand. Whimpering, he grabbed his wounded wrist.

John hauled off with a roundhouse punch, clipping Cobb in the face. The old man collapsed like a broken doll, the back of his head thumping the concrete.

John looked around for Cobb's friend but saw no one.

He decided this friend was no doubt the one who had slammed the basement door on his way out. He was now probably standing in the doorway, ready to make the next move.

John snuck up the stairs. His penknife out, he cautiously pushed the door open and tensed himself for immediate action.

Erika was lying on the floor just beyond the window. She lay on her side and was trying to sit up.

Quickly pocketing his knife, he rushed to her and gingerly felt for a pulse. It was racing. Then he squatted and wrapped an arm around her back to brace her.

She shook herself and smiled. "One of these days, you're gonna get tired of saving my life."

"You hit your head." He noticed slight bruising on her forehead and a few drops of blood. "Are you all right? I mean, dizzy or anything?"

"I'm just fine."

"What are you…what did you do?" He noticed the opened window. "You opened up the window and slid through?"

She shrugged. "The door was locked."

He shook his head. "You could've really hurt yourself. Why'd you do this?"

"I wanted to help."

He was furious with her but decided to give her a break. After all, she'd managed to keep Cobb away from him for nearly half an hour. "You've already helped a *lot*."

"I just didn't like him locking the door. I was worried."

"You *really* wanna help?"

She nodded eagerly.

"I'm gonna help you up and you're gonna leave this place. Through the front door, this time. Understand?"

"But—"

"I mean it, now…"

"John—"

"This is something I have to do."

"You're gonna kill him, aren't you?"

"Not unless I absolutely have to."

She studied his expression. Then she sighed and said, "All right. But just to set the record straight—"

"I know." He helped her up. Still obviously weak, she lost her footing, but he wrapped his arm around her waist and kept her from falling. Their faces were only a few inches away. They looked into each other's eyes.

John knew in that single moment that he never wanted to kiss a woman so much before in his life. But it wasn't the right time. Not while he had to deal with the man who had killed his friend.

He forced himself back to reality. "Can you walk all right?"

"I *think* so…"

"I won't be long."

"I'll wait."

"Go back to your car and wait, all right?"

She didn't reply.

He groaned. "Erika…"

The right side of her mouth twisted upward. "All right…"

He pulled away and tried very hard not to gaze at Erika's parted lips. It was nearly impossible, but he kept thinking of Cobb and what he had to do, and he managed to turn away from Erika and head back down the stairs.

Cobb lay in a heap, his expensive suit wrinkled and blotched with dirt and grease. His imports were smudged and scuffed. The Windsor knot of his tie had come undone. The tie lay in bunches across his right shoulder. Glass shards and bits of metal from his gold pocket watch lay beside him on the concrete floor.

John picked up the knife, noting the exceptional sharpness of the blade. After a very quick search of the area, he found a box tied securely with thick strands of twine. He glanced briefly at Cobb, then began slicing away at the twine.

When he had gathered enough loose twine, he pulled an armchair from the stack against the wall, dragged it across the concrete, put the chair directly beneath the light bulb, and picked up Cobb by the armpits.

John decided that it was now time for Cobb to face the consequences for having Buster murdered.

***

Cobb opened his eyes and groaned.

After a few cloudy, disorienting moments, he discovered he could not move. He realized, in horror, that he was tied to a chair. His wrists were

325

fastened securely to the wooden arms with twine, his ankles similarly fixed to the front legs. Several strands of twine encircled his midsection, passing through the chair slats and obviously knotted behind his back.

He could feel his pulse racing. His left wrist throbbed painfully with the beating of his heart. His jaw ached. The deafening pounding in his head made it nearly impossible to think clearly.

Then he heard movement behind him.

He tried turning, but the side of his head began vibrating unmercifully, and he cringed and squeezed his eyes shut. A whimper escaped his throat.

When he opened his eyes, the man was standing in front of him, looking at him with the same ferociousness one would expect to see in the eyes of a predatory jungle cat. He stood terrifyingly close, the butcher knife in his hands.

Norton's friend!

"You!" The throbbing in Cobb's head increased.

"Yeah. Me." The man's voice was soft, unemotional. And defiant at the same time.

"Wh-What are you...d-*doing* here? Wh-Why am I...*tied*...in this *chair*? Wh-Why d-did you...*attack* me? I d-d-demand you release me, right here and now!"

"Shut up." The man slid over a rocker and positioned it directly in front of Cobb. "You're not exactly in the world's best bargaining position right now."

"B-B-But...what...why are you — "

326

"I said *shut up*!" The opened palm came from out of nowhere, cracking Cobb viciously in the face and driving a harsh wail from him. Cobb sagged in the chair. A fresh onslaught of red-hot pain sliced up the side of his head before moving down and settling in his jaw.

Cobb's head drooped forward. A soft groan escaped his throat. The twine around his midsection cut into him, making it difficult to breathe.

"You'll speak when I want you to, and only then," the man said. "Understand?"

Cobb continued to groan.

"I *said*, understand?"

Cobb looked up. The monster's hand slowly raised again. Cobb managed a quick nod. The sudden movement filled his head with an onslaught of excruciating pain.

"You're going to tell me why you had my friend murdered, and you're going to give me every detail. Every last fucking scrap of information. Your assassin is dead—just like the Murphy's. He's next door, wadded up in the dumpster with the rest of the garbage." The monster's eyes blazed. "Understand?"

In the dumpster.

Rbow. In the dumpster.

My God...

Rbow. Dead!

No hope!

Everything...gone!

Cobb swallowed the sob that was fighting its way out.

This doesn't make sense. None of it makes sense. First, the Murphy twins are killed by this...this monster...

Then Rbow. A professional assassin for many years...and this creature comes along and kills him...then stuffs him in a dumpster!

What kind of devil stands before me?

What evil monster has Hell unleashed upon me?

When Cobb opened his mouth to scream, a filthy rag appeared in the monster's hand. In a flash, it was stuffed into Cobb's mouth. The disgusting taste of grease and oil made him gag as the sourness filled his throat, then oozed slowly down to his stomach.

The monster sat watching him, an amused expression on his hard features. All the while, his hands played with the butcher knife.

"You ready to behave?"

"*You've got to humor him,*" Cobb's friend said, appearing quickly. "*Make him think he is in control. Appeal to his human side. If you can distract him, I might be able to get the knife from him and slit his throat.*"

"I asked you a question."

"*Do it, Nathaniel. I know you can. Distract him!*"

Cobb nodded.

The monster reached out and yanked the rag from Cobb's mouth.

"Listen," Cobb said urgently, his heart pounding. "You must untie me. Right now. It is

328

hard for me to breathe. The ropes around my chest
— "

The hand slammed into his cheek again, in the same place. Cobb closed his eyes and watched a kaleidoscope of beautiful colors racing before him. The throbbing in his head had become deafening. The heavy weight in the back of his head seemed like a bowling ball had slammed into his skull. An intense heat exploded inside him. He gasped; the tears squeezed out from between his eyelids.

"I just told you to speak only when I tell you to. Did you forget? Or are you just stupid?"

Cobb kept his eyes closed and waited for the colors to go away. They were blinding, splashing everywhere.

"Well?"

A rough hand cupped his chin, jerking his face up. The sudden motion turned the colors into a blinding splatter of white. The room jerked before him. The thumping grew faster, louder. The bowling ball bounced frantically.

"Please!" he moaned through the horrible pain. "I can't *stand* this — "

"Cobb, if you don't start cooperating, I'll tell you what I'm gonna do." The monster let go of Cobb's chin. He leaned forward in the chair and began playing with the butcher knife again.

"I'm going to break one of your fingers." The monster began staring at Cobb's bound hands. He seemed to be studying them. Just then, he sat back and looked Cobb right in the eye. "I think I'll break the little finger of your right hand. The one with the expensive ring. How does that sound?"

The monster crossed one leg over the other. He seemed very relaxed. It was almost as if he were discussing sports, or the stock market. "Anyway, that's the game plan. Understand now?"

Oh my God...

My friend...

Where are you, my very dear friend?

"Understand, Cobb?"

I need you so much right now!

Silence.

Nathaniel Cobb began to whimper. Then, without warning, his jaw dropped.

His scream rang loud and clear.

***

Erika had just unlocked the front door of Cobb's Collectibles when she heard the screaming.

It came from the basement.

John?

No. Not John. This one was high-pitched and sounded like a woman.

The old man, most likely.

Was John torturing the old man? Making Cobb suffer for what had been done to John's friend?

Would John *murder* the old man after all?

She clearly remembered what they had talked about just minutes earlier, when he came up the stairs to see what had happened.

"You're gonna kill him, aren't you?"

"Not unless I absolutely have to."

330

His expression suggested that he'd been sincere. John was no longer a killer. He'd killed three men in the last two days, but that had been necessary. They'd tried to kill him, hadn't they? If he hadn't killed them, they would have killed him—right?

John is not *a killer!*

Images of what had happened in the alley thundered past. John's scuffle with the man dressed as a priest. What happened when she distracted them. John abruptly changing, turning from a sweet, considerate, personable man into something cold and inhuman. Something beastlike.

The memory of the scream trickled right back. John was torturing the old man. And she needed to stop it—somehow…

Her thoughts racing, Erika rushed down the cluttered aisle and down the hall, to the door leading to the basement. She stood in the open doorway, swaying a little, still trying to regain her equilibrium since her crash-and-burn from the window. After a few moments, she knew she'd be okay. She'd probably have another bruise or two, but that was no big deal.

Confident she'd regained her equilibrium, she took a few tentative steps. Then, after steadying herself, she crept down the stairs.

What she saw made her bite her lower lip.

John was sitting in a chair facing Cobb, who was tied to another chair. Some sort of cloth or rag was stuffed in the old man's mouth. John sat just a few feet away, a large knife in his hands.

Both men turned in her direction.

"I thought I told you to leave." John's expression was fierce. His eyes had turned into a white fluorescent in the dim basement lighting.

"John —— "

"Please do as I say."

"But —— "

"Please?"

She stared at him, trying to see through the depraved eyes that had once belonged to the man she had been falling in love with. Eyes that now resembled that werewolf that had scared her years ago, in a stupid horror flick.

But just then, the whiteness began dimming, and after a couple of very long, tense moments, Erika could see the soft brown orbs of John Callen, the man she knew was no longer a killer. And when his eyes turned back into the soft pools she recognized so well, the look on his face was unmistakable. This look said:

Erika, this bastard killed my good friend, and I really need this moment. Please trust me.

Without another word, she turned and went back up the stairs.

***

His eyes never left the woman, even when the filthy rag was yanked from his mouth.

That bitch!

Trollop!

She distracted you while her friend—this monster—snuck down here.

Yes. I know that now.

332

That trollop! Just like your bitch of a mother —

"Don't *say* that about her! I told you not to *say* that about her!"

But it is true, Nathaniel...

"I told you not to *talk* about her like that!"

Nathaniel —

"No! *Stop* it! *Stop* it!"

The monster was saying something. His head was tilted; a vertical crack had appeared between his brows.

Cobb was much too distraught to listen. His one and only true friend had suddenly turned on him...for the very first time!

Look what that bitch has gotten us into!

His friend was beside himself. For the very first time, Cobb's soulmate was not the figure of calm rationality that had been the cornerstone of their relationship for more than sixty years.

"*Look at this!*" Suddenly his friend was speaking aloud, regardless of their earlier plan. "*We're tied to this chair, this beast has us at his mercy, and you're still defending that disgusting pile of feminine waste you call your —* "

CRACK!

Another cascade of bright stars.

Fireworks.

Distant thunder.

The colors ebbing, fading away...

Growing dimmer, darker...

Even darker.

Black.

Blank.

333

Empty. A total void.

Cold.

The hard wooden floor was cold against his naked bottom. The small, stuffy room was slowly suffocating him in the darkness.

You've wet the bed again...

You're a nasty, nasty child!

Filthy. Foul. An embarrassment.

I'm here. Where is my friend?

I'm here, too.

I'm so glad. I've missed you.

There's someone here with us.

Who?

Don't know. He keeps asking us questions.

What sort of questions?

Strange questions.   About someone named Buster.

Buster?

Yes.

Are you sure?

What else could it be?

Are you sure it's not Alexander?

Now that you've mentioned it, I'm not so sure anymore.   Maybe it is Alexander.   They sound similar, do they not?

Why does he want to know about him?

I don't know.   Nor do I care.   That ghastly, drooling bastard is dead.

Are you sure?

Positive.

And Mother?

She's dead, too.

No! She went away! She ran out because the monster was doing things to us and she could no longer bear to watch when he grabbed my penis and did that disgusting thing he liked so much that made me cry —

No. Dead.

No!

Yes!

No! No!

She's dead, Nathaniel. I'm sorry, but your mother is —

NO! NO! NO! NO-O-O-O-O-O! —

CRACK!!!

***

Cobb slumped helplessly, head dangling.

John faced the chair, looking down at the old man and trying to figure what was going on.

After the first slap, Cobb started blubbering. He'd been incoherent, chattering away furiously. Then, after a strange conversation in two distinctive voices, John interrupted the old man's tirade with another slap.

"The old man's insane, isn't he?"

John turned sharply at the sound of her voice.

Erika was leaning against the banister at the bottom of the stairs. A sad expression covered her face.

"There are two of them."

"Sounds like it. Scary, huh?"

John suddenly noticed a pungent, ammoniac odor. He turned back to Cobb.

335

A large dark stain had saturated the material of the old man's expensive slacks.

Cobb's eyes opened; there was a glazed look in them. He stared straight ahead but didn't seem to notice John or Erika.

"Who are you?" John asked.

"I'm Nathaniel," the old man said in a little boy's voice. "I've wet the bed again, and Mother will be very angry — "

"*No*!" Cobb barked in a different voice, this one brash, lower-pitched. The man's face had changed: the eyes had turned cold, defiant. "I told you. Your mother's dead!"

"No!"

"Yes!"

"No!"

John slapped Cobb again, but not nearly as roughly as he'd done earlier. This one was merely to stop the quibbling. "Listen to me. Both of you."

Cobb went silent.

"Why did you kill Buster?"

Cobb's face had become defiant again. "*He* did, *I* didn't."

"Who are you?"

"I am the one who does things right. The one who gets things done. Nathaniel is the one you want. He is the one who paid to have your moronic friend killed."

John cringed at the blistering heat crawling up his spine. "Why?"

Cobb laughed. "For the painting, of course."

"Why the painting?"

336

"Because of what that bastard Summerville had scribbled beneath the cardboard backing."

"Where's the painting?"

Another laugh. "In the safe."

"How do I open it?"

A chuckle. "By using the combination, Einstein."

"What's the combination?"

This laugh was both long and hysterical. "You really expect us to tell you?"

"If you don't, I'll — "

"Yes. I know. You'll break one of his fingers."

"How do you feel about that?"

Cobb shrugged. John could tell by the nature of the shrug what was to follow.

"I don't really give a healthy shit, as a matter of fact. It'll be Nathaniel's finger you'll be breaking. I'll just go away again and come back when the stupid fuck's boo-boos are all better. All these years, I've been trying like hell to get this pitiful sack of shit to stand on his own two feet. Since he obviously won't do it, I'm just going to have to make him pay."

John turned to Erika. "This isn't going very well."

Cobb laughed. "You *are* a genius, aren't you?"

John turned back to Cobb and cracked the old man viciously in the face.

Erika cringed and turned away.

Cobb's head dangled again. Moments later, he began to whimper. When he opened his eyes, he sniffed and turned to John. A glazed look filled his

337

eyes when he opened his mouth and said, "Where did..."

***

"...you go?"

Silence.

Cobb turned his head. The harsh brightness of the light bulb made him squint his eyes. As he squinted, his tears distorted the figures in front of him, casting strange shadows, making them look frighteningly familiar.

Mother! And Summerville!

They were standing there, so frighteningly close, watching him!

He'd wet himself again, and they'd tied him to a chair for his punishment.

Now they were getting ready to lock him in the closet. They'd simply drag the chair into the tiny room next to his bed and close the door. Then they'd go back downstairs and forget about him.

"They're dead," his friend said. *"You're seeing things."*

Trying to trick me. Suddenly, my very dear, wonderful friend is trying to trick me. Telling me things that aren't true.

Then he remembered: the man with the white fury in his eyes. The beautiful, dark-haired woman who had become an evil decoy.

The tears stopped. The figures before him became clearer. He knew then that his mother and Summerville weren't standing there, weren't standing there at all.

338

But something else became the big issue here. Something even more frightening, more horrible, than the return of his mother and Summerville...

"I heard what you said. You said you didn't care what this beast does. Is this true?"

More silence.

"I thought you were my friend! Friends don't treat one another like this. Friends — "

"Don't tell me what friends do. I have been your friend all your lonely, miserable life."

"Then why don't you care what this beast does to me?"

"I care. But sometimes you are so naive, Nathaniel. Sometimes —"

"What does that have to do with your telling this beast you don't care what he does?"

"Sometimes I have been forced to do and say things. You are not in control, Nathaniel. You are still a helpless little boy. Look at you. You have placed yourself in one hopeless, impossible situation. You have wet your pants again. You are at this bastard's mercy, with no idea how to get out of it."

"But what you said—"

"I am bluffing him, Nathaniel, because he will not actually hurt you. He can't afford to because he needs you right now. In fact, he needs you very much. He wants to open the safe. And when he opens it, he will — "

"Let him open it, then. I am tied to this chair, and he will kill me — kill *us* — if he does not get what he wants."

"He…can't know…about Summerville's treasure, Nathaniel."

"But he will *kill* us if we don't cooperate!"

Silence.

"Did you hear me?"

More silence.

"Please! Let him — "

"No."

"Wh-*What*?"

"There is…no treasure, Nathaniel…"

"*What* did you say?"

"There is no treasure."

"What are you saying?"

"There is no treasure. It's…not there. Nothing is there. It's all…a lie. A hoax. Summerville was not only an evil bastard, but a clever one. He –"

"But Mother always said — "

"She is dead, Nathaniel."

"Stop *saying* that!"

"She is dead!"

"No!"

Yes!

"How do you--"

"I know she is dead, Nathaniel."

"How can you possibly—"

"I know. And so do you. She is dead because I …could no longer stand what was happening to--"

"What did you do?"

"I—"

"What did you do?"

"I was the one who –"

"N-N-N-N-N-O-O-O-O-O!"

340

The blackness came quickly.

EPILOGUE - Friday

Dressed in his dark suit, John was in the middle of packing when someone knocked on his motel room door.

It was Erika. She was wearing slacks, a white blouse, plaid jacket, and open-toed heels, and looked fabulous. Her hair had just been washed. It hung loose, shining brightly in the late afternoon sun.

"You look very nice." She smiled. "May I come in?"

"Thank you. So do you." He opened the door wider. "Make yourself at home while I finish packing." He turned and headed for the bathroom. And while he gathered up his shaving things, he struggled to think of what he could tell this beautiful lady, who had come into his life so suddenly and changed so many things even before he realized what was happening.

Erika came in and closed the door. While he was at the sink, he heard her ask, "You're flying back to Orlando after the funeral?"

"That's the plan." He left the bathroom, his shaving gear in one hand, a hair blower in the other. He put everything on the bed, which was covered with his opened suitcase and clothes he had folded and laid out in a neat row. He looked at her. She was standing just a few feet from the door, gazing at the bed. The darkness covering her face was unmistakable. "What's wrong?"

She looked up at him. A vertical line split her brows. "It looks like I'm going to win my court battle. The private investigator my attorney hired caught my husband with his new girlfriend. There are pictures, motel room receipts, and bunches of other incriminating things. I guess I won't have much to worry about from now on."

"That's great! It's what you wanted, isn't it? Now the house is all yours. You can write your own settlement."

Erika sat down on the edge of the bed and looked down at her lap. When she looked back up at him, her eyes were moist. "Yes. It's what I wanted. I've got the house. It's all mine, now."

John sat next to her and watched her, noting the darkness clouding her fine features. Despite the good news about the divorce settlement, something very bad had obviously happened. She didn't look like someone who wanted to celebrate. She looked like someone who had lost something very special.

"You don't exactly look victorious, if you want to know the truth."

A deep sigh. "Don't *feel* victorious."

"Why not?"

She stared at the floor. John could feel the tension emanating from her. For an instant he felt as if he'd done something loathsome.

Just then, she straightened and looked directly at him. Her wet eyes glinted at him. "Don't you know?"

It was his turn to stare at the floor. The time had finally come.

Yes, Erika. I know. Believe me.

"You do know, don't you?"

He got up and hurried back to the bathroom. He paused in the doorway, glimpsing his reflection in the bathroom mirror. It showed clear evidence of his cowardice, and he truly despised himself. This beautiful woman had not only saved his life, she'd managed to make him fall in love with her...but all he could think of was flying back to Orlando, where his existence awaited his return. Where things were familiar and manageable.

Where his life remained safe and predictable.

Coward.

Without turning around and looking at her, he faced the shower curtain as if his explanation lay within its folds. "All I know is that my old Army buddy is dead, and after I pay my respects to his family, I have to go back to Orlando. My life is there. My life, my business. My contacts. Everything about me is down there."

"Everything?"

He remained motionless in the doorway, concentrating on the shower curtain so he could avoid his own accusing stare.

"My business here is finished, Erika. And since the people responsible for Buster's death are either dead or put away..."

Turn around and look at her. You owe her that much.

He turned. And discovered she was no longer sitting on the bed.

344

She was standing beside the bed. Facing him, hands behind her back, head tilted, lips parted. Her eyes were still wet, but the dimples at the corners of her mouth had returned. "I just asked you a question."

He turned away again. The warmth was crawling slowly up his back. And an uncomfortable tightness had been forming in his gut. "I was getting to that."

Erika took two steps closer. "Why so nervous?"

"I'm…not nervous." He tried to ignore the minty smell of her shampoo, the sweet scent of roses radiating from her skin. Tried to ignore the outfit, the round breasts hiding beneath the frilly blouse. The glistening brightness in the beautiful almond eyes.

"Please answer my question…"

"Which one?"

"You're really nervous, aren'tcha?" Her tone told him she was enjoying this.

He turned around and faced her.

She was now less than a foot away. And her hands rested on her hips.

"I don't…really need to tell you…do I?"

"No. You don't. But I would like to hear it, anyway."

"I just…" He sighed. The words just wouldn't come.

She moved closer, until they were pressed together. He wrapped his arms around her and clung tightly to her. She kissed him, her warm, full lips caressing his.

Moments later, he went to sit down on the bed. He felt drained. Deflated.

And realized right then that Orlando was the last place he wanted to be right now. But he had to face facts. And so did she.

"I've...*got* to go back," he said in a soft voice.

Erika sat down beside him. "Yes."

"My business...is there."

"You don't sound like you really want to go."

She's right, Callen. You want to stay here with this gorgeous woman, rip off her clothes, and have your way with her, again and again...

He sighed. "My business is there."

"You've already said that."

"Erika, you're a beautiful, kind, caring, sensitive lady, and I've fallen in love with you...but my business...it's—"

"Can't you move it?"

"Too many contacts down there."

Erika rested her head on his shoulder. "Then why don't you ask me to go with you?"

The feeling of her head on his shoulder made him dizzy. It was getting much more difficult to concentrate on the issue. "But...your divorce. The house. Your job. Your life is here."

She smiled. "It's a *house*, John. A *building*. Four walls, a few rooms, a front porch, a small yard. It's not a home unless there's a family living in it. There hasn't been a family living there in quite a while. And I can always find another job."

346

"And all that bullshit and heartbreak you went through to keep it. It doesn't matter?"

"Not now, it doesn't."

He went silent.

Her closeness and the sweet smell of her were making the heat unbearable.

"Nothing to say?"

"I screwed up before," he managed stiffly. "I was married before. To a girl I nearly destroyed."

"Tell me what happened."

"Are you sure…do you really want me to—"

"Yes."

"But it's not—"

"Tell me, John. Right now."

He took a breath and forced himself to stick to the issue. "I'd brought Iraq back with me but didn't realize it. I'd done something very bad back there and was trying to keep it from coming up again. I didn't know it at the time, but I do now. Now that Buster's gone, I can finally face it. And now I realize that it's not gonna kill me."

"Tell me what happened…"

"I killed…I killed some kids…back there. When Pam and I were married, I was really messed up. I put pressure on her. I wanted kids, but she didn't because she knew I wanted them for the wrong reasons. I didn't realize that at the time. It took me quite a while before I did, but by that time, it was too late. She had already gone. I blamed her for a lot of other things I couldn't quite understand. I sort of…went crazy. Subconsciously, I wanted kids to replace the ones I'd killed." He shrugged. "I guess I was blaming her for.. for what I did back there."

"Would you still like to have kids?" Erika asked softly, after a long pause.

He shook his head. "I'm over it now. And too damned old to be chasing after them."

Erika smiled. "Then there's no problem, is there?"

He couldn't speak; he just looked at her.

"John? Talk to me…please?"

"Iraq is still with me. Look what I did last week. I killed…I killed two more kids. Then another guy, and I stuffed him into a—"

"He tried to kill you, John… And he almost did."

He sighed. She was right. But even so, he knew that what happened in this quiet little town would stay with him forever.

"Well?"

"Then there was Cobb."

"You didn't kill him. You—"

"I tortured him."

"You didn't torture him. He tortured himself."

"I *wanted* to kill him… Badly…"

"But you didn't, did you?"

"I almost—"

"You know what they say about that, don'tcha? Horseshoes and hand grenades?"

"It was still there, Erika. Deep down in my gut. I could feel it."

"What was still there?"

"The darkness. The chills. The creepy feeling running down my spine."

"You didn't kill him, John. You called Sheriff Grubb. He same right over. They arrested Cobb and took him away. He was chattering away like the crazy man he is. The Sheriff and the two deputies were right there, watching. They knew—"

"But it was still there." He couldn't convince her what all this meant to him.

"It didn't matter, did it?"

"Whaddya mean?"

"It might have been there, but you were the one in control."

"How can you possibly think—"

"You just said you wanted to kill the old man."

"More than anything."

"But you didn't."

"No…"

"But you knew it was there, right?"

"Yes…"

"Yet you didn't let it come out and take over."

He didn't know how to respond. He wanted her to be right; he just didn't trust himself. "But what if—"

"What if what?"

"What if it comes back?"

"What if it does?"

"What if it comes back…when I'm with you?"

"Why would it?"

"I just don't think I have any control over it."

Erika smiled once again. "You may not think you do, but you do."

"How can you tell?"

"What brought it back in the first place?"

"Rage. Anger. Revenge."

"How about the guy with the priest's collar?"

"Survival."

"You don't feel any of those things with me, do you?"

"No…"

"Do you think you ever will?"

"Hell, no."

"What *do* you feel when you're with me, John?"

"Happy."

"Anything else?"

"Contentment. Relief."

"Is that all?"

He sighed.

"*Please* tell me…"

"Well, lust."

Erika smiled. "Funny. I was thinking the same thing."

This time, he smiled back. And for the first time in ages, he could sense the promise of happiness heading his way.

"It's not part of you anymore, John. Trust me."

He thought once again about what had happened the past week. That, despite Buster's senseless murder and the killing of three vicious men, something wonderful had occurred. A new love had developed from a background of death and murder.

He had finally found happiness after burying his old friend — and the past — and the terror that had plagued him more than half his life.

"Ask me, John," Erika said softly, her face close. "Ask me to come with you."

John pulled her closer. They kissed, long and passionately. And with this kiss, they both knew where their destiny lay.

THE END

OTHER WORKS BY
DAVID BERARDELLI

THE APPRENTICE
THE WAGON DRIVER
STEPPING OUT OF MY GRAVE
ESCAPE CLAUSE
FATAL INNOCENCE
COLORS
IN ANOTHER REALM
BEYOND RECOGNITION
THE NIGHTMARE COLLECTOR
HIDDEN
BEYOND GUILT
A RIPPLE IN TIME
YESTERDAY'S JOURNEY
ENLIGHTENMENT
REDEMPTION
AWAKENED
THE PLANNING COMMITTEE

Titles available through:
Gravestone Press
Fiction4All